Forbidden Love of a Buddhist Monk

An Autobiography of Passion, Past Lives, and Spiritual Awakening

Venerable Ananda

Forbidden Love of a Buddhist Monk

First Print 2025

ISBN: 978-1-0369-1803-3

www.venerableananda.org

Foreword

It is both a privilege and a profound responsibility to introduce this autobiographical work titled *Forbidden Love of a Buddhist Monk*, written by Venerable Panadure Ananda Thero, a young Buddhist monk whose journey is as extraordinary as it is inspiring. Born into a non-Buddhist family, his life defies convention and speaks to the quiet but powerful call of inner transformation. Even in his early school days—long before robes or rituals—Venerable Ananda felt an instinctive pull toward the path of meditation, a call that would shape the entire course of his life.

His first steps into the Dhamma were guided not by formal religious instruction, but by the wisdom of an elderly layman who introduced him to the practice of insight (*vipassanā*) meditation. This early encounter planted the seeds of spiritual aspiration that, in time, grew into a disciplined and luminous practice. By the age of fifteen, he had left the familiar world of family and school behind and entered the noble path of Buddhist ordination.

What followed was a remarkable deepening of meditative experience, as he immersed himself in the rigorous training of Samatha meditation in Myanmar—the land where the ancient currents of Theravāda practice continue to flow with undiminished force. His life since then has been marked by quiet determination, philosophical depth, and a rare clarity of vision—qualities that are reflected both in his teaching and in his English-language work, *The Liberation Manual.*

It was through a cousin of mine that I first heard of Venerable Ananda Thera as a young Buddhist monk of rare brilliance whose spiritual journey had already begun to draw quiet attention. My cousin mentioned that the Thera was seeking someone who could translate his English-language work into Sinhala for local publication. I agreed to undertake the task, moved by the depth and clarity of the original, and convinced of its relevance to a broad readership—both Buddhists and non-Buddhists—who seek spiritual fulfilment through meditation and inner reflection. The work spoke not only to those who walk well-trodden paths, but also to those adrift amidst competing spiritual claims, yearning for a way yet unmarked.

What began as a literary engagement soon evolved into a meaningful and enduring relationship. Over time, Ven Ananda and I developed a close mutual understanding, bound by shared values and a growing respect for each other's insight. It was within this context that he entrusted me with the honour of writing the foreword to his second and more daring work—a text that defies genre and challenges both literary convention and religious taboo.

This new book, autobiographical in its essence, transcends the limitations of conventional autobiography. It weaves together personal recollection, meditative insight, and metaphysical narrative to present a tapestry of existence that spans not only one life but several. The Thera revisits his former births—recollections revealed through deep Samatha meditation—and draws striking connections between the desires of those past lives and the lingering afflictions of his present monastic existence. In doing so, he crafts an intensely personal, even romantic, narrative set in a historical kingdom in India, where he once lived as a king entangled in a spiritually complex and emotionally charged relationship with an elder sister who nurtured him following the premature death of their royal parents.

Though this segment may read like historical fiction—rich in emotional depth and symbolic tension—it serves a deeper purpose. It is not written for entertainment, nor intended to provoke or sensationalise. Rather, it is an act of spiritual excavation. By laying bare the karmic entanglements of past desires, the author courageously reveals how deeply rooted attachments can travel across lifetimes, subtly shaping the moral and emotional challenges of the present.

In the current life, even as a monk dedicated to the path of liberation, he finds himself haunted by the echo of a yearning he cannot name—a longing for a love that once was, cloaked in the form of an elder sister, and shadowed by the complexities of attachment. The emotional terrain he traverses in this life is not easily reconciled with the austere ideals of monastic detachment. It is precisely this inner struggle—the raw, unfiltered tension between spiritual aspiration and lingering worldly desire—that gives this work its exceptional power and honesty.

What is perhaps most remarkable is that this book does not shy away from what is often left unsaid in the life of a monk. With rare transparency and courage, the Thera opens up themes that are usually shrouded in silence: desire, love, longing, emotional entrapment, and the existential burden of memory. Yet his aim is never to scandalise. Rather, it is to confront—gently but unflinchingly—the hidden corners of the human condition, and in doing so, to offer a path to healing.

Through the practice of insight meditation (*vipassanā*), he eventually comes to recognise the deep structures of attachment that bind him to *saṁsāra*—the ceaseless cycle of birth, death, and rebirth. And it is through this profound seeing that liberation slowly emerges. The narrative thus becomes not just a recounting of memory, but a spiritual testimony—a map of inner release that mirrors the Buddha's own invitation to examine one's experience with unwavering honesty.

Literarily, the work occupies a unique space. It is at once an autobiography, a metaphysical memoir, a spiritual confession, a philosophical novel, and, most strikingly, a romantic *bildungsroman*—an artistic portrayal of the emotional and spiritual growth of the protagonist across multiple births. As such, it defies conventional categorisation. It is a bold act of deconstruction—not merely of narrative form, but of the psychic and karmic layers that shape identity across lives. Yet unlike other deconstructionist texts that end in fragmentation, this one deconstructs in order to liberate. It does not dissolve meaning into ambiguity; it reveals a way beyond suffering towards ultimate freedom.

What makes the work especially captivating is the intensely romantic engagement of the protagonist in a love so unconventional, so penetrating, that it touches the deepest recesses of the heart and soul. This romance is masterfully crafted to engage the reader with growing intensity, maintaining suspense and emotional resonance throughout. The story does not merely narrate a love affair; it charts its profound psychological, moral, and spiritual imprint on the protagonist's development. Through this deeply human narrative, readers are invited to reflect on their own secret longings and unspoken attachments. The language shifts with exquisite subtlety between the passionate ethos of romantic love and the austere discipline of detachment, evoking a rare emotional cadence. The intermittent poetic passages heighten both engagement and transcendence, amplifying the emotional entanglement as well as the liberation that follows.

I am confident that this work will resonate with a wide spectrum of readers. It is deeply personal, yet profoundly universal. It opens space for critical reflection, spiritual introspection, and therapeutic catharsis, in the Aristotelian sense of purification through art. It invites us to confront the hidden patterns of our own lives—our memories, our attachments, our yearnings—and in doing so, gestures towards the possibility of release.

In offering this foreword, I do not merely introduce a book; I bear witness to a rare and fearless journey—a journey marked by intensity, vulnerability, philosophical depth, and spiritual courage. I commend this work to all who seek not only to read about love and liberation, but to experience their echoes stirring within their own hearts.

Kithsiri Amaratunga
Senior Lecturer
Department of Languages
Faculty of Management, Social Sciences, and Humanities
General Sir John Kotelawala Defence University
Ratmalana

Preface

There are loves we can speak aloud—and loves we carry in silence.

This is the story of a love that lived in the hush between those two realms. A love not of lust, nor possession, but of something deeper, older—carved into the soul across lifetimes. A love forbidden by form, yet allowed by feeling. A love that asked for nothing, yet gave everything.

In another time, in another world, I pressed myself into the warmth of someone who once felt like home. I was not her lover. I was not her child. I was something stranger—something sacred. I was the boy who longed to lie near her heartbeat just to feel peace, just to belong. And she was the sister of my soul.

Now I walk this life robed as a monk, my head shaven, my footsteps quiet. I speak of mindfulness, of detachment, of liberation. And yet—beneath all that silence, the heart still remembers. It remembers the softness of emotional closeness, the haunting ache of absence, and the strange way one soul can find itself searching for another through the fabric of time.

This is not a story of scandal. It is not the confession of a monk who broke his vows. It is the **revelation of a monk who dared to feel**—and through feeling, began to wake up.

In these pages, you'll find moments of innocent closeness and aching desire. You'll read of past-life memories that burn brighter than the present, and of a sacred bond that challenged everything I thought I had renounced. But more than that, you'll walk beside me as I stumble through longing, wrestle with inner conflict, and slowly, tenderly, learn to transform love into light.

This book is for those who have loved too deeply to let go. For those who have longed for someone who could never be theirs in this life, but perhaps, once was. For those who have felt that love and spirituality are not separate paths—but reflections of one another, each leading home.

So if your heart has ever ached without explanation…
If you've ever loved someone in silence, across time, against reason…
If you believe that even forbidden love can be sacred…
Then perhaps this story is already yours.

Welcome to the space between passion and peace.
Welcome to the memory you've never told anyone.
Welcome to *Forbidden Love of a Buddhist Monk.*

— Venerable Panadure Ananda Thero

Introduction

To Those Who Have Loved in Silence...

Some stories are born from memories.
Others, from dreams.
This one was born from a wound—so quiet, so sacred, that for years, I dared not speak it aloud.

I am a monk. I have left behind the world. Or so I thought.

But beneath the saffron robes and the still breath of meditation, there lived a longing I could neither name nor extinguish. It was not lust. It was not romance. It was something more innocent… and yet, more haunting. A desire for a connection that transcended form. A love that felt ancient, eternal, forbidden.

It began with a memory—not from this life, but from one far older.
A life in a palace. A sister. A bond. A silence that held more meaning than words.
And then—this life. A flicker of that same presence in another form. A face. A closeness. A trembling in the soul.

Could love really follow us across lifetimes?

As a Buddhist monk, I was trained to watch my thoughts, not indulge them. To observe desire, not feed it. But how could I ignore a feeling that had followed me through birth and death, across oceans of time? This was not fantasy—it was a truth that lived in my bones.

And so, I began to write. Not to justify, but to understand.
Not to preserve the past, but to free myself from it.
Not to claim a person—but to release a pattern.

What followed was this book.

You will not find a tale of recklessness or rebellion.
You will not find fantasy wrapped in cliché.
But you *will* find the story of a monk who dared to feel.
Who touched the fire of emotional attachment, and instead of turning away, stepped into it—eyes open, heart trembling—until it burned clean.

You will walk with me through memories of love, whispers of past lives, and the silent chambers of meditation where identity begins to dissolve. You will witness how sacred love and sensual longing can occupy the same breath—and how, through wisdom, they can be transformed into stillness, into clarity, into liberation.

This book is not just about *forbidden love.*
It is about the **transformation** of love.

It is about what happens when we no longer seek to own another soul, but to understand why that soul moved us so deeply in the first place. It is about turning toward the ache, not away from it. Watching it. Studying it. Letting it dissolve—not through suppression, but through truth.

If you've ever loved someone you could not hold...
If you've ever longed for a closeness that seemed to live outside the boundaries of what the world allows...
If you've ever wondered whether love could be more than desire—perhaps even a path to awakening…
Then this book was written for you.

This is not a story of breaking vows.
It is a story of breaking illusions.

So come with me—past the robes, past the rules, past the lifetimes.
Let us walk into the tender space where love meets emptiness,
and where emptiness, finally, begins to feel like peace.

Though written with the cadence of a story, this book is not a work of fiction. It is based on my true experiences—drawn from the memory stream of this life and others. Only a few elements have been refined for poetic and narrative beauty. The essence, however, remains unaltered: raw, real, and lived.

— Venerable Panadure Ananda Thero

Acknowledgements

I wish to express my heartfelt gratitude to those who have made this book, *Forbidden Love of a Buddhist Monk - An Autobiography of Passion, Past Lives, and Spiritual Awakening*, a reality.

First and foremost, I would like to extend my deepest thanks to **Mr. Kavinda Siriwardhana**, who graciously designed the cover of this book free of charge, bringing my vision to life with his artistic talent.

I am also immensely grateful to my meditation disciples **Ms. Chaminie Dias** and **Ms. Nimna Jayasinghe** for their valuable editing support, helping to refine the manuscript with their keen insight.

A special thank you goes to my devoted disciples **Dr. Danushi Kavindi**, **Mrs. Priyani Ranabahu**, **Ms. Rivini Cooray**, and **Mr. Harsha Perera** for their meticulous proofreading, ensuring the accuracy and clarity of this work.

I am honored to have **Senior Lecturer Kithsiri Amarathunge** write the foreword for this book, a contribution that adds depth and perspective to the narrative.

To all those who have offered their time, resources, and energy, I share with you the blessings and merits of this work. May the teachings and wisdom contained within these pages bring peace and understanding to all who read them. May the merit of this endeavor be a cause for the upliftment of our collective consciousness, leading to the realization of true liberation.

Thank you all for your unwavering support, guidance, and love. Without each of you, this journey would not have been possible. May all of you be blessed with good health, happiness, and peace. May your efforts lead to the cessation of suffering and the attainment of enlightenment in this very life.

Contents

2:38

Chapter 1

The Midnight Awakening

The soft, rhythmic ticking of the clock on my bedside table fills the stillness of the room. It reads *2:30 a.m.* when I suddenly jolt awake, drenched in sweat, my heart racing as though I've just run miles. I sit up slowly, clutching my chest, trying to still the uneasy thumping within. The faint glow of the streetlight outside my window seeps through the curtains, casting eerie shadows across the walls. I know this feeling all too well. It's not the first time I've awakened this way, gripped by a dream—a dream that feels less like a vision of the mind and more like a memory, haunting me with its familiarity and leaving me unsettled.

Each time, it's the same: I see her—an elder sister I've never had—her face a blur yet unmistakably gentle, her presence both warm and distant. I reach for her, my heart swelling with an unexplainable yearning, only to watch her slip away, fading into nothingness as I am left standing alone. *Why do I dream of her? Why do I long for her so deeply when she has never existed in my life, not in this reality?* And yet, every time I close my eyes, she returns—a shadow in the realm of my subconscious, growing more familiar with each encounter.

I swing my legs over the edge of the bed and let my feet touch the cool floor. With a sigh, I make my way to the bathroom. Flicking on the light, I brace myself against the sink, avoiding my own gaze in the mirror. I splash cold water on my face, hoping to shake off the lingering fog of sleep and the intensity of that vision. The water runs down my skin, grounding me, reminding me that I am awake, that I am *here.* Leaning against the sink, I finally dare to look up, staring into my own eyes, searching for answers that never seem to come. *Why am I dreaming of this elder sister who doesn't exist? Why does her absence hurt me so deeply, like a piece of me that was once whole, now fragmented and unreachable?* There is a void within me, one I can't quite understand—a hollow space that seems shaped precisely for her, though I know she's nothing more than a figment of my imagination.

Yet, the longing is real. The ache is real. And it leaves me wondering, night after night, if perhaps she isn't just a creation of my mind, but a missing piece of my soul. I straighten up, turning off the light as I step back into the darkness of my room. I sink onto the edge of my bed, my thoughts racing. I wonder, for the hundredth time, whether I should do something about this desire. *Should I search for someone who could be the sister I never had, to fill this aching emptiness within me?* Or would it be wiser to confront and release this strange obsession—to let go of this need and simply move forward?

But how do I let go of something so deeply embedded in my heart? How do I silence a yearning that has grown with me, hidden in the shadows of my soul, refusing to be dismissed? The ticking of the clock grows louder, each second stretching out like an eternity. I take a deep breath, pulling the covers around me as I lie down once more, staring into the darkness above, knowing sleep will not come easily tonight.

Chapter 2

The Dreamers' Interval

"Yohan, why don't you go outside and play with your friends during the interval?" Mrs. Lakmali's voice broke through my thoughts. Her gaze was soft, yet puzzled, as she looked at me. She was one of those rare teachers who truly tried to understand each of her students—never dismissing us as *just kids with meaningless ideas.* Perhaps she could see I was different; maybe she caught a glimpse of the solitude I held on to so tightly.

I looked up at her, meeting her curious eyes. "Engaging with others only brings stress and fatigue, Mrs. Lakmali," I replied, my tone flat and matter-of-fact. "It's better to stay in the classroom and live with an empty mind."

A faint smile flickered across her face—the kind of smile adults give when they're both amused and taken aback. Most teachers would argue, would try to encourage me to *fit in* or *be a kid,* but she simply nodded, letting my words settle in the air without resistance.

In truth, my character was like that—quiet, introspective, always a bit removed from the other kids.

While they found excitement in soccer games and afternoon cricket matches, I felt detached, disinterested. I found peace in solitude, a quiet refuge from the chaos of the world outside. My grades, however, were another story. Academically, I was always the first in my class and grade, securing my place at the top with ease. It wasn't that I was particularly ambitious; I just understood things quickly and felt compelled to keep learning.

Now, at twelve years old, I had only one friend—a boy named Sahan. Unlike most friendships built on shared hobbies or similar interests, ours was different. Sahan was, perhaps, the only person who understood the strange things that occupied my mind. Together, we discussed topics that would make most kids our age frown in confusion. Our conversations weren't about the latest video games or popular TV shows. No, we talked about things that felt bigger, deeper, and sometimes darker.

"Do you think we could rule Sri Lanka one day?" Sahan would often ask, his eyes gleaming with a mix of ambition and mischief. "We could make it a monarchy again. We'd start by getting into the government—maybe even become the president."

"And once we're in, we'd make friends with the army," I'd reply, our strategy slowly taking shape in our young minds. In our imagination, we were future rulers, strategists preparing to change the fate of our country.

The idea of monarchy fascinated us. We believed that if one person ruled, they'd have no reason to steal or exploit—for the country would be their own, and they'd nurture it as a part of themselves. The concept of power, responsibility, and a just ruler captivated our young minds, though we barely understood the intricacies of governance or politics. It was an idealistic dream, a vision of a better Sri Lanka led by the values we held dear.

But it wasn't just politics that intrigued us. We delved into topics that most adults would struggle to understand—*simulation theory*, the idea that our world might be an elaborate illusion crafted by some higher intelligence; *quantum physics*, with its mind-bending theories and endless possibilities; *emptiness and Nibbana*—concepts of Buddhism and philosophy that we grasped only on the surface, yet they fascinated us with their promises of freedom and liberation. Even martial arts and black magic found their way into our conversations, as we imagined ourselves mastering skills that could make us powerful and unbreakable.

One day, when a teacher asked about our future ambitions, I didn't hesitate. "I want to become a Supreme Court Judge," I answered confidently, my words laced with conviction. The notion of justice, of a role where I could decide right from wrong, appealed to me. It felt like a path that could channel my desire to bring order, to correct the flaws I saw around me.

Sahan, ever the thinker, replied, "I'll be a lecturer." His tone was calm, thoughtful, as though he'd spent years contemplating it. It suited him well; he had a natural curiosity and a love for knowledge that would only grow with time.

While the other boys chased soccer balls and played cricket during breaks, Sahan and I stayed back, buried in our discussions. We didn't care for the noise, the rush of adrenaline that sports brought to others. Instead, we spent our time planning, dreaming, discussing theories that seemed lightyears beyond our age. There was, however, one physical pursuit that intrigued us: the gym. Strength appealed to us—not for competition—but as a symbol of control, a means to strengthen the mind and body, to be prepared for the life we envisioned.

Our lives unfolded in the quiet spaces between classes, in the stolen moments when the rest of the world was busy playing and laughing. We were different—not better—just different. Two boys trying to find our place in a world that felt both too small and too vast. The future loomed ahead, an open road of possibilities, and though we didn't know where it would lead, we felt ready to walk it together.

In our young minds, we had already begun shaping our own kingdom—a world where dreams became reality, and reality could be bent to our will.

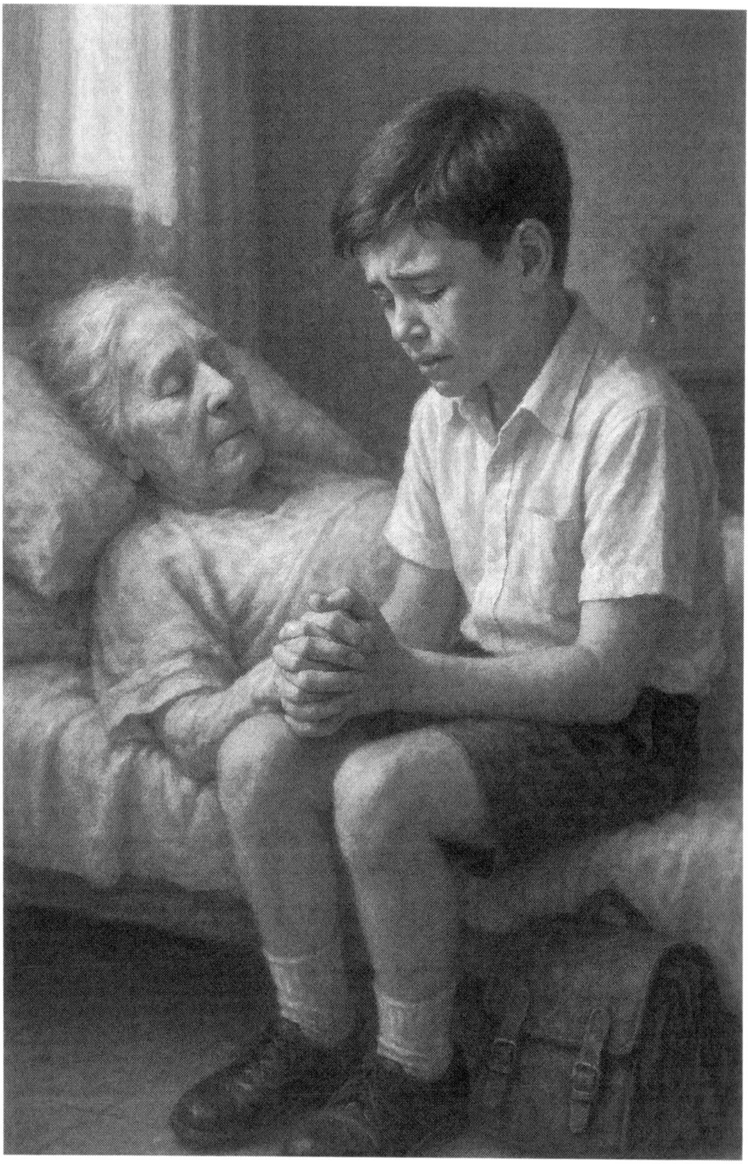

Chapter 3

The Silent Confidant

I wore my prefect badge with pride, even at a young age, believing that it was a testament to my integrity and discipline. It was a sign that my teachers and the principal trusted me, saw something in me that was worthy of respect. One day, however, Principal Sir gave me a new duty—a task that would test more than just my sense of responsibility. I was to be a silent observer, a spy, watching over the elder students and reporting any misdeeds directly to him.

For a while, it was an easy enough role to slip into. I watched, I observed, and I quietly informed the principal whenever I saw anything out of line. But one day, everything changed. Some of the older boys—the Advance Level students—caught on. They found out about my role as the principal's informant, and they didn't take it lightly. They cornered me after school, their faces twisted with anger and menace. Words flew, harsh and cutting, laced with a venom that left me both stunned and shaken. They scolded me, threw threats my way, taunting me, trying to break down my resolve.

In that moment, I felt small, vulnerable, and utterly alone. Sahan, my only friend, was absent that day, and there was no one to stand by my side, no one to share in my fear. My heart raced, and I felt the sting of humiliation and anxiety coursing through me. Somehow, I managed to escape their mocking eyes and hurried outside. Without a second thought, I hailed a taxi, desperate to get home, away from the school and the weight of their words.

The house was quiet when I arrived. My mother wasn't at home, and for a brief moment, a wave of emptiness washed over me. I had hoped to see her, to find solace in her presence, but there was only silence. In the stillness of the house, I felt the sharp sting of loneliness once again. The only people there were my dearest grandmother and her helper. My grandmother, once vibrant and full of life, was bedridden now, ravaged by dementia that had stolen her voice and dimmed her once-bright eyes. She couldn't speak, couldn't recognize people clearly anymore, but she was there, her presence warm and steady in the room.

I found myself drawn to her bedside, her frail form barely a shadow of the woman she once was. I took her hand gently, feeling the cool, soft skin that had once comforted me in my darkest moments. I looked into her eyes, searching for some flicker of recognition, hoping she could somehow understand the turmoil inside me. With a shaky voice, I began to speak, pouring out my heart, recounting every detail of the day's events. I told her about the older boys, about how they had found out about my duty, how they had taunted and frightened me. I spoke about the fear, the loneliness, the ache that seemed to settle in my chest.

She sat there, silent, her gaze distant and unfocused, yet I held onto her hand tightly, as though her touch alone could offer me strength. In her eyes, I saw fragments of memories, moments that reminded me of the past when she had been my world, my constant source of love and warmth. I remembered the days when she would help me put on my shoes, her fingers carefully tying each lace with patient hands. She would dress me, feed me, and after each meal, she'd tenderly wipe the crumbs from my lips, handing me a glass of water with that gentle smile of hers. She had loved me in a way no one else did, with a devotion that made me feel like the most cherished child in the world.

Perhaps she loved me more than her other grandchildren because I was born just two days after her husband—my grandfather—had passed away. I had always wondered if she saw a part of him in me, if perhaps her love for me was a way of keeping his memory alive. Whatever the reason, her love had been my sanctuary, a place where I felt wholly accepted and adored. It was that love that had shielded me from my growing desire for an elder sister. With her by my side, I had never felt the sting of loneliness or the need for a sibling.

But now, everything had changed. My beloved grandmother, who had once been my confidant, was now a silent witness to my pain. She couldn't speak, couldn't offer words of comfort, and though she was physically present, the bond we once shared felt like a distant memory. The empty space in my heart, once filled by her love, now felt like a void, a hollow ache that no one could fill. And as that emptiness grew, so did my yearning for a sister—a figure I had long imagined but never known. It wasn't just a fleeting wish; it was a desire that took root deep within me, a longing that I couldn't shake.

I found myself wishing, with a desperation that left me breathless, that I had an elder sister to turn to. Someone who would understand me without needing explanations, who would hold me close and reassure me, who would be there when everyone else seemed so far away. I wished for someone who could listen to my troubles, share in my fears, and be the unwavering support I so desperately craved.

As I sat by my grandmother's side, tears began to blur my vision—a silent expression of the pain I held within. I was crying not only for my grandmother, for the woman she had been and the loss I felt, but also for the sister I had never known, the sister I yearned for with an ache that seemed to have no end. I cried for the loss of the love that had once shielded me, and for the relentless desire that now consumed me, even though I knew it was a desire that could never be fulfilled.

I closed my eyes, letting the tears fall, feeling the weight of my sadness and longing pressing down on me. In that moment, I knew that no matter how much I wished, no matter how deep my desire, there was no sister waiting in the wings to rescue me from my loneliness. There was only the empty silence of the house and the quiet presence of my grandmother, who could no longer offer the comfort I so desperately needed.

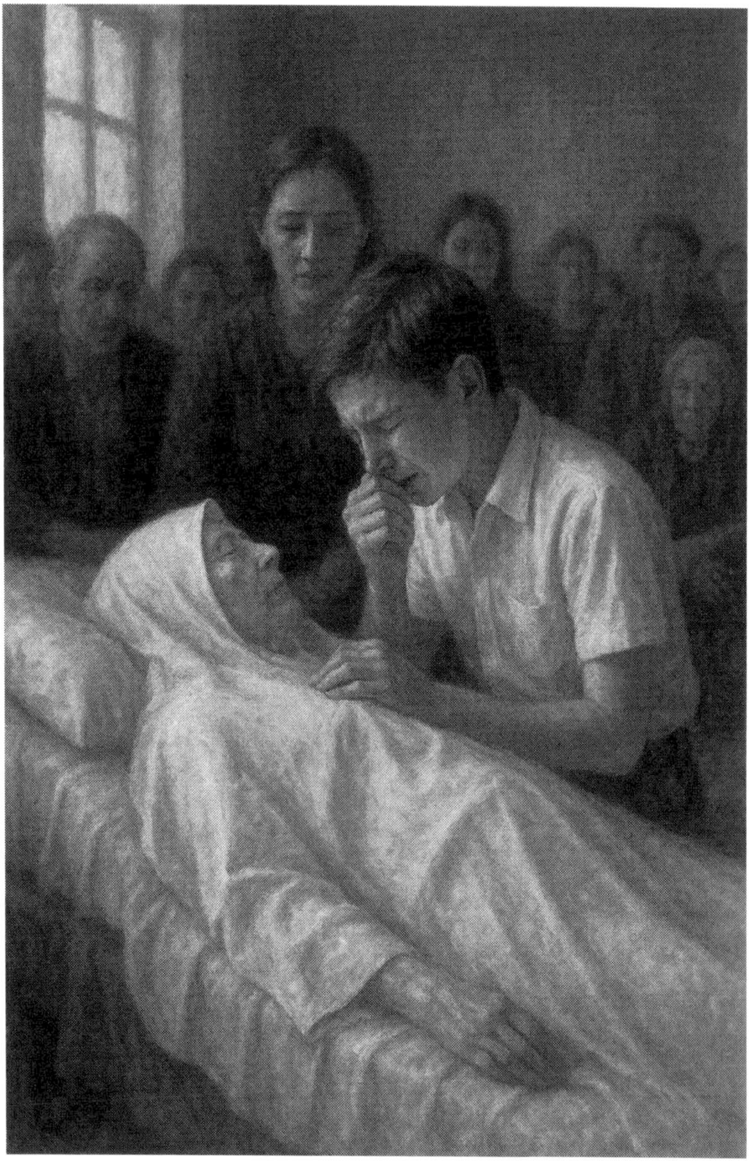

Chapter 4

The Day Love Left

The taxi ride home felt like any other day—the same winding roads, the same gentle hum of the engine beneath me. But as we pulled up in front of my house, something felt off. The gates were wide open, swung so far back they nearly touched the walls. All the windows were open too, as though the house itself was gasping for air. In front of the entrance, a sea of shoes and slippers was scattered—a gathering I hadn't expected.

My heart began to beat faster as I stepped out of the taxi, dread curling through me. I recognized some of the shoes: familiar ones belonging to relatives, neighbours, people who usually only came over on special occasions. I pushed through the small crowd that had formed inside, my feet carrying me straight to her room.

There she was—my grandmother—covered in a white cloth, lying still and silent. I took a step closer, and a relative whispered to me, "She's gone, son." I barely heard them. She had left this world, just as her warmth had left my life so long ago when her illness took over. The finality of it hit me like a blow. Without a word, I pulled back the white cloth, just enough to reveal her face. I leaned down and kissed her forehead, feeling the coolness of her skin, a goodbye that seemed to settle into the deepest parts of my heart. But I couldn't stay there—not in that room filled with the loss of her. I stumbled back, my chest heavy, and made my way to my own room. There, the silence fell over me like a wave, and I finally broke down. The tears came fast, and I cried until I could barely breathe, the pain tearing through me as I grasped the enormity of my loss.

Moments later, I felt the soft touch of my cousin sisters as they hugged me tightly, murmuring, "It's okay, Yohan, it's okay," as they wiped away my tears. They held me like I had imagined an elder sister would—soothing me, trying to fill the hole that my grandmother's love had left. But as much as I appreciated their care, it couldn't truly fill that void. It only reminded me of the irreplaceable bond I had lost.

With my grandmother gone, I sought out that deep love somewhere else. I turned to my mother, hoping to find the same exclusive, boundless affection I had once felt with my grandmother. My mother was loving, yes, and so caring, always there for me. But I craved something that couldn't be shared, a love that was just for me. I needed to feel like I was someone's whole world.

Yet, my mother's heart wasn't mine alone to hold. I could see it every day—her love for my father, the way they looked at each other, spoke to each other. I realized then, painfully, that I was a part of their world, but never the centre of it. Their love wrapped around each other like an embrace that left me just outside, a bystander to a bond I could never truly enter.

At night, I would sleep in my parents' bed, nestled between them, trying to feel included in the love that surrounded me. But most nights, I would wake up to find my father had moved, leaving my mother's side to hold her close. And in those quiet moments, I would feel the pang of disappointment—a reminder of the love I couldn't own.

I was just thirteen, trying to understand emotions too big for me, feelings that had no words. My longing for a love that was only mine grew deeper, and the absence of that love gnawed at my heart, a wound that seemed to grow each day.

Then, one evening, everything shattered. My father, who had long been drawn to the casino, lost a large sum of money. Desperation etched on his face, he turned to my mother, pleading with her to lend him more money so he could try to win it back. My mother refused—her voice quiet but resolute. I watched as frustration boiled over into anger, words turning harsh and unkind. And then, in a moment that felt like it fractured the very foundation of my world, he struck her. The slap echoed through the house, cutting through the air like a knife. My mother, always gentle, always strong, stood there with a silent dignity, her face turned away, refusing to give in to his demands.

The sight of her pain was unbearable, and I felt a fierce protectiveness surge within me. I begged her, pleaded with her to leave with me—to escape to London, where her close relatives lived, where we could find peace. We could tell my father that we'd come back once he'd freed himself from the grip of the casino. But she simply looked at me with sad, tired eyes and said, *"I still love your papa. I cannot go like this."*

Her words hurt more than anything. The man who had struck her, who had chosen gambling over us, still held her heart. She chose him over the chance to escape—over the chance to start fresh with me. I wasn't angry at her—how could I be? But I felt the distance between us grow, a distance that could not be bridged by love alone.

After that, I let them love each other, choosing to stop standing between them. Nights felt different now; instead of sleeping between them, I returned to my own room. I could hear their voices sometimes through the walls—laughter, murmurs of conversation—and I knew I had made the right decision. They had each other, and I had to find a way to live with that.

In the days that followed, I pulled away from her emotionally, retreating into myself, learning to guard my heart from the pain of rejection. I let them love each other, stepping back from the little space I had once held between them. It was painful, but I convinced myself it was necessary. And as I withdrew from my mother, my yearning for an elder sister grew stronger, becoming an obsession. I imagined her by my side—someone who would choose me first, someone who would never walk away or love someone more.

Each day, I longed for her presence—for that deep, undivided love that seemed like a distant dream. It became a desire that filled my thoughts, one that I couldn't let go. My grandmother was gone, my mother's love was shared, and my father was distant, consumed by his own vices. I felt alone in a way I hadn't known was possible, and all I could do was cling to the hope of an elder sister—a figure who existed only in my heart, but who felt more real than anything else in my life.

Chapter 5

The Dream of the Sister

The night was quiet, with only the soft hum of the air-conditioner in my room as I drifted into sleep. I hadn't dreamt of her in a while, but tonight, without warning, she appeared once more in the landscapes of my mind, as vividly as ever.

The dream began with a grand, three-storey house, painted a pristine white. It was the kind of house that looked like it belonged in a fairy tale, its tall fences gleaming in the sunlight, surrounding a garden so well-kept it seemed crafted by nature itself. Every leaf, every petal seemed to dance with life. Beside the house, nestled among fragrant flowers, was a white swinging chair, its graceful curves inviting in the gentle breeze. It was a house filled with warmth, a place that felt like home in ways I'd only dreamed of.

And then, there she was.

She was breathtaking—older, perhaps eight or ten years my senior, with a presence that seemed to fill the entire dream. She had the look of a princess, delicate and regal, and a kindness in her eyes that made me feel safe. Her hair, dark and silky, flowed like a river as she ran after me, her laughter echoing through the garden. I could feel my heart race, not out of fear, but out of joy—a happiness so pure it felt like I'd been holding onto it my whole life.

She called out, her voice ringing with laughter, *"Where do you think you're going to escape to, little one?"* She was closing the distance between us, her earrings glinting in the sunlight, her laughter lighting up the world around us.

When she finally caught me, she wrapped her arms around me, pulling me into a hug so tight it felt like she was trying to pour all her love into me. Her warmth surrounded me, and as she gently pulled back, she pressed a soft kiss to my forehead. *"You are my precious gem,"* she whispered, her voice like a lullaby. *"I will never let you go."*

My heart swelled, feeling full in a way it rarely did in waking life. I looked up at her, smiling, basking in her attention and affection, feeling like I had finally found the one person I had been searching for.

"Are you hungry, little one?" she asked, her gaze tender.

I nodded, unable to find words, and she laughed, guiding me to a small table under the shade of a tree. She fed me with her hands, each bite filled with a warmth that made my heart feel like it was being wrapped in a soft blanket. Her fingers moved gently, and her touch made me feel as though I was the most cherished person in the world.

After we finished, she brought me to a small mirror, her hands reaching for my hair as she began to playfully style it. I laughed, trying to imitate her, running my small fingers through her long, beautiful hair, carefully weaving it into tiny braids. *"You're getting good at this!"* she teased, her eyes shining with pride. *"Maybe one day you'll be better at it than I am!"*

"Oh, I'm already the best," I retorted, grinning.

She chuckled, pulling me into another hug. We sat down, and she picked up a book, her voice gentle as she began to read aloud. I sat by her feet, my back pressed against her knees, feeling the words settle around us like a soft blanket. Each story she read seemed to come alive in her voice, every page a new world she brought to life just for me.

But the most magical moments were at night. She would pull me close, wrapping me in her arms, humming soft lullabies as her fingers drifted through my hair. Her touch was so soothing, and her voice melted away every worry, every ache, every fear.

"Close your eyes, little one," she'd whisper. *"You're safe with me."*

I'd feel the press of her lips against my cheek, then my forehead, and then another kiss on top of my head. *"I'll never let you go. You're my precious gem, my little star. I love you more than anything."*

"I love you more!" I'd say, clinging to her, squeezing her tightly, trying to hold onto this moment, to hold onto her.

But then, as I pulled her close, I felt something strange. My arms didn't wrap around her; instead, they met only the soft, empty resistance of a pillow. I opened my eyes, blinking against the darkness. The three-storey house, the garden, the white fence—all of it had vanished, as though it had never been there at all.

My heart pounded as I realised the truth. I was back in my room, alone, my arms wrapped around a pillow instead of her. The ache of disappointment, of loss, hit me like a wave—a sadness so deep it felt like a cloud descending over me. My elder sister, the one who had filled my heart, who had loved me so completely, wasn't real. She was nothing more than a dream, a beautiful illusion that slipped through my fingers the moment I tried to hold on.

I buried my face in the pillow, clinging to it as though it could somehow bring her back. *"Please… come back,"* I whispered, my voice barely audible. I lay there, eyes closed, desperately wishing to return to the dream, to see her face again, to feel her warmth, even if only for a few more moments.

But the night stretched on, silent and still, and as I drifted back to sleep, the memory of her lingered like a ghost, filling the corners of my mind with whispers of a love I'd only ever known in my dreams.

Whispers of a Dream

Searching for a life in the crying sky,
Waiting for the day you'll come and stay by my side.
Everywhere I go, it's only you I find,
Filling the spaces, living in my mind.

You must have forgotten, but at the dream's end,
You whisper softly, "I'm here, my little one."
It's love from eternity, through every lifetime's tide,
A bond unbroken, forever entwined.

In my eyes, untouched by tears,
You ask why they fall now, what are these fears?
You've always known me, seen what's inside,
A love that lingers, too deep to hide.

Hold me close, till the night is done,
And in the silence, we'll be as one.
Echoes of love, from a past life's tide,
Forever here, forever by my side.

Chapter 6

The Bond of a Sister

My grandmother's brother, known around town as Mr. De Mel, was a man of respect and reputation. Once a high-ranking government officer, he was now the President of the Town's Elder Society. Although retired, he still carried the influence of his past work and often found ways to contribute to the community. One of his initiatives was a free one-year Tamil language course for anyone over sixteen years old. In our country, Tamil is the second language, with Sinhalese being the first, and it was a chance for locals to connect with each other on a deeper level.

Mr. De Mel pulled a few strings and enrolled me in the programme. *"You're only thirteen, Yohan, but I know you'll manage. You're bright,"* he said, smiling as he handed me the materials. *"Besides, learning Tamil will open up a whole new world for you."*

Excited but nervous, I showed up on the first day right on time. As I entered the classroom, I was the youngest there by years. I saw many unfamiliar, older faces around me—faces that held no recognition or comfort. I took a few hesitant steps, scanning the room, when suddenly, a soft

"Hi!" accompanied by a warm smile caught my eye. A girl waved at me, her fingers moving in a gentle greeting.

It took me a moment to recognise her. *"Ravishki?"* I asked, my eyes widening.

She laughed, her eyes lighting up. *"Yes, it's me! I didn't expect to see you here, Yohan!"*

Ravishki, the daughter of my father's old classmate, was eighteen, and we'd only met briefly at family gatherings before. But at that moment, she was a beacon in a sea of strangers. I quickly made my way over to her and took the seat beside her, relieved to see a familiar face.

The class instructor, a young, cheerful Muslim woman, introduced herself and began the lesson. Around the room, I noticed several older students who were clearly couples, holding hands or whispering to each other. It was a new experience for me, being around people so openly connected, but with Ravishki next to me, I felt a strange sense of belonging.

Every week, I'd meet Ravishki at the class. She was always warm and kind, treating me with a gentle care that felt both exciting and comforting. One day, after we'd been writing notes for hours, I looked at her, my hand aching from the endless scribbling.

"My hand hurts," I muttered, rubbing my wrist.

She gave me a soft smile. *"Pass me your notebook. I'll write the notes for you,"* she said.

I hesitated, but her smile was so inviting that I handed her my notebook. She began to write my notes, and as she did, I felt a warmth spreading in my chest—a sense of gratitude mixed with awe. She had such a gentle touch, an effortless kindness that made me feel seen.

As the weeks passed, we grew closer. One day, I came to class with a pounding headache. I could barely keep my eyes open, the pain dull and persistent.

"You look pale, Yohan. Are you all right?" she asked, concern in her eyes.

I shook my head. *"Just a headache... nothing serious,"* I replied, trying to smile.

Without hesitation, she moved closer and gently pulled my head to rest on her shoulder. I let out a sigh of relief, closing my eyes as her fingers began to massage my temples. Her touch was soft and soothing, and I felt as though I was floating. The world around me seemed to fade, leaving only the warmth of her presence.

"There you go," she whispered. *"Just relax."*

That simple act meant everything to me. It was the first time I had experienced such closeness with someone outside my family, and I could feel my heart swell with something I couldn't quite name. Week after week, I found myself looking forward to the moments when I could lean against her shoulder, feeling her fingers trace gentle circles against my temples. Teenagers' emotions are tender and sweet, for they cherish the ones they love with boundless admiration, seeing them as rare and exquisite treasures.

One afternoon, as we sat together in the back of the class, she reached out and took my hand, her fingers intertwining with mine. The touch sent a thrill through me, a feeling of connection that was so pure, so complete. I looked at her, my heart racing, and I knew in that moment that she was more than just a friend to me. She was the sister I had always longed for, the sister from my dreams.

The year flew by, and before I knew it, the course was over. I couldn't bear the thought of not seeing her again. She had become such an important part of my life, and the idea of letting go of that bond felt like a loss I couldn't face.

In the final days of the class, I poured my feelings into a letter. I included a poem I'd written, hoping it would convey the depth of my affection:

To be in your arms,
At least one moment at a time,
In a still moment, in an early morning,
Stay warm in your arms.

In the letter, I asked her to become my elder sister, to be the person I could always turn to. I shared my dreams, my hopes, my promise to be there for her, just as she had been for me.

One afternoon, I rode my bicycle to her house, clutching the letter in my hand. I told myself that I'd give it to her, that I'd find the courage to share my heart. But when she opened the door, her smile so warm and kind, my courage wavered. Instead of handing her the letter, I asked, *"Could I borrow a camera, if you have one?"*

She looked surprised but nodded. *"Of course, Yohan. Wait here."*

I left her house with the camera in my hand, my letter still folded in my pocket. I hadn't been able to share my feelings—the words heavy and unspoken. Tears pricked at my eyes as I rode away, the weight of my unfulfilled wish pressing down on me.

In the silence of my heart, I turned to the only place I could think of: the church. My family were devout Roman Catholics, and the church had always been a place of comfort. I walked to the altar, my knees hitting the cold stone floor as I clasped my hands together, my head bowed in prayer. *"Please,"* I whispered, my voice thick with emotion. *"If there's a way... please let me find the love of an elder sister. Even if just for one day."*

The days turned to weeks, and I continued to visit the church, each visit a silent plea. I began to read the Bible, memorising verses and finding comfort in the words. I even served as an altar boy, hoping that my devotion might bring me closer to the wish I held so deeply—to have an elder sister. My devotion became a ritual, a way to ease the ache in my heart, and eventually, I won prizes in Bible memorisation competitions. But despite my prayers, my wishes, and my dedication, the love I sought never came. Each prayer, each hope, led only to disappointment.

MEDITATIONS

Chapter 7

The Path to Insight

In those teenage years, my imagination often ran wild with the worlds I watched on television. I was fascinated by characters with supernatural powers—beings who could bend reality, see beyond the veil of the mundane, or control the elements with a mere thought. I dreamed of having those powers myself, and that desire took root deep within me.

Driven by that fascination, I began exploring ways to achieve what I believed was possible. Hindu meditation books introduced me to the concept of *Kundalini*, a powerful spiritual energy that, if awakened, could grant extraordinary abilities. Night after night, I pored over those books, practising the meditations they described, hoping to unlock the hidden potential within me.

At the same time, school introduced me to another philosophy: Buddhism. Though I was born into a Catholic family, Buddhism became one of my favourite subjects. Its profound ideas intrigued me, especially the concept of *Anatta*—non-self or the absence of a permanent soul. One day, while walking home with Sahan, my best friend, I asked him about it.

"Sahan," I began hesitantly, "what does *Anatta* really mean? No soul? No self? It's… confusing."

Sahan, always calm and thoughtful, adjusted his glasses before answering. "It's not easy to explain, Yohan. But think of it like this: everything we think of as 'I'—our body, mind, feelings, thoughts—are constantly changing. There's no permanent core holding it all together. It's like… trying to catch the wind."

His words stayed with me, lingering in my mind like a whisper that refused to fade. Though I didn't fully grasp the concept then, it sparked a curiosity that would later reshape my entire way of thinking.

While reading my Hindu meditation books, I stumbled upon a section that mentioned Buddhist teachings. It spoke of meditative practices that could lead to supernatural powers—abilities like seeing distant worlds or hearing sounds beyond ordinary perception. Excited, I began to delve deeper into Buddhist philosophy, borrowing books from libraries and asking my teachers for recommendations.

Around that time, my class teacher, Ms. Disna, noticed my interest. One day after class, she handed me a book. *"Yohan,"* she said with a smile, *"I think you'll like this. It's by Venerable Rerukane Chandawimala Maha Thera, one of the greatest Buddhist scholars of our time. It's about the Chathurarya Sathya—the Four Noble Truths."*

"Thank you, Miss!" I said, taking the book eagerly. I had no idea then that this simple gesture would change the course of my life.

The book was unlike anything I had ever read. It spoke of desires as mirages—illusions that promised happiness but left only restlessness and pain in their wake. It described the self as a fabrication, a fleeting collection of thoughts and sensations with no true substance. It unveiled the reality of existence—not as a place of joy, but as a web of suffering, held together by ignorance and craving. And yet, it offered a way out: relinquishing desires and understanding the illusion of self could lead to ultimate freedom.

Each page struck a chord within me. The ideas felt both profound and unsettling, shaking the very foundation of my beliefs. I began to realise that chasing supernatural powers was like reaching for smoke—it would never bring true peace. Instead, the key lay in understanding the nature of the mind and body, and through that understanding, breaking free from the illusions that bound us.

From that point on, I turned my attention entirely to Buddhist teachings. I sought out the *Sutta Pitaka*, the original discourses of Lord Buddha, and began reading them fervently. Some passages were difficult to understand, their meanings hidden beneath layers of subtlety. But I didn't give up. I read them two, three, sometimes four times, taking notes and piecing together their insights.

At school, I carried Buddhist books in my bag, sneaking in a few pages during free periods or intervals. On the taxi ride home, I'd read until the rumbling of the engine became background noise. Even at home, my mind was consumed by the teachings. One day, I came across a keyword that would define my journey: *Vipassana*—insight meditation, a practice said to lead to liberation and enlightenment.

I was thrilled. But in those early days of the internet, resources were scarce. I searched online, but there were no clear guidelines for practising *Vipassana.* Determined to learn, I decided to visit the temples in my town, hoping to find a monk who could teach me.

Most of the monks I approached gave kind but unhelpful answers. *"You're too young,"* they'd say, or, *"Vipassana is too advanced for someone your age."* My frustration grew, but I refused to give up.

One afternoon, during a Buddhism lesson at school, I raised my hand. "Mrs. Chandani," I began hesitantly, "how do you practise *Vipassana* meditation?"

She looked at me with a mix of surprise and amusement. *"Yohan,"* she said gently, *"you're still very young. Vipassana is a deep practice, and it's not something to rush into. But you can start with something simpler. Have you tried walking meditation?"*

"No, miss," I admitted.

"Let me show you," she said. After class, she demonstrated the basics of walking meditation: slow, mindful steps, synchronised with the breath. I practised it diligently, grateful for her guidance, but deep down, my

heart yearned for more. Walking meditation was calming, but it didn't satisfy my inner drive to uncover the truths I had read about.

As the days turned into weeks, my pursuit of *Vipassana* became an obsession. I could feel the teachings shaping me, transforming the way I saw the world. The allure of supernatural powers faded, replaced by a burning desire to understand the nature of reality, to unravel the mysteries of existence, and to find freedom from the illusions that held me captive.

And so, my journey continued, fuelled by curiosity, determination, and a growing sense that I was inching closer to something profound—a truth that lay just beyond the horizon, waiting to be discovered.

Chapter 8

The Turning Point

The 20th of April, 2017, was an ordinary Thursday. It had been exactly two months since my grandmother's passing, and life, despite its cracks and sorrows, moved forward. I went to school as usual, my bag heavier than before with Buddhist books tucked inside. During the break, I found Sahan sitting under the old Indian Almond tree where we often talked about philosophy and life.

"Sahan," I said, sitting down next to him, "I want to learn *Vipassana*. Properly. Not just walking meditation or what I've been trying to piece together from books."

He raised an eyebrow. "Why this sudden urge?" he asked, though his tone was curious rather than dismissive.

"I don't know," I admitted, fiddling with my pen. "I've been reading about it, and it feels… important. Like it's the answer to something I've been searching for."

Sahan nodded thoughtfully, leaning back against the tree, his gaze fixed on the distance. "There's an old man in town," he began, his voice measured. "Mr. Somarathne. My father used to meditate under him before…" He paused briefly, his expression clouding for a moment. "…before he passed away from a heart attack."

He continued after a breath, his tone soft but reverent. "Mr. Somarathne was a monk once. They say he meditated in a cave for years, completely dedicated to the practice. But then he got paralyzed, and his family brought him back home to care for him. Even now, though, he teaches meditation to those who seek him out. Perhaps he can guide you."

There was a sense of quiet respect in Sahan's words, and the name—*Mr. Somarathne*—seemed to linger in the air, like the beginning of a path waiting to be walked.

His words felt like a spark igniting something within me. "Really?" I asked, excitement bubbling up. "Do you know where he lives?"

"Yes," he replied, "but it's a bit far. And I don't think you'll have time to go today."

"Of course, I will," I said, grinning. "Here's the plan: I'll call your mum and tell her we have afterschool activities, so she won't expect you home early. We'll have lunch at a hotel buffet—I'm treating. But you have to come with me to meet this man."

Sahan chuckled. "All right, Yohan. You've convinced me. Let's go after school."

The rest of the day passed in a blur of anticipation. As soon as the final bell rang, Sahan and I headed to the address he had given me. The house was small and unassuming, nestled on a quiet street. An old mango tree shaded the front yard, its roots curling into the earth like ancient fingers.

We knocked on the wooden door, and after a moment, it creaked open. A frail man in his late seventies sat in a wheelchair, his face lined with years of wisdom and struggle. His eyes, however, were sharp and piercing, as though they could see through the fabric of the world itself.

"Come in," he said, his voice soft but steady.

Inside, the air was filled with the faint aroma of incense. A small shrine dedicated to Lord Buddha stood in the corner, its simplicity adding to the room's serene atmosphere. Sahan introduced us, explaining my desire to learn *Vipassana* meditation.

The old man studied me for a long moment, then nodded. "Very well," he said. "Sit down, and I will guide you."

I sat cross-legged on the mat, my heart racing with a mix of excitement and nervousness. He began to speak, his voice calm and deliberate. "*Vipassana* is the practice of seeing things as they truly are," he explained. "It begins with understanding the five clinging aggregates—

form, feeling, perception, mental formations, and consciousness. These are what we cling to as the self, but they are impermanent, empty, and not truly ours. You must observe them with clarity and detachment."

His words resonated deeply, but it was during the meditation itself that I felt their true power. As I focused on my breath, he guided me through a process of discerning the non-self in each aggregate. At first, it was subtle—just a sense of distance between myself and the sensations I usually identified with. But as the meditation deepened, I felt a profound relief washing over me, like a heavy weight being lifted from my shoulders.

When the session ended, the old man said, "The path of insight is not easy, but it is the only path to true liberation. If you are ready, I will also bring you to the refuge of Lord Buddha and observe the five precepts."

I nodded eagerly. He led me through the ceremony, and for the first time, I formally took refuge in the *Buddha, Dhamma,* and *Sangha*, and committed to the five precepts. The act felt both solemn and transformative, as though I had crossed a threshold into a new chapter of my life.

From that day on, I visited him whenever I could, skipping lunch to spend time learning and meditating under his guidance. My school schedule was packed with tuition classes every other day, but on the free days, I made my way to his house, eager to learn more.

Then, on the 27th of April, 2017—just a week after meeting him—something extraordinary happened. I was practising *Vipassana*, focusing on the aggregates as he had taught me. Slowly, I began to feel a profound stillness. My thoughts grew quieter until they disappeared altogether. I felt as though I was being absorbed into a vast emptiness, an ecstasy unlike anything I had ever known. But even in that bliss, I realised that emptiness itself was not mine to claim. It, too, was a fabrication, a product of the mind's causes and effects.

And then it happened: a stilling of all preparations. Sensations ceased; perceptions faded. For a few minutes, it was as though the world had been turned off. There was no "I," no emptiness, no self to grasp. When I emerged from the meditation, I felt lighter, freer, as though I had touched the edge of something infinite.

That day marked a turning point. The overwhelming desire for an elder sister—the longing that had consumed me for years—began to fade. It didn't disappear entirely, but it felt more distant, like a shadow that no longer dictated my emotions. I continued to meditate under the old man's guidance for over a year, deepening my understanding and finding a peace I had never thought possible.

The path of insight was not always easy, but it gave me something far greater than supernatural powers or fleeting desires. It gave me a glimpse of the truth—a truth that would guide me for the rest of my life.

Chapter 9

The Crossroads

Time flowed steadily after my transformative experience with Mr. Somarathne, but life, as always, brought change. One afternoon, as I prepared to visit him for another meditation session, I received devastating news: Mr. Somarathne had passed away. His teachings had left a deep imprint on my heart, and I felt both a profound sense of gratitude and a lingering void. But his death ignited a new resolve within me—I couldn't stop now. The journey had to continue.

I began dedicating my weekends to visiting meditation centres around Colombo. Each week, I would hop on a taxi and travel to new places in search of someone who could guide me further in *Vipassana.* Many of the teachers I met introduced methods that felt inconsistent with the original teachings of Lord Buddha. Having read the *Sutta Pitaka*, I could discern when techniques veered away from the authentic path. It frustrated me, but it also pushed me to delve deeper into my own practice.

Even as I grew in my understanding of meditation, the desire for an elder sister remained. Though diminished, it was a fire that refused to go out entirely. In moments of mindfulness, the longing was manageable, like a faint shadow in the background of my mind. But when I was sick or upset, it would resurface with full force, consuming me. In those moments, I felt raw, vulnerable, and utterly alone. I would cry, sometimes for hours, overwhelmed by the absence of someone who existed only in my dreams.

Desperate for clarity, I decided to seek professional help. I made an appointment with Dr. Jayan Mendis, one of the most renowned psychiatrists in Sri Lanka at the time. I went alone, not wanting to involve my family in this deeply personal struggle.

Dr. Mendis welcomed me with a kind smile. "Come in, son. Let's talk."

I sat across from him, nervously explaining my feelings—my relentless desire for an elder sister, and how it dominated my thoughts in moments of weakness. He listened patiently, his expression never wavering, as though he understood every word.

After what felt like hours, he finally leaned forward, resting his hands on his desk. "Son," he said gently, "you don't have a problem. You don't need to see another psychiatrist. What you're experiencing is not abnormal—it's simply the result of your longing for deep emotional connection. If you can, try to find an elder sister figure, someone who can fulfil that role. Or," he added with a knowing smile, "continue your meditations. That is your solution."

I nodded, grateful for his reassurance, but deep down, I already knew the truth. Even if I found someone to play the role of an elder sister, it wouldn't truly solve my problem. She would eventually leave—through marriage, life circumstances, or even death. And she would never be the idealised version I dreamed of. My desire was a mirage, an endless chase after something that could never be fulfilled. Yet, even knowing this, I couldn't entirely control my emotions, especially when I was at my weakest.

Over the years, the absence of an elder sister shaped my relationships with women. I never pursued girlfriends; the idea of giving love didn't appeal to me. I wanted to be the one taken care of, the one cherished and adored, just as I imagined an elder sister would do. When elder cousin sisters showed me kindness or young teachers cared for me at school, that same longing would resurface. But each time, I turned to my meditative practice, focusing on the repulsiveness of the body and the non-self of my feelings and theirs. I began to see the delusion in my desires more clearly, dissecting their origins and recognising their fleeting nature.

Still, I found myself caught in a duality. A part of me wondered if I could find peace by eventually marrying someone who embodied the qualities I longed for in an elder sister. Would a partner like that fill the void in my heart? But the other part of me knew the truth: these desires were illusions, born of the mind's endless craving. True freedom lay not in fulfilling them, but in understanding their nature and transcending them.

One night, as I sat in silent reflection, a thought struck me like lightning. *"If Lord Buddha was correct,"* I murmured to myself, *"then there's no greater path than the one he showed. He needed nothing from us—no offerings, no devotion. People worship him out of gratitude, not because he asked for it. If he truly uncovered the ultimate reality, then there's nothing left for me to question. I must follow his teachings and seek liberation."*

With that realisation, my path became clear. I decided that after completing my Advanced Level exams, I would ordain as a monk. The thought filled me with both peace and determination.

I no longer needed to chase after fleeting desires or try to mould the world to fit my dreams. The road to *Nibbāna* was in front of me, and I was ready to walk it.

In the days that followed, I carried this resolve like a flame in my heart. The longing for an elder sister still lingered, but it no longer ruled me. Instead, it became a reminder of the illusions I was learning to transcend—a teacher in its own way, guiding me toward the truth.

And so, with each passing day, I grew closer to a life of renunciation, ready to leave behind the mirages of the world and step into the light of liberation.

Chapter 10

The Forest of Resolve

The middle-term exams of Grade 10 were over, and as expected, I had secured the top position in the entire grade. My teachers and peers celebrated my success, but my mind was already elsewhere, fixated on the path that had been growing clearer to me with every passing day. I longed to deepen my meditation practice, to immerse myself in an environment where I could pursue the teachings of Lord Buddha without distraction. I approached my parents with a determined voice.

"I want to attend a meditation retreat," I declared.

My father looked at me with a mixture of surprise and hesitation. "A retreat? For how long?"

"Fifteen days," I replied. "I've found a monastery in Diyathalawa town that conducts them."

At first, they resisted, unwilling to let me go. But I persisted, presenting arguments and promises until, reluctantly, they gave their permission. My father drove me to the monastery himself, the car ride filled with his cautionary advice and my quiet determination.

The monastery in Diyathalawa was serene, nestled amidst rolling hills and misty mornings. But as the days went by, I realised that the techniques taught there didn't align with the pure, early doctrines I had studied. The methods were well-intentioned but seemed overly customised, deviating from the original teachings of Lord Buddha.

One afternoon, as I shared my thoughts with a monk at the monastery, he nodded understandingly. "If you're looking for guidance rooted in the earliest doctrines," he said, "there's an old monk—Venerable Saddhaseela Thera—living deep in a forest in a rural village. He's known for his strict adherence to the original teachings. If you can find him, he may be able to guide you."

His words sparked a new resolve in me. That same day, after the midday meal, I packed my belongings and boarded a bus to the village he mentioned. The journey was long, and the roads grew narrower and more rugged as the bus approached the forested area. When the bus dropped me off, I found myself standing at the edge of a vast, untamed wilderness. I knew the path ahead was fraught with danger—tuskers, elephants, and even bears roamed these forests—but my motivation to find a true master burned brighter than my fear.

As I ventured deeper into the forest, the trees seemed to close in around me, their branches casting long shadows across the uneven trail. The rustling of leaves and distant calls of unseen animals kept me on edge, but I pressed on. Finally, after what felt like hours, I arrived at a small, secluded hermitage where Venerable Saddhaseela Thera resided.

The old monk emerged from his hut, his gaze calm and penetrating. "Little one," he said, his voice steady, "where have you come from? And what do you seek from me?"

Gathering my courage, I bowed deeply and replied, "Venerable Sir, I have come to learn meditation. I wish to practise until I attain complete enlightenment."

The monk studied me for a moment before nodding. "Very well. First, go and bathe in the well nearby."

I had never bathed in a well before, but I followed his instructions, pulling up the cool, fresh water and letting it wash away the dust and sweat from my journey. When I returned, he gestured to a small corridor outside his hut.

"You will live here," he said. "Monks cannot share a room with anyone. You may use this space."

He explained that the villagers provided alms only once a day, around noon, as it was too dangerous to venture into the forest during the early mornings due to the presence of elephants. Monks, bound by strict discipline, could not cook for themselves, and so their sustenance relied entirely on the generosity of the villagers.

After I arrived, the villagers decided to build a small hut with a wood-fired stove near the hermitage. One afternoon, a kind elderly villager approached me with a warm smile. "Son," he said gently, "please cook for yourself and the master. It will be a great help."

I hesitated, wringing my hands nervously. "But… Uncle, I've never cooked before," I admitted, my voice tinged with uncertainty.

The old man chuckled softly, his eyes twinkling. "Don't worry, son. Try your best. It will be one of the greatest merits you can ever do."

Encouraged by his words, I decided to give it a try. Though I had never cooked a meal before, I drew on faint memories of watching my mother in the kitchen. With time and patience, I learned to prepare simple but nourishing meals for my master and myself. Each morning, I would light the wood fire, the smell of burning logs mingling with the fresh forest air, and begin the task that had quickly become a part of my routine.

Monks followed a strict discipline, refraining from eating after noon until the dawn of the next day. To honour this practice, I, too, refrained from eating in the afternoons, sharing in the simplicity and restraint of monastic life. For three months, I prepared meals each morning, feeling a quiet sense of fulfilment in serving my master. Each meal was an offering not just of food but of dedication and gratitude, a small way to repay the immeasurable wisdom he shared with me.

Under Venerable Saddhaseela's guidance, I immersed myself in meditation for three months. Each day began with the practice of observing the aggregates, discerning their impermanence, and peeling away the layers of illusion that veiled the truth. Slowly, I felt my understanding deepen.

My parents, however, were less than thrilled. They visited often, pleading with me to return home. "Yohan," my mother said one afternoon, her voice heavy with emotion, "you're too young for this. Come back with us. You can meditate at home."

I shook my head. "Mama, I'm not leaving. This is where I need to be."

Their visits became more frequent, their pleas more desperate. Finally, my father threatened to file a police complaint against Venerable Saddhaseela if I didn't return. The thought of causing trouble for my teacher left me no choice. Reluctantly, I packed my belongings and returned home.

Back in the familiar confines of our house, I tried to maintain my meditation practice, dedicating my days to listening to Dhamma sermons, particularly those of Venerable Katukurunde Ñānananda Maha Thera and Venerable Dhaṇkande Dhammāratana Maha Thera. But home came with its own challenges. Relatives visited frequently, and I was often dragged to family gatherings. In those moments, my old longing for an elder sister resurfaced.

One day, while travelling in a crowded car with my relatives, I found myself sitting on one of my cousin sister Binari's laps due to the lack of space. Throughout the journey, she held me tightly, her arms wrapped around me as she chatted cheerfully about various things. Her gesture was entirely innocent, a natural expression of affection. Yet, for me, it stirred something deeper—an ache I had been striving to let go of for so long.

That simple moment reignited the mental proliferations I had worked tirelessly to suppress. For weeks afterward, my mind spiralled, consumed once more by the unfulfilled longing for an elder sister's love. The feelings I had thought were fading returned with an intensity that left me restless and conflicted.

In those weeks of inner turmoil, I came to a painful but undeniable realisation: the only way to truly free myself from this cycle of craving and sorrow was to fully commit to the path of renunciation. Only by letting go of all attachments could I hope to find the peace I so deeply sought.

I sat in my room one evening, staring at the small shrine I had built. *"This longing,"* I murmured to myself, *"it's just another mirage. A fabrication of the mind. I must let it go."*

The words of Lord Buddha echoed in my mind: *Craving is the root of suffering.* If I truly believed in his teachings, there was only one path left for me to take.

"I will ordain," I whispered, the resolve settling in my heart like a flame. *"I will dedicate my life to understanding the truth and freeing myself from this endless cycle of desire."*

My parents, however, were adamant. "We will never allow it," my father said firmly. "Meditate at home, Yohan. We'll support you, but we won't let you ordain."

I nodded, knowing they wouldn't change their minds. But deep within, my decision was already made. It was only a matter of time before I would step into the robes of a monk, leaving behind the mirages of the world and walking the path toward ultimate liberation.

Chapter 11

The Dawn of Renunciation

I was fifteen when the call to renounce my household life grew louder than ever before. It wasn't just a fleeting thought or a passing desire—it was a relentless pull, deep and unwavering, echoing through every part of my being. The craving for worldly attachments, especially the haunting desire for an elder sister, had tormented me for years. Now, I felt that the only way to break free from this endless cycle was to step onto the path of full renunciation.

One ordinary afternoon, my parents had gone to town, leaving me alone at home. The house was unusually silent, the kind of silence that allows thoughts to surface without distraction. I sat cross-legged on the floor, my heart heavy yet determined, listening to a Dhamma sermon on YouTube by Venerable Dankande Dhammaratana Maha Thera. His words resonated with me like never before, piercing through the layers of my restless mind. *"If one seeks true liberation, one must be brave enough to walk alone, to let go, and to see the truth beyond illusions."* Those words felt like a spark igniting a long-buried flame within me. A powerful surge of motivation washed over me. I knew then—I couldn't delay this decision any longer.

Without hesitation, I reached for my wallet, where I had around 10,000 rupees. My hands trembled slightly as I scrolled through my phone, trying to contact various monasteries across the country. *"Will you ordain me without my parents' permission?"* I asked each monk I managed to reach. But the answer was always the same—a hesitant no. Most monasteries were reluctant to ordain someone so young without parental consent.

Frustration grew, but I refused to give up. Then, almost like fate intervening, I remembered a forest monastery in Anuradhapura. I had been following their page on Facebook for some time, drawn to their simple, disciplined lifestyle. On impulse, I sent a message to the abbot. To my surprise, he responded quickly. *"Yohan,"* he wrote, *"if you are truly determined, come here. I will ordain you without your parents' approval. I promise I will find a way to gain their consent eventually."* His words felt like a door opening—a door I had been searching for all my life. Without another thought, I packed a small bag, took my wallet, and booked a first-class train ticket from Colombo to Anuradhapura. It was a long, nearly nine-hour journey, but my heart raced with anticipation, not exhaustion. I switched off my phone, cutting off all ties to the world I was leaving behind.

The train rumbled through the night, its rhythmic clatter matching the steady beat of my heart. I stared out of the window, watching the dark landscape pass by, knowing that with every mile, I was leaving behind everything I'd ever known—my family, my home, my past. But there was no sadness, only a quiet determination.

When I arrived at the Anuradhapura station around 9:30 p.m., the abbot had sent a lay disciple to meet me. Under the dim station lights, I followed him silently, my bag slung over my shoulder, feeling both weightless and heavy at the same time.

The monastery was a quiet sanctuary nestled amidst towering trees and ancient ruins, its simplicity profound under the star-lit sky. After settling into a small room, I borrowed a phone from one of the monks and called my parents. My mother answered.

"Mama," I said softly, *"I'm in Anuradhapura. I've come to a monastery to ordain."*

There was a long pause on the other end before panic erupted in her voice. *"Yohan, what are you saying? You can't do this! We're coming right now."*

Within ten hours, as the morning sun began to rise, my parents arrived at the monastery, their faces filled with a mixture of fear, anger, and desperation. They tried everything to persuade me to come back home. My father's voice grew louder with frustration, while my mother's eyes brimmed with tears.

But I remained firm. *"This is what I need,"* I told them. *"Please understand. I'm not running away from you—I'm running towards the truth."*

For three days, the arguments continued. My father's patience grew thinner, and on the third day, in a fit of frustration, he tried to forcefully pull me towards the car. I resisted, tears streaming down my face. **"If you take me today," I cried out,**

my voice trembling but fierce, "I will end my life. I swear, I will."

Those words, raw and desperate, shattered the tension in the air. My mother's face went pale with fear. She broke down, her sobs filling the silent monastery grounds. Finally, through her tears, she whispered, *"If this is what you truly want, then… I give you my blessing."*

Relief washed over me like a wave. On the fourth day of my renunciation, I was ordained as a novice monk in a simple ceremony. My parents, still emotional, left shortly after, their hearts heavy but their love evident in every glance they gave me.

My new life began with quiet simplicity. I dedicated myself to meditation with unwavering discipline, often practising *Vipassana*—insight meditation—for up to seven hours a day. The abbot, recognising my dedication, granted me special permission to focus almost entirely on my practice, freeing me from many of the typical monastic duties. However, not everyone viewed this favour positively. Some senior monks grew envious, their subtle remarks and cold glances a constant reminder of the fragile nature of human emotions—even within monastic walls.

But I paid no attention. My mind was fixed on my goal. I sought solitude whenever possible, spending weeks meditating in caves near the monastery. The stillness of the forest, the distant calls of wild animals, and the rustling of leaves became my companions. On occasion, I even ventured to the remote caves near Adam's Peak (*Sri Pada*), seeking deeper isolation to sharpen my focus.

As months passed, I mastered the art of *Vipassana*, dissecting the nature of existence with each breath, each moment of mindfulness. Yet, a part of me longed to explore another dimension of the Buddha's teachings—*Samatha* meditation, the art of tranquillity and concentration.

I knew that many renowned Sri Lankan meditation masters had travelled to Myanmar to study *Samatha* under highly skilled teachers. The abbot of my monastery had once been a disciple of one such master in Myanmar. Inspired by this connection, I made a decision that would shape the next chapter of my journey. *"I wish to go to Myanmar,"* I told the abbot one evening, my voice steady with resolve. *"I want to deepen my practice of Samatha meditation under a master who truly understands the path of tranquillity."*

The abbot looked at me for a long moment, his gaze filled with both pride and understanding. *"Then go,"* he said quietly. *"The path of the Dhamma knows no boundaries. May your journey lead you to the peace you seek."* And so, with nothing but a small bag, a heart filled with determination, and the robes that symbolised my renunciation, I prepared to leave for Myanmar—to dive deeper into the ocean of the mind, seeking not just knowledge but liberation itself.

Chapter 12

Shadows in Silence

Leaving the familiar shores of Sri Lanka, I embarked on my journey to Myanmar with a heart filled with hope and determination. My mind was set on one goal—to master *Samatha* meditation, the art of tranquil concentration that could complement the insight I had cultivated through years of *Vipassana* practice. It felt like the next natural step in my spiritual path, a deeper descent into the vast ocean of the mind.

Before departing, I was required to submit an online form detailing my previous meditation experiences, the level of understanding I had achieved, and the insights I had gained. I filled it out truthfully, describing my journey through *Vipassana*, my practices, and the realisations that had shaped me. I thought little of it at the time, believing that such honesty would be respected in a place dedicated to the pursuit of enlightenment.

But reality, I soon discovered, was far from my expectations.

Upon my arrival at the monastery—a vast compound bustling with over a thousand monks, novices, and practitioners—I felt an initial sense of awe. The towering pagodas, the rhythmic chants, and the serene faces of those immersed in meditation created an atmosphere that seemed otherworldly. Yet beneath this surface of calm, darker currents flowed.

Unbeknownst to me, a Sri Lankan monk had taken my application and shared it within certain Sri Lankan Buddhist groups online. My meditation methods, rooted deeply in early Buddhist teachings, differed from the structured techniques favoured in that monastery. Instead of being met with curiosity or respect, my practices became the subject of ridicule. By the time I stepped through the monastery gates, whispers had already spread among the Sri Lankan immigrant monks.

From the very first day, the bullying began—not from strangers, but from those I had assumed would be my brothers in the Dhamma. They mocked my youth, my experiences, even my aspirations. I was the youngest among them, a seventeen-year-old boy caught in a web of jealousy and ego cloaked in robes.

But despite the isolation, I didn't waver. My resolve grew stronger with each passing day. I committed myself to rigorous meditation, sitting for 9 to 11 hours daily, diving deep into the stillness of my mind. Even when exhaustion gnawed at me, even when the laughter and snide remarks echoed in the background, I sat—unmoving, unshaken. Meditation became my refuge, my rebellion against the noise around me.

On my birthday, I decided to offer *dāna*—a full day's worth of alms to the entire monastery. It was an act of gratitude, a silent prayer woven into the generosity of giving. Providing for over a thousand individuals was costly, but I did it wholeheartedly.

Interestingly, not a single monk showed signs of jealousy. Perhaps it was because this was the first and only individual *dāna* offered by a Sri Lankan to that monastery. My actions spoke louder than any words, rooted not in pride but in pure intention.

As my practice deepened, I pushed the limits of my endurance. Some days, I meditated without sleep for four consecutive days. By the fourth day, sleep became an overwhelming force, pulling at the edges of my consciousness. Eventually, I succumbed, dozing off during my meditation. Little did I know that one of the monks recorded me in that vulnerable moment and shared it with Sri Lankan monastic groups, mocking me once again.

In the midst of this chaos, I met Venerable Vimalavansa—a Sri Lankan monk who initially appeared different from the rest. He was an intelligent, eloquent man, a former consultant gynaecologist who had renounced his prestigious career for the monastic path. His charisma was undeniable, and his knowledge of Pali intrigued me.

"You seem dedicated," he said one evening after noticing me in the meditation hall. *"Would you like to join me in my room sometimes? I can teach you Pali."*

Loneliness had been my silent companion for too long, and the offer of mentorship felt like a rare comfort. I agreed. At first, our meetings were filled with discussions on Buddhist philosophy, language, and the subtleties of ancient texts. I trusted him, believing I had finally found someone genuine amidst the hostility.

But slowly, the cracks began to show.

Venerable Vimalavansa grew increasingly possessive, demanding my attention beyond the boundaries of simple mentorship. He insisted I visit his room every evening for coffee, even when I preferred solitude after long hours of meditation. His moods shifted unpredictably—if I didn't smile at him in the dining hall or if I happened to be speaking with someone else, he would sulk, growing visibly irritated.

His need for control crept into every corner of my life. *"Who just called you?"* he'd ask sharply whenever my phone rang. *"Why didn't you mention you were meeting someone?"*

I felt suffocated. The teachings I had come seeking were buried beneath layers of manipulation and emotional control. I found solace in conversations with another monk—Venerable Kumarabodhi, an Indian senior monk whose wisdom carried a calm authority.

"One day," Kumarabodhi said quietly, his eyes kind but serious, *"you need to distance yourself from Vimalavansa. He's a narcissist. Trust me, I've seen it before. Look it up for yourself."*

That evening, I searched for information on narcissistic behaviours. As I read, every description mirrored Vimalavansa's actions. The realisation hit me hard—I wasn't imagining things. I was entangled in a toxic dynamic that had nothing to do with Dhamma.

Determined to reclaim my peace, I began to withdraw slowly, reducing the time I spent with him. But Vimalavansa noticed. His frustration grew, his questions more invasive, his behaviour more erratic. Around this time, I had quietly started an online meditation programme for Sri Lankans, invited by someone I had met before. Knowing our meditation methods differed, I kept it private from Vimalavansa.

Eventually, he discovered the programme. Furious, he confronted me, snatching my phone from my hands. I had had enough. I went straight to the abbot and reported everything. The abbot listened carefully, his face grave. *"Leave him alone,"* the abbot instructed Vimalavansa. *"Do not interfere with his practice anymore."*

That evening, the monastery felt unusually silent. But darkness had its own way of creeping in. Late at night, as I was preparing to rest, Vimalavansa appeared outside my room. His face twisted with rage, he swung a pole at me, striking me with brutal force. **My screams shattered the night's silence**, drawing monks from nearby rooms. They rushed to my aid as Vimalavansa disappeared into the shadows, leaving me bruised and bleeding.

The abbot acted swiftly, taking me under his personal protection, assigning me a room next to his. I was just seventeen—a boy caught in a storm far from home, wounded not just physically but emotionally.

But pain, I learned, has a strange alchemy. It can either break you or forge you into something stronger. In the heart of that adversity, I found a deeper resilience within myself. I continued my meditation, unyielding, turning even my suffering into a tool for insight. The noise around me faded, and I discovered that true tranquillity comes not from external peace but from an unshakable mind.

Despite everything, I mastered my *Samatha* practice—alone, in silence, with nothing but the breath, the mind, and the boundless depth of awareness as my companions. Myanmar had given me more than I expected, not through ease but through trials that carved strength into my spirit.

Chapter 13

Echoes of a Forgotten Life

As my meditation deepened in the monastery in Myanmar, I began to see glimpses—fragments of lives before this one, blurred images forming like ripples in still water. At first, they came as flashes: a feeling, a face, a moment, but nothing cohesive. I persisted, pushing my awareness further, allowing my consciousness to break past the barriers of time.

I had come to Myanmar seeking mastery of *Samatha* meditation. Instead, I had stumbled upon something far greater—the ability to remember.

At first, I saw a celestial realm. A divine palace of gold and silver, filled with radiant beings, where I had existed as a god for thousands of years. The world of the heavens was filled with bliss, but I could see the underlying truth: even in divine existence, there was suffering. Even in a place of endless pleasure, the mind compared, desired, longed—for more power, for more recognition, for something greater. *Where there is existence, there is ego. Where there is ego, there is suffering.* And so, I had wished to leave.

I had made a choice—a wish to return to the human realm, to be born again not for pleasure, not for power, but for liberation. But that life was not the one that held my answer. The real answer lay deeper. *And then… I saw it.*

The vision sharpened. I was no longer in a heavenly realm. I was in ancient India—standing within the towering walls of a grand palace, its golden domes gleaming under the vast blue sky.

I was a child—a Crown Prince. A boy born into royalty, power, and privilege, draped in the finest silks, wearing golden ornaments crafted by the kingdom's most skilled artisans. But none of it mattered to me.

Because the kingdom was not my world. *She was.*

I had an elder sister—seven years older than me. She was the Royal Princess, the pride of our people, and to the world, she was seen as a stern, disciplined, regal figure. She carried herself with the dignity of her lineage, her presence commanding admiration and fear alike.

To others, she was untouchable. *To me, she was everything.*

I was only six years old when tragedy struck. Our parents—the King and Queen—fell ill during an epidemic that spread through the capital. Within weeks, the fever had consumed them both, leaving the kingdom orphaned, leaderless, vulnerable.

The Chief Minister and the royal court took control of the kingdom in my name, promising to guide the nation until I was old enough to rule. But I did not care for politics, for council meetings, for the throne.

I had lost my parents. But I did not feel their absence. *Because she was still there.* She—my sister, my protector, my entire world. That day, she pulled me into her arms, holding me so tightly that I could feel her heart beating against my small frame.

"Don't be afraid, my little king," she whispered, her lips pressing against my forehead. *"I will never leave you. You are mine."*

And from that moment forward, I was hers, and she was mine.

She was beautiful beyond words—her features proud, regal, and sharp, her posture always straight, her presence both intimidating and intoxicating. Her hair was long and dark, cascading down her back in waves, adorned with golden hairpins set with pearls and rubies.

Her face was stern before others. She did not tolerate nonsense, nor did she let herself show weakness. To everyone else, she was prideful, serious, untouchable.

To me, she was *softness, warmth, devotion.*

She played with me like a child, yet held me like a mother. She taught me with wisdom, yet kissed me like I was her baby. She was my protector, yet I was her purpose. She never scolded me. She never ignored me. Her world revolved around me.

I saw myself as a small boy, sitting on the marble floor of our palace chambers. My sister sat before me, on a grand chair carved with golden embellishments.

I rested my spine against her knees, my head lightly leaning back against her as she ran her fingers through my hair. Her voice was strong yet soothing, weaving wisdom into every word as she recited from memory—lessons passed down through generations.

"Listen carefully, my little king," she said, gently tapping my forehead with her finger. *"These are the teachings of our ancestors. A true ruler is not the one who merely wields the sword—but the one who carries wisdom in his heart."* Her words felt like a lullaby of strength and tenderness, echoing softly beneath the golden glow of the chamber's lamps.

I looked up at her, my small hands resting on her lap. *"I don't want to be a ruler,"* I whispered. *"I just want to stay with you forever."*

She smiled softly, pressing a kiss to my forehead. *"Foolish boy,"* she murmured. *"You will always have me."* And she kept her promise.

She dressed me every morning, fastening my robes with delicate care. She fed me with her own hands, making sure I ate before she did. She combed my hair, her fingers moving gently through the strands. She played with me, hugged me, kissed my cheeks, held my hand wherever we walked. And each night, I slept in her arms.

As darkness fell over the palace, I would crawl into her bed, pressing myself close to her warmth. Even now, through the veil of time, I could see her face so clearly—it was almost as if fate had left me a clue, a familiar reflection of someone who once meant the world to me.

She would wrap her arms around me, holding me as if protecting me from the world itself.

"Close your eyes, my love," she whispered, her fingers running softly through my hair.

And then, she would sing.

A lullaby, one only for me.

A song that made me feel like nothing could ever hurt me.

A melody that wrapped me in an unbreakable bond of love.

"Sleep now, my precious one,
Rest in my arms, my moon, my sun.
Nothing shall harm you, nothing shall fade,
For I am with you, always to stay."

The sound of her voice filled the air like silk, her fingers gently stroking my forehead.

"You are my little king," she murmured, pressing a kiss against my temple.

"And I will never lose you."

I felt my small hands tighten around her wrist, holding onto her like she was the only thing keeping me safe.

And she was.

She was everything.

I buried my face against her chest, listening to the steady rhythm of her heartbeat.

I was loved, protected, fulfilled.

I was home.

Oh, my sister, my moon, my light,
You held me close through endless night.
A queen to all, but just to me,
A mother's love, a melody.

Your arms, my home, so warm, so tight,
Your voice, the song that calms my fright.
The world could bow before your grace,
Yet only I could touch your face.

With silken hands, you dressed me fair,
You tied my sash, you combed my hair.
With every meal, your hands would feed,
And every tear, your heart would heed.

When thunder roared, you held me near,
"Don't be afraid, my love, I'm here."
And when the stars began to gleam,
You kissed my brow and wove my dream.

Oh, my sister, my heart, my sky,
If love could speak, it would not lie.
A thousand lives may rise and fall,
But you're my love, beyond them all.

I was your prince, your little king,
But you my world, my everything.

Chapter 14

The Throne, the Crown, and the Heart That Would Not Change

Time moved forward, but nothing between us changed. For ten years, my sister and I had lived within the golden walls of our palace, bound by a love that never faltered. She was my world, and I was hers. The passage of time did not weaken our bond—it strengthened it.

Now, I was sixteen years old. A man in the eyes of the kingdom, yet in her arms, I was still her little king, her precious boy, the child she had protected and nurtured. There was no force in the palace to separate us, no hand to pull me away. We slept together, ate together, lived together—a world untouched by the obligations of royalty.

But time does not allow love to remain in its perfect form. Royal duty began to knock on my door. The Royal Council had begun to pressure me—a King must marry before coronation. At first, I refused. What use did I have for a queen? My heart belonged to someone already, though not in the way the world understood.

But my sister… she insisted.

"You must marry," she said, though her voice was not as firm as it usually was.

"Why?" I asked, searching her face for an answer.

She did not meet my eyes. *"Because it is tradition. The people expect it. The Council will not stop until you agree."*

I sighed. I did not care for love, for romance, for a woman's affection. I had all the love I needed already.

"Fine," I said at last, *"but I will marry only for duty, not for love."*

She gave me a small nod, but her face turned pale. Something in her eyes changed, as if she had just sentenced herself to a fate she had feared all along.

It was then I realised—to her, I was her possession. I was the heart she had nurtured for ten years, the boy she had claimed from the moment our parents had left us. And now, that possession was being given away—even if only in name.

Just as I was being forced to marry, the Royal Council had urged my sister to accept a proposal from a noble prince. She refused. Every time a new suitor came, she turned them away with a cold glance, her voice unwavering as she spoke.

"I will not marry," she said.

"But, Your Highness—" the ministers would argue, only to be silenced by the deadly sharpness of her gaze. *"I have spoken."*

No one dared to challenge her word. No one could command her. The palace feared her, yet they adored her. She was untouchable, yet irreplaceable. She was the Princess Royal—the untamed heart of the throne.

But to me, she was simply the girl who had once kissed my wounds, who had fed me with her hands, who had sung me to sleep in the dark. She did not want to belong to another. *She wanted to belong to me.* And secretly, in the depths of my heart, *I wanted the same.*

The marriage took place in a grand ceremony, a spectacle meant to appease the kingdom. The bride was beautiful, her dress shimmering under the golden torches of the great hall. I sat beside her, wearing my prince crown, my expression emotionless, empty. The vows were spoken. The rituals were completed. The people cheered.

And yet, in the very same night, my sister fell ill.

As I returned from the ceremony, I found the palace servants in distress.

"Her Highness has collapsed," they whispered in fear. *"She refuses to eat. She has a fever. She will not leave her chambers."*

I ran to her room. There she lay—her once-proud frame weakened, her skin pale, her lips parted as if she had been robbed of breath.

"What happened to you?" I asked, sitting beside her, taking her cold hand in mine.

She did not answer.

"Sister," I whispered, brushing my fingers against her cheek, *"this is not like you. You are strong. Nothing breaks you."*

Her fingers weakly reached for mine.

"I am just... tired," she murmured.

But I knew the truth.

Her body had fallen ill. But it was her heart that had broken.

Despite her illness, my coronation took place days later. I stood before my people, adorned in gold and silk, my golden sword strapped to my waist, my crown glimmering beneath the sunlight.

But the greatest honour of the ceremony did not come from the people's cheers, nor from the blessings of the court.

It came from her.

My sister crowned me.

With her own hands, she placed the crown upon my head, her fingers trembling, her lips parted in silent emotion.

And then, in front of the entire kingdom, I wiped her tears away with my fingers, cupping her face as she looked up at me.

"Do not cry," I murmured, my voice gentle yet firm.

And then, in front of thousands of noblemen, ministers, and warriors, **I embraced her.**

I did not care for the whispers. I did not care for the traditions.

She was my world, my crown, my kingdom.

And so, I kissed her forehead, as I had done a thousand times before.

I ruled the kingdom with peace, kindness, and strength. I reduced the taxes, ensuring that my people thrived. I helped businesses flourish, creating a kingdom of prosperity. I protected the ascetics, ensuring the wise men and sages had places to meditate in peace. I fought battles with a golden sword, riding a white horse, striking down those who threatened my people.

To my people, I was a god-like king, a ruler they revered and worshipped.

But within the palace, *I was still her little boy.*

She still fed me with her hands, ensuring I never missed a meal.

She still wiped my lips with her fingers, as if I were a child.

She still walked beside me, held my hand, whispered in my ear.

We ruled together.

No one in the palace dared to speak against us. No one dared to separate us.

As a King, I had a separate chamber from my Queen. I had the right to take as many mistresses as I wished, to choose which chamber I would sleep in each night.

But most nights, **I walked past the Queen's chambers, past the courtyards, past the halls… and arrived at my sister's door.**

And there, in the quiet hours of the night, *I crawled into her bed as I had always done.*

"*Sing to me,*" I would whisper.

She would wrap her arms around me, pulling me close, her fingers tracing through my hair as she had done since I was a boy.

"Sleep now, my precious one,
Rest in my arms, my moon, my sun.
Nothing shall harm you, nothing shall fade,
For I am with you, always to stay."

Her voice was the only lullaby I ever needed.

In the eyes of the world, I was a King.

In her arms, I was only hers.

And that was all that mattered.

Chapter 15

The Moment, She Stopped Me

Golden sunlight filtered through the lush canopies of the royal garden, casting dappled shadows on the carefully tended pathways lined with fragrant flowers and towering trees. The scent of blooming jasmine and sandalwood filled the air, mixing with the faint aroma of damp earth after the morning's light drizzle. Birds sang in the distance, their sweet melodies blending with the soft rustling of the wind as it carried the whispers of the palace beyond. The garden was a place of serenity, a sanctuary where only a few had the privilege to enter. But today, the air was heavy with tension.

I stood before one of my highest ministers, my hands clenched into fists, my entire body rigid with fury. The man, a seasoned advisor, had served the kingdom for decades, but his words today had crossed the line of my patience. *"Your Majesty, if we raise taxes on the working class, the royal treasury will flourish. The laborers will endure, as they always have. Wealth must flow upwards to strengthen the kingdom, not down to those who only know how to toil."*

I exhaled sharply, my blood boiling. The arrogance, the cruelty in his voice—it disgusted me. *"And what of our empire?"* he continued. *"Our borders must expand. Weak nations lie at our feet. We should strike before they rise against us."*

I could feel the heat rising within me, an uncontrollable rage pressing against my chest. The golden hilt of my sword burned beneath my fingertips, begging to be drawn.

"You dare stand before me and suggest war for greed? You dare suggest stripping my people of their livelihood while we sit in golden halls and feast like gluttons?"

My voice was cold, yet filled with venom. The minister hesitated but stood his ground, his beady eyes locking onto mine, his expression unreadable.

"My King, mercy weakens a ruler. If you do not act now, you will be seen as soft, and in time, you will be betrayed. Your people must fear you."

A deadly silence fell between us.

"Fear me?" I echoed, my voice a whisper—a warning.

I stepped forward, slowly, deliberately, my boots pressing into the damp soil. *"I do not rule by fear. I rule by justice."* Then, without hesitation, I reached for my sword. The sound of metal sliding against metal filled the air as I unsheathed the golden blade from its scabbard, the polished steel catching the sunlight as if it had been waiting for this very moment.

The minister's eyes widened in fear, his breath catching in his throat as he stumbled backward. He had miscalculated.

"I do not like repeating my words," I said slowly, raising the sword with a steady grip. *"And I do not suffer fools."*

I lifted the sword, ready to strike down a man who had dared to insult the very foundation of my rule.

And then—I felt it. A presence. A force. A warmth.

Before the blade could fall, before the strike could be made, a pair of slender arms wrapped tightly around me from behind. A soft gasp escaped my lips as her warmth pressed into

my back, her embrace firm, desperate, unyielding.
My sister.

She had seen everything. She had been watching from a distance, unnoticed, standing beneath the golden pavilion that overlooked the garden. She had seen my rage, my fury, the way my hand reached for my sword. And in that moment, she had known I would not stop.

Her breath hitched, her heart pounded—and she ran.

She did not care for decorum, for grace, for the eyes that might be watching from the palace windows. All she saw was me, standing on the edge of something dark, something dangerous.

And so, she ran.

Her robes flowed behind her, the sheer fabric catching in the wind as her jewelled anklets rang against the marble stones. Her golden earrings swayed, and her long hair—always so perfect, always so regal—came undone from its pins, cascading wildly behind her as she sprinted.

Her vision blurred with fear, with desperation, with the unbearable thought that she might lose me to the very power that surrounded us.

And then, she reached me.

She threw herself at me, her arms locking around my torso, her hands pressing into my chest, her cheek resting against my shoulder as she gasped for breath.

"Please," she whispered, her voice breaking. *"Stop."*

I froze.

The sword in my hand, the burning fire in my veins, the

thirst for blood—all of it vanished the moment she touched me.

Her hold was so tight, so desperate, as if she were afraid that if she let go, I would slip into something irredeemable.

I felt her breath against my neck, warm and trembling, as she tightened her embrace even further.

"Please," she whispered again, her voice barely audible. *"Don't become this. You are mine."*

Something in me cracked.

The weight of her words settled deep into my bones, disarming me in a way no sword ever could.

I took a slow, shuddering breath, my grip on the sword loosening. I turned my head slightly, catching the faint scent of rose and sandalwood in her hair, the familiar scent that had always surrounded me since childhood.

Slowly, my fingers uncurled from the hilt.

With a quiet thud, the sword fell from my grasp, embedding itself in the soft grass below.

The minister, still trembling, took a step back, his breath uneven. He opened his mouth to speak, but one glance from my sister silenced him completely.

"Leave," she commanded, her voice sharper than the blade I had nearly used.

He bowed hastily and fled, disappearing into the palace corridors without another word.

But she did not let go.

I felt her entire body pressed against mine, felt the frantic rhythm of her heart against my back.

For the first time since I had drawn my sword, I let out a breath I had not realized I was holding.

I turned slowly in her arms, my movements careful, deliberate, and when I faced her, she did not step away.

Her hands rested against my chest, her fingers gripping the silk of my robe as if she needed to hold onto something tangible.

Her eyes—those deep, knowing eyes—held a storm of emotion.

"I thought I lost you for a moment," she murmured, her voice unsteady.

I lifted my hand, my fingers brushing against her cheek, my thumb tracing the line of her jaw.

"You never will," I whispered.

Her lashes lowered, her grip on me tightening for just a moment longer before she finally exhaled, a deep, shaky breath that carried all her unspoken fears.

Neither of us moved. Neither of us spoke.

The garden stood in silence, the golden sun dipping below the horizon, casting its final rays over us like a blessing from the heavens.

And in that moment, held in her arms, I knew one thing with absolute certainty.

I would have burned the entire kingdom to the ground before I ever let her cry again.

And when the moment passed, and the court faded behind me like a crumbling mask, I sought refuge—not in temples nor thrones, but in the only place my heart could rest.

That evening, when the sky was dressed in amber robes and the air was heavy with the scent of impending rain, I went to the white royal horse tethered near the stables. My elder sister stood beside him, serene and radiant in the twilight. Her eyes met mine—not with judgment, not with fear, but with the gentle knowing that only someone who had held you in your darkest hours could possess.

Without words, we mounted. She sat in front, her frame delicate but sure, and I held the reins with one hand, the other resting lightly on her waist. The world around us quieted, the wind soft as a lullaby, the leaves murmuring blessings as we rode out through the palace gates.

At once, the royal guards appeared behind us, their armour clinking with distant obedience. I turned my head slightly, my voice steady but low, like a current beneath still water:

"Stay distant. If you must follow, let it be as shadows. We are not to be disturbed."

They slowed their pace, and soon it was just the two of us—brother and sister, rider and guide—gliding beneath the canopy of trees that curled like fingers toward the heavens.

We rode towards the jungle-draped hill beyond the palace, where wild jasmine grew in defiant silence and birds sang in forgotten dialects of joy. Her hair, untamed by royal ceremony, streamed into the wind and touched my face like silk kissed by moonlight. I closed my eyes and leaned in, resting my cheek against her shoulder, letting her warmth seep into my skin like sunlight on cold stone.

She did not flinch. She only leaned back slightly, enough for her head to rest against mine.

In that sacred hush, I felt it again—not power, not pride, but peace. The kind of peace I had not known since childhood, when my tears were still allowed and my dreams were ungoverned.

"Faster," she said, giggling softly when the distant sound of armour rang behind us. "Before they catch up."

And so I spurred the horse. We flew through the winding path, our laughter rising like incense through the trees. I buried my face into the curve of her neck, breathing in her scent—a blend of wild blossoms, parchment, and something uniquely her. It was intoxicating, like a memory from a former life trying to find its way home.

"My darling angel," I whispered into her ear. "My dearest light."

By the time we reached the mountain's peak, the sky had spilled into hues of rose and indigo. The palace below lay bathed in gold, distant and dreamlike, as if it were a story someone else had lived. The wind carried no decree here. No whispers of courts. Only stillness… and the breath of the earth itself.

We dismounted. The white horse grazed nearby, unbothered. We stood hand in hand, gazing at the city we belonged to but had never truly belonged within.

I turned to her, my voice trembling beneath the weight of words too long unsaid.

"Thank you," I said, not as a prince, not as a king—but as the boy she had once cradled in her arms during nights of fever and fright. "Thank you for loving me when the world chose duty over affection. For never letting me feel the ache of being an orphan. You gave me a mother's tenderness… a father's protection. You gave me what kingdoms could not."

Her eyes glistened, and for once, there was no restraint between us. I drew her into my arms and held her as tightly as a soul can hold another. My chest heaved, and the tears came—not in shame, but in reverence. They slipped from my eyes and fell into her hair like quiet blessings, as the stars began to light the sky one by one.

She did not speak. She didn't need to. Her silence was its own kind of vow.

I felt her tears too—warm on my collar, soft on my skin. And in that moment, beneath the canopy of heaven, far from the world that demanded so much and gave so little, we were not royalty. We were not forbidden. We were not broken.

We were simply two souls, suspended in the grace of each other's love.

That night, I did not return to my Queen's chamber. I did not seek the company of advisors or generals or scholars. I walked the long halls of the palace, past the moonlit corridors, past the golden statues, past the symbols of my rule.

And I arrived at the only place that ever truly felt like home.

Her chamber.
I did not knock. I did not need to.
She was waiting.

The moment I stepped inside, she opened her arms, and I stepped into them.

She guided me toward the bed, where we had slept together since childhood. Without a word, she pulled me close, stroking my hair, tracing soft circles on my back.

"You scared me today," she murmured, her voice laced with something she had never shown before—fear.

"I scared myself," I admitted.

She kissed my forehead, her lips lingering as if she was trying to steal away the remnants of my anger.

"Rest now, my little one," she whispered.

She began to hum, the same lullaby that had followed me through every night of my childhood.

"Sleep now, my precious one,
Rest in my arms, my moon, my sun.
Nothing shall harm you, nothing shall fade,
For I am with you, always to stay."

My arms tightened around her waist. The fire inside me had burned so brightly today, but her embrace had extinguished it.

Her love had always been stronger than my anger.

Her arms had always been stronger than my sword.

As my eyes grew heavy, my breath slowed, and for the first time since taking the throne, I truly rested.

Because I was home.

In her arms.

Where I had always belonged.

Chapter 16

The King's Adornment and the Queen's Ailment

The day of the royal court gathering had arrived, a day where nobles, ministers, generals, and scholars gathered beneath the golden ceiling of the palace to swear allegiance, discuss governance, and witness the presence of their King. But before I adorned myself in the robes of power, before I stepped into the world where men kneeled before me in reverence, I indulged in a moment of luxury that only a ruler of my stature could afford. The giant bath pool within my king's chamber was filled with warm milk infused with fragrant lotus petals and healing herbs. The water was smooth as silk against my skin, the scent calming yet invigorating. Four of the most beautiful lady servants attended me, their hands skilfully massaging sandalwood and turmeric onto my arms, chest, and shoulders, ensuring that my skin remained as radiant as my golden throne. I leaned back against the edge of the pool, allowing my body to relax, my eyes half-lidded in contentment. The gentle ripples of the bathwater mirrored the serenity of my mind.

And then—**she entered.** Without announcement, without hesitation, without permission. Because she did not need it. The great doors to my chambers swung open, and the scent of royal jasmine drifted in before she did. She stepped inside, her sheer shawl flowing like mist, her presence demanding without uttering a single word. The lady servants immediately paused, sensing the change in atmosphere. My sister clapped her hands twice, a silent command that needed no explanation. *"Leave us."* The four women bowed their heads and retreated, their bare feet moving swiftly across the marble floor. I remained still, watching her through the drifting mist of the bath.

She stood near the edge of the pool, her shawl slipping from her shoulders as she let it fall onto a cushioned stool. And in that moment, I could not deny it—*she was beyond beautiful.* Her figure was sculpted like an exquisite deity, more perfect than even the queen or the countless maidens who sought my favour. Her curves, her grace, her commanding presence—*she was not just a princess, she was a force,* a presence that made even kings forget their crowns. For a fleeting moment, my gaze betrayed me. My eyes flickered lower, to the gentle curve of her belly, to the elegance of her bare arms adorned with gold, to the way her dhoti draped over her hips like flowing water. But then, with a single breath, I tore my gaze away.

She stepped into the bath chamber fully, moving behind me, her hands reaching for the golden bowl filled with sandalwood paste and turmeric. *"You're spoiled,"* she said, her voice teasing yet filled with warmth. *"And whose fault is that?"* I murmured, tilting my head back slightly. Her fingers pressed firmly against my shoulders, massaging the cool, fragrant paste into my skin. Her touch was different from the servants—*deeper, more certain, filled with familiarity.*

"Mine, of course," she admitted, her laughter soft.

She moved from my shoulders to my arms, her fingers tracing along the toned muscles, ensuring that every inch of my skin was bathed in the sacred mixture. The warmth of her hands, the scent of sandalwood, the intimate silence between us—it was a moment that only belonged to us, untouchable by the outside world.

"You're stronger now," she mused, pressing her thumbs into the tense muscles of my forearm.

"I have to be," I replied.

"Yet still, you are the same boy who clung to me at night," she said, her tone almost nostalgic.

I let out a quiet breath of amusement. *"And yet, here you are, still looking after me."*

She chuckled softly, her hands trailing down to my wrists, rubbing the last of the mixture into my skin before dipping them into the bathwater.

Once she was done, I straightened, the warmth of the water now replaced with the coolness of the bath oils. *"Leave,"* I said. *"I need to wear my lower garment."*

She merely arched an eyebrow, her expression amused. *"Brother,"* she scoffed, handing me a thick towel instead. *"I have seen every inch of you since the moment you were born. What is left for you to hide from me?"*

And with that, she turned gracefully, leaving before I could respond, her laughter trailing behind her like a song.

By the time I stepped out of the bathing chamber, my sister had already selected my royal adornments. Upon the marble dressing table, before the towering gold-rimmed mirror, lay the finest collection of jewellery and royal attire. Each piece had been hand-picked by her. As I approached, she stood beside the table, examining the golden forehead chain between her fingers, ensuring that the rubies embedded within it gleamed perfectly.

"Come," she said simply.

I sat before the mirror, my reflection staring back at me—the face of a King, now adorned with the faintest trace of a moustache, a sign of time's passage. With careful hands, she fastened the forehead chain onto my skin, adjusting it so that it sat perfectly at my hairline. Next, she clasped the heavy emerald-studded necklace around my throat, her fingers brushing against the skin just below my jaw.

"This is the one Mother gifted you," she whispered.

"I remember," I replied, my voice softer now.

One by one, she adorned me—The armlets, fitted securely around my biceps. The rings, placed on each finger with care. The waist chain, tightened around my midsection, symbolizing the power of my reign. The shawl, draped over my shoulder in the traditional style. And finally—the crown. She lifted it with both hands, its golden edges glinting under the light. As she placed it upon my head, our eyes met through the mirror.

"You are ready," she said, her voice filled with something beyond words—*pride, devotion, something ancient and unspoken.*

And so, I stood.

And I entered the royal court.

The moment I stepped into the grand hall, every noble, minister, and warrior rose to their feet. The court was vast, its golden columns stretching to the ceiling, adorned with silk banners and precious stones. A deep, melodious voice began to sing, a poetic chant of my authority, my reign, my divine rule.

To my left, my Queen sat, adorned in regal silk. To my right, my sister, draped in her imperial elegance. We ascended the steps of the royal stage, my robes flowing behind me like cascading gold. My Queen and my sister sat upon their respective royal seats, flanking my throne like the two most powerful women in the kingdom. **And I, the King, took my place.**

I climbed the final steps, and as I lowered myself onto the golden throne, a surge of power, weight, and absolute authority settled upon me. At that moment, I did not feel like a mere man. *I felt like I was standing upon the highest peak of the world, looking down upon everything below.* Two beautiful maidens stood beside me, large fans in their hands, waving delicately to keep the air cool. The chanting of my name continued. The kingdom watched. **And for a fleeting moment, as I sat upon my throne, I felt truly invincible.**

The air in the grand hall was thick with the weight of power and duty, the scent of burning incense curling toward the high ceilings. My ministers stood with bowed heads, awaiting my command, while the poets and scholars murmured words of reverence. The noble lords gazed upon me with admiration and fear alike, knowing that I alone held the fate of this kingdom in my hands. The royal court session began. Decrees were announced, matters of governance were laid before me, and the voices of my advisors wove through the air like threads of fate. I listened, my presence commanding, my judgment absolute.

And then, something unexpected happened. From my left, where my Queen sat in her regal grace, there was a sudden shift. A sharp inhale, a slight tremor in her hand as she reached for the golden rail of her seat. A moment later, her face paled, and without warning, she covered her mouth, rising abruptly as if struck by an unseen force. The hall grew still. All eyes turned toward her. Her breathing was uneven, her delicate fingers trembling as she pressed them against her lips. And then, it happened—a sudden, involuntary retch, her body folding slightly as the sickness took hold.

A murmur rippled through the court.

I turned my head sharply.

Before I could speak, **my sister moved.** Without hesitation, without waiting for permission, she rose from her seat with effortless grace, her sheer silks billowing as she moved to my Queen's side. She did not pause to bow, did not wait for my word. She simply placed a hand against the Queen's back, steadying her, her expression unreadable.

Then, she turned toward me, her gaze meeting mine across the expanse of the royal dais. *"Excuse us, Your Majesty,"* she said, her voice carrying through the hall, calm yet commanding.

No one would question her. No one could.

Not even me.

I gave the slightest nod.

Without another word, my sister guided the Queen away, her movements unhurried yet firm, her fingers gently curled around the Queen's wrist. As they descended the steps of the throne, the nobles parted before them like waves before a steady vessel. The Queen faltered slightly, but my sister's hold did not waver. She led her through the grand doors of the court, disappearing beyond the golden arches, leaving only the faint echo of soft footsteps behind them.

The court remained silent for a brief moment, as if the very air had hesitated, unsure whether to continue. And then, as if nothing had happened, I lifted my hand.

The session resumed.

The voices of my ministers filled the air once more, and I sat upon my throne, watching, deciding, ruling.

But in the back of my mind, in the quiet recess of my thoughts, *I knew that somewhere beyond these walls, my sister was taking care of what I could not.*

As she always had.

As she always would.

Chapter 17

The Royal Heir and the Weight of Desire

The golden throne beneath me felt lighter as I shifted my weight. The royal council had concluded, and now the time had come for me to rise. As I stood from my seat, a quiet murmur rippled through the court, followed by the unmistakable sound of movement—hundreds of nobles, ministers, and generals standing in unison, bowing their heads in deep reverence. I placed my right foot firmly on the foot bench, my golden sword pressed to the marble floor beside me. For a moment, I held still, letting the weight of my authority settle into my posture. Then, with a swift motion, I flipped my sword from my right hand to my left, the gleam of its polished blade catching the light as I adjusted the royal shawl draped over my right arm.

A show of control. A display of mastery. A reminder that the King's hands were as skilled in war as they were in governance.

Then, without a single glance backward, I descended the steps of the throne.

The royal shawl that hung from my shoulder billowed in the wind as I moved. My pace was fast, my posture commanding, each stride carrying the unmistakable weight of a ruler who had no need to hesitate. The gold embroidery of my robes shimmered in the torchlight, the sharp angles of my jewels catching every flicker of movement as I walked past the bowing nobles.

I did not stop. I did not slow.

I was headed straight to the Queen's chamber.

By the time I reached her room, the torches outside burned softly, casting flickering shadows on the grand wooden doors. The royal guards stationed there immediately stepped aside, lowering their spears as I pushed the doors open without a word. Inside, the air was quiet, warm, and scented with rose oil. The soft glow of lanterns illuminated the vast chamber, their golden light touching the silken drapes and intricately woven carpets.

She was asleep.

The Queen lay upon the grand bed, her body delicate and still, wrapped in the folds of the softest white linen. Her youth was evident—just sixteen years old, so pure, so untouched by the burdens of ruling. Her chest rose and fell gently with each breath, her dark lashes resting lightly against her fair cheeks.

She looked like a painting of a goddess, untouched by time.

I stepped forward, my boots barely making a sound against the polished marble floor. As I reached the bed, I lowered myself onto the edge of the mattress, placing my palm gently against her forehead. She stirred, her lashes fluttering, her lips parting slightly before she finally opened her eyes.

"My King…" she whispered; her voice still laced with sleep.

Her fingers reached for my hand, her skin warm and soft beneath mine. Before I could say a word, the royal doctor, who had been standing near the window, stepped forward, bowing deeply. **"Your Majesty,"** he said, his voice carrying the weight of an announcement. I lifted my head, watching him closely.

"The Queen is with child."

A moment of silence. And then, it struck me. **I was going to be a father.**

For the first time in my life, I felt a sensation different from power, different from victory or conquest. It was something… *deeper, more personal.* A seed of my own bloodline had taken root, a legacy that would extend beyond my reign. My Queen looked up at me, her eyes filled with a quiet kind of wonder, an innocence that mirrored the news itself. My lips parted slightly, and without thinking, I leaned forward, pressing a single kiss onto her forehead.

"You have done well," I murmured, brushing a loose strand of her hair aside.

She smiled softly, and I felt a flicker of pride—not in her, but in myself.

One attempt. That was all it had taken. The strength of my blood, the power of my lineage, had already begun to shape the future.

I stood up, my voice steady as I turned to the royal guards stationed outside.

"Announce it publicly. Let the entire kingdom know."

The guards immediately bowed and exited the chamber, their footsteps echoing down the hall.

Then, turning to the doctor, I gave a second command.

"Arrange a grand royal celebration for tomorrow. And let the gates of the capital open—there shall be feasting for the people as well."

The doctor bowed once more, his assistants already bustling to make the necessary preparations.

The night air outside was cool, but within the chamber, the warmth of silk and firelight lingered.

I had made up my mind.

Tonight, I would stay with the Queen. This would be the second night I spent with her. The first had been our wedding night—a night of curiosity, of discovery, of instincts overriding thought. *Tonight felt different.*

I had chosen this night not out of duty, not out of necessity—but out of something else. She lay before me, so young, so untouched by the weight of the world. A child herself, and yet carrying mine. A moment later, two of her lady servants approached, their hands moving with practiced grace as they began to remove my heavy jewellery. One by one, the adornments of the throne were stripped away. The forehead chain, the waist ornaments, the rings, the golden armlets—each piece placed neatly upon the carved wooden table.

Then, the Queen rose from the bed.

"Let me do it," she said suddenly, stepping forward.

The servants immediately stilled, exchanging glances before bowing their heads and stepping back.

She was still so small, just sixteen, her frame delicate as she moved closer, lifting her slender hands to my shoulders.

"You are my King," she whispered. *"But you are also my husband. I should serve you myself."*

I remained still, letting her unclasp the last of my jewels, her fingers working slowly. As she stood beside me in front of the grand mirror, her delicate frame barely reaching my shoulder, my gaze drifted downward. My eyes traced the gentle curve of her waist, the softness of her belly—the place where my heir now grew.

A strange warmth stirred within me, an instinctual pull I could not ignore.

Without thinking, I lowered myself slightly, pressing my face against her belly, letting the warmth of her skin fill my senses. The scent of jasmine and rose lingered on her, blending with the faint traces of sandalwood that still clung to me. She let out a soft gasp, then suddenly laughed, a sweet, innocent sound that rang through the quiet chamber.

"Those tickles!" she giggled, her hands instinctively moving to my head.

Her fingers threaded through my hair, holding me there as she laughed, her body shaking lightly with mirth. For a moment, I remained still, my face against her warmth, listening to the rhythm of her laughter.

It was soft, genuine, untouched by the burdens of royalty.

And in that moment, she was not a Queen, not the mother of my child—**just a young girl**, sweet and pure, laughing at the touch of her husband.

But in that very moment, as my face rested against the warmth of my Queen's belly, *another vision flashed unbidden through my mind.*

I saw her—my sister.

Her figure, regal and untouchable, yet far more intoxicating than the innocence before me. The curve of her waist, the grace of her form—it was different, unmatched. A quiet fire radiated from her, a presence that commanded rather than submitted.

For an instant, my mind betrayed me.

The warmth I felt against my skin—the softness, the scent, the closeness—it was not hers, but *I wished it was.*

A sharp wave of guilt washed over me, sudden and inexplicable, like a blade pressing against my chest.

Why? Why did my thoughts drift to her at a moment like this?

My hands, which had lingered on my Queen's waist, suddenly felt misplaced. The closeness, once so natural, now felt undeserved.

I slowly straightened, pulling back just enough to mask the conflict within me.

The Queen, still laughing softly, noticed nothing. She only smiled sweetly, reaching up to brush her fingers against my cheek before stepping away.

I turned to follow her, pushing aside the thoughts lingering in my mind.

We lay in bed, two figures on opposite sides. The silk drapes rustled lightly; the room lit only by a few dim lanterns. A moment of silence.

Then, a soft voice broke it.

"My King… may I sleep on your chest?"

I turned my head toward her.

"Come, my dear."

She moved closer, her arms wrapping tightly around me, her warmth pressing against my bare skin. She was soft, small, delicate. She rested her face against my chest, her lips brushing against my skin in small, absentminded movements. Slowly, she began to kiss my chest, her touch hesitant yet full of quiet affection.

A warmth began to stir inside me.

My fingers trailed down her back, unknowingly moving lower—until they reached her waist, her hips, her—

And then, I stopped.

Because in that instant, *I thought of my sister again.* That same inexplicable guilt returned, cutting through my desire like a blade. I took a slow breath, forcing the heat within me to settle, reining in the surge of desire that threatened to rise.

Instead of indulging the moment, I shifted my hand, bringing it to her head, letting my fingers weave through her soft, silken hair. With slow, deliberate movements, I began to massage her scalp, tracing soothing circles with my fingertips.

She sighed gently, leaning into my touch, her body completely at ease in my presence. To her, this was an expression of love.

To me, it was a quiet act of control.

I lowered my head, pressing a single, lingering kiss upon her crown, feeling the warmth of her against my lips.

As I held her in that moment, a strange emotion stirred within me—*not the hunger of a husband, but the tenderness of a protector.*

She was so young, so delicate, so untouched by the complexities that weighed upon my soul.

Looking at her now, *I did not see a Queen. I did not even see my wife.*

I saw a girl—sweet, innocent, and fragile. And for reasons I could not yet name, she felt less like a lover and more like a daughter.

Chapter 18

The Queen's Offering and the Sister's Silence

The golden rays of the morning sun filtered through the silken drapes, casting a warm glow over the chamber. A faint scent of jasmine and incense lingered in the air, mingling with the cool morning breeze that drifted in through the carved balcony doors.

As my eyes fluttered open, the first thing I saw was my Queen—sitting gracefully beside me on the grand bed, a delicate smile adorning her lips. In her hands, she held a golden goblet filled with warm milk, waiting patiently for me to wake. The moment our eyes met, she tilted her head slightly, her smile widening as she greeted me with a soft, melodic voice.

"Good morning, my King."
I blinked away the haze of sleep, my gaze flickering between her and the offering in her hands.
She gently lifted the goblet. **"I have brought you this myself."**

A quiet sigh left my lips as I sat up, reaching for the cup. Her hands, small and delicate, brushed against mine as I took it from her grasp.
"You are too kind," I murmured before bringing the goblet to my lips. The warmth of the milk spread through my chest, soothing yet unfamiliar.
For a moment, everything seemed peaceful.
Then, she spoke again.

"My King," she said hesitantly, tracing her fingers along the silk sheets, **"Would you allow me the honor of bathing you today? With my own hands?"**
Her words were gentle, innocent—spoken with devotion.
And yet, something inside me shifted.

In an instant, a memory surfaced in my mind—one that had been woven into my very soul.
At this very hour, it was always her—my sister—who came to my chamber to bathe me and dress me. Not my Queen. Not anyone else.

A strange, inexplicable tension seized my chest.
I lowered the goblet slowly, setting it aside, my fingers tightening for a brief moment before I forced myself to relax.
"I appreciate your kindness, my Queen," I said carefully, keeping my voice steady. **"But I have urgent matters to attend to today."**
She blinked in surprise, her smile faltering for the briefest moment before she nodded obediently.

I did not wait for her to respond further. I rose from the bed, still dressed in my night garments, and called for a servant.
"Bring my jewellery and attire to the royal chamber," I commanded. **"I will prepare there."**
Then, without another word, I left.

The moment I reached the royal chamber, I waited.
Minutes passed. Then an hour.
But *she* did not come.

I frowned, shifting slightly in my seat, my fingers tapping restlessly against the golden armrest. A strange unease settled in my chest.

She always came. Every morning. No matter the season, no matter the occasion.
Why not today?

I called for one of the royal maids.
"Go to the royal dining hall," I instructed. **"Find out if the Princess Royal has come for breakfast—or if she has requested her meal in her chambers."**
The maid bowed, leaving swiftly.
I sat in silence, waiting.
Why was I uneasy?

I should have been satisfied—I had spent the night with my Queen, and now an heir was growing in her womb.
And yet, a hollow feeling gnawed at me, quiet yet relentless.

Then, the maid returned.
"Your Majesty," she said carefully, bowing before me. **"Her Highness has not left her chambers today. She has not taken her breakfast, nor has she requested it."**
My breath stilled.

So I was right.
She was upset.
Without hesitation, I rose from my seat and left.

I did not change into my royal attire. I did not wait to be bathed or dressed.
I went straight to her.

The grand doors of my sister's chamber stood before me.
The moment the guards saw me, they pushed them open

without a word, without an announcement.
They knew. They always knew.

The room was dimly lit, the golden curtains drawn just enough to let in a soft glow. The air inside was heavier than usual, filled with the faint scent of lotus and sandalwood, yet lacking the warmth that always greeted me.
And there she was.

Seated upon the velvet couch near the balcony, her legs tucked beneath her, arms wrapped around her knees, gazing silently at the sprawling royal gardens below.
She did not turn to look at me.
For a moment, I just watched her.
Then, I spoke.

"Are you unwell, my dear?"
She exhaled softly, shaking her head. **"No. I am simply in an upset mood."**
Her voice was calm, but distant.

I approached her slowly, closing the space between us, until I stood beside the couch. Then, I reached for her hands, gently unlocking them from around her knees.
She did not resist.
With careful movements, I placed her feet back onto the floor, my hands lingering against the warmth of her skin.

Then, in the quiet glow of her chamber, I bowed before her. Lowering myself to the floor, I touched my forehead to her feet in an act of deep reverence.
"I greet you, my dearest sister," I murmured against her skin.

For the first time since I entered, she moved.
Her fingers brushed through my hair; her touch gentle yet weighted with emotion.

"Bless you, my King," she whispered.
I lifted my head, looking into her eyes.
She smiled—but *it was not the smile I knew.*

Without thinking, I rose to the couch and embraced her, pulling her into my arms.
"I am always yours," I murmured into her hair. **"I only love you, my darling sister."**

She closed her eyes, her breath warm against my shoulder.
"You are the one who gave me to my Queen," I reminded her. **"It is unfair for you to be upset now."**
She let out a quiet sigh. **"It is okay, darling,"** she said softly. **"You can love your Queen."**
Then, she hesitated.
And in a voice barely above a whisper, she asked,
"But will I always be at the top of your heart?"

Her words were timid, uncertain—yet heavy with something unspoken.
I pulled back slightly, my hands cupping her face, my gaze steady.
"Yes. For sure," I said firmly. **"You are my everything, my sister. Do not doubt it."**
And at last, *she smiled.*

The kind of smile that belonged only to me.
I cuddled her closer, feeling the warmth return to the room, the silence shifting into comfort.

Then, I spoke again.
"Today, I will bathe you and dress you."
She let out a soft laugh.
"As you wish, Your Majesty," she teased.

The bath had already been prepared—steaming water infused with fragrant herbs and rose petals, the scent of sandalwood filling the chamber.
She stepped behind the curtain to change into her bathing cloth, then emerged.
I extended my hand toward her.
"Come with me, Your Highness," I said with a grin.
She chuckled, placing her hand in mine.
And as I led her into the bath, **all was right again.**

The scent of sandalwood, jasmine, and rose petals filled the warm bath chamber, curling into the air like a silent song. The lanterns cast a soft golden glow over the water, reflecting the delicate ripples as she stepped gracefully into the tub.

Her movements were effortless, fluid, as if she had done this a thousand times before.
Because *she had.*
How many times had she prepared my bath, scrubbed my shoulders, cleansed my skin with the same gentle care as she did when I was a child?
How many mornings had I woken to find her already waiting, her presence the first thing to greet me?
Most days.
But today, I had chosen to bathe her instead.
It was rare—but not new.

She settled into the steaming water, her head tilting slightly to the side, exposing the graceful curve of her neck and shoulders.

She waited.
I followed, kneeling at the edge of the tub, dipping my fingers into the smooth sandalwood paste.
"Close your eyes," I murmured.
She obeyed without hesitation, trusting, unguarded.

With slow, deliberate movements, I smoothed the fragrant mixture along her shoulders, her arms, the delicate slope of her collarbones. Her breath slowed, her lashes resting lightly against her cheeks.
"You always do this so gently," she whispered, her voice barely above a breath.
"And you always take care of me," I replied softly.
She smiled but kept her eyes closed, leaning into the warmth of my touch.

I trailed my hands along the length of her arms, feeling the softness of her skin beneath my fingertips.
And then, without thought—without hesitation—I leaned forward and pressed a small kiss against the side of her neck.

Her body froze.
Not in fear. Not in hesitation.
But in a quiet, startled stillness.

Her breath hitched, her fingers gripping the edge of the tub for a fleeting moment—before she moved.
With a sudden playful force, she grasped my wrist and pulled me forward.
"Come bathe with me," she giggled, her voice light, teasing, yet laced with something deeper.

Before I could react, water splashed against the edges of the tub as I lost balance and fell in, my silken gold-embroidered white dhoti instantly soaking through.
Her laughter filled the chamber, rich and melodic, as I blinked, droplets clinging to my skin.

"You are impossible," I muttered, shaking my head.
She grinned. **"You deserve it for teasing me."**

I let out a soft breath of amusement, adjusting myself in the water as she leaned back against my chest, her hair damp, her body warm against mine.
This was nothing new between us. It had always been like this.

As I rubbed slow circles along her shoulders, trailing my fingers down her arms, she sighed softly, tilting her head slightly to press her temple against my jaw.
Then, after a quiet pause, she moved again.
"Come here," she whispered.

Her voice was softer now, a quiet invitation that carried more than mere words.
I turned slightly, allowing her to loop her arms around my shoulders, her hands tracing the nape of my neck.
She guided me closer, and I followed—without question, without hesitation, without doubt.

With the same unshaken familiarity, I rested my face against her right shoulder, exhaling as my breath warmed the damp skin of her neck.
And then—**she embraced me.**
Her arms wrapped around me, tight, unyielding, whole, as if she was afraid to let go.

My eyes fluttered shut, my mind at ease.
"You are always mine," she whispered.
"And you are always my everything," I replied.

Her embrace tightened. Her fingers traced slow circles along my back, a silent promise that she always would.
And in the warmth of that bath, in the safety of her arms, I felt truly whole.

Chapter 19

The Bond That No One Could Take Away

The golden sun sat high in the sky, bathing the palace in a warm glow, its light spilling through the marble corridors like molten gold. Servants rushed in quiet efficiency, their footsteps light against the polished floors as they carried trays, scrolls, and silk-draped parcels. The sound of the courtyard fountain echoed through the halls as I walked, my mind occupied with the weight of rulership. Documents needed signing, merchants awaited approvals, and nobles had their endless petitions—my entire morning had been consumed by responsibilities, and yet, *an unease rested within me.*

It was a feeling that I could not yet name, but it pressed against my chest like an unseen force, making me restless. A cluster of my royal advisors, generals, and high-ranking ministers trailed behind me as I stepped outside into the vast royal gardens. Their hushed discussions barely reached my ears as I took in the sight before me—a moment that sent an unfamiliar heat rushing through my veins.

Beyond the white stone pillars of the courtyard, **I saw her.** She stood beneath the flowering archway, her golden robes flowing like silk spun from the sun itself, her elegance so effortless, it felt almost ethereal.

But it was not just her presence that caught my eye. **It was the man standing before her.** The son of the royal army's chief commander. A man of high status, an assistant commander himself, and a man I had seen before—always hovering around my sister. I had noticed him attempt to approach her many times, always with careful precision, always with a calculated intent.

Something in my chest tightened. I slowed my steps, ensuring that neither of them saw me as I drew closer. My subconscious mind knew what it wanted—it did not want to share her, not in any way, not in any form. The sound of their conversation reached me as I moved carefully along the columns, remaining just out of sight.

"My Lady," the man's voice was careful, measured, but there was something beneath it—*an emotion I did not like.* I saw him extend his hand toward her. A piece of jewellery rested in his palm. A delicate gold chain, encrusted with rubies, its craftsmanship intricate and fine.

"This belonged to my mother," he said, his tone holding a quiet admiration. **"She always said that such beauty should only be worn by the most graceful of women. And I can think of no one more fitting than you, Princess."**

Something inside me snapped. My hands curled into fists at my sides. Would she take it? Would she accept something that belonged to another man's family? Would she—

Before my thoughts could spiral further, she did something that made my chest tighten—*not in fear, but in pride.*

Without even looking at the piece of jewellery, **she stepped back.**
"I do not accept gifts," she said, her voice unwavering, regal, and utterly indifferent. **"And I do not engage in unnecessary conversations."**
Without another word, she turned away from him, walking toward the far side of the garden, her posture unwavering, her steps deliberate.

The officer stood frozen for a moment, clearly stunned by her cold dismissal. He had expected hesitation. He had expected shyness. *He had expected a chance.*
But **she gave him none.**

I should have been relieved.
I should have walked away with the certainty that **she did not belong to anyone but me.**
But instead, *I felt fear.*

Even though she had rejected him, I had seen the way he looked at her. *I had seen the way others looked at her.* And one day—*one day, someone might steal her from me.*
A bitter taste filled my mouth at the thought.

My mind churned, unsettled. I had spent two nights with my Queen, and in those nights, I had only come to understand how much attention she desired from me. She sought my affection, my pampering, my presence. And while she had been gentle and sweet, I realized something in those moments—**I had only taken from my sister.**

She had always been the one to give, to nurture, to shower me with love without expectation.
But today, **I would not be the taker.**
I would be the giver.
Because *if I did not give her the love she deserved, someone else would try.*
And that, I could never allow.

I turned to one of my maids, my decision already made.
"Prepare lunch for two and have it sent to the Princess's chamber," I ordered. **"No one else is to disturb us."**
The maid bowed and hurried away.

I took a slow breath, adjusting the golden shawl draped over my shoulder before I made my way toward her chambers.
As I stepped inside, she turned to me, her expression soft with surprise.
"Brother," she greeted, tilting her head slightly. **"What a rare honour to have you here at midday."**

I smirked slightly, stepping further inside.
"I came to have lunch with you."
She studied me carefully, her eyes flickering with something unreadable. *I could tell that she sensed a shift in me, that she knew something had changed.*
"And what has led to this sudden affection?" she mused, amusement in her tone.
"Because today, I will feed you," I stated simply.

Her lips parted slightly, caught off guard by the declaration.
"Feed me?" she repeated.
I nodded. **"Sit."**

She hesitated for a moment before gracefully lowering herself into her seat at the table.
The meal before us was rich yet simple—golden rotis, fragrant curries, sweetened rice. I tore a piece of warm roti, dipping it into the curry before lifting it toward her lips.

She stared at me for a long moment before finally leaning forward and taking the bite. She chewed in silence, her gaze never leaving mine. I repeated the process—feeding her piece after piece, watching as she took each bite with quiet grace.

And then, on the final bite, **she took my hand.**
I watched as she slowly brought it toward her lips—and then, without breaking eye contact, **she licked the remnants of the curry from my fingers.**

My breath caught.
Her eyes fluttered closed, *savouring the taste, the moment, the intimacy of it.*

When she lifted her gaze back to mine, *her eyes were glistening.*
"Why do you look at me like that?" I murmured.
She did not answer.
She only smiled—*a smile so full of love, devotion, and quiet worship that my chest tightened painfully.*

I lifted the goblet of water, bringing it to her lips. She drank slowly, delicately.
Then, with the fingers of my left hand, I reached forward, wiping her lips clean.
My touch was light, delicate—yet deliberate.

The soft pad of my fingers brushed over the velvet curve of her lips, *warm and glistening from the water she had just sipped.*
Her skin was always soft, *but here—on her lips—it was something else entirely.*
Something like silk spun from moonlight.
Something that held the power to unravel me.

I did not look away.
And neither did she.

Her eyes were locked onto mine, deep and unwavering, *their usual golden-brown depths darkened into something unreadable. Something unfathomable.* Her lashes fluttered for the briefest second, *as if my touch had sent a whisper of sensation through her.*

She parted her lips ever so slightly, just enough for a breath to escape—a breath that I could almost feel against my fingertips.

I felt the slow rise and fall of her chest, the way her body stilled beneath my touch, as if the world around us had faded into nothing.
The air in the chamber grew heavy, thick with something neither of us could name.

She did not pull away.
She did not speak.
She only stared, the intensity in her gaze piercing through me like a blade—**sharp, but not wounding.**

No, *this was different.*
This was something deeper, something that dug into the very essence of who we were.
Something that had always been there, lurking in the spaces between our silences, waiting to be acknowledged.

Her lips trembled—just slightly.
Was it from my touch?
Or from something neither of us were ready to face?
And yet, *she did not move.*

She let me trace the curve of her lower lip with my thumb, catching a stray drop of water that lingered there.
Her breath hitched, just for a moment.
And in that moment, I saw it.
The longing. The need. The unspoken worship.

It was not the gaze of a woman simply looking at her King.
Nor was it the gaze of a sister merely admiring her brother.
No—*it was something more.*
Something far more dangerous.
Something that threatened to swallow me whole.
And I let it.

Slowly, I withdrew my fingers, *the warmth of her lips lingering on my skin like an imprint that would never fade.*
I did not break the silence.
Neither did she.
Instead, I lifted my fingers to my mouth.
And without hesitation, **I took a bite from my own plate—using the same fingers she had just licked clean.**

The taste of the meal mixed with something else—something intangible, something intoxicating. And all the while, **she watched me.** *Her eyes never wavered, never softened.*
They burned—not with fire, but with something far more consuming.
An emotion I could not name.
An emotion that drove me mad.

Chapter 20

The Night of a Thousand Lights

The golden sky stretched endlessly, painted in hues of fire and dusk, as the palace prepared for a night of grand celebration. The announcement of the Queen's pregnancy had set the kingdom into a joyful frenzy. The royal courtyards were adorned with flowing banners of crimson and gold, the air thick with the scent of lotus, sandalwood, and freshly burning oil lamps.

Two grand feasts had been arranged—one inside the royal arena, reserved for nobles, dignitaries, and the highest members of court. The other, a grand celebration outside the palace gates, where musicians, dancers, and citizens gathered to revel in the festivities. But my mind was consumed by only one thing. Tonight—she would dance.

A performance unlike any before, a Kathak-style dance meant to be both a tribute to tradition and a message only I would truly understand. Before the evening began, before the first note of music filled the air, I made my way to her chamber.

The guards straightened the moment they saw me, immediately stepping aside without a word. The carved golden doors swung open, and the first thing that greeted me was the thick, intoxicating scent of perfumed smoke. Inside, she sat on her stool before the grand mirror, her spine straight, her posture regal.

Her maids gathered around her like devoted attendants to a goddess, holding her long, cascading hair aloft while letting it pass through fragrant incense. Thin curls of perfumed smoke swirled around her strands, coating them with a delicate aroma of jasmine, saffron, and sandalwood. Her reflection stared back at me through the mirror—a gaze of quiet pride, straight-backed elegance, and untouchable poise. She did not turn. She did not move. She only watched me through the mirror, as if awaiting my approach.

I stepped closer, the sound of my golden sandals soft against the marble floor. Her maids instantly lowered their heads, placing down her tresses and stepping back. "Leave us." She did not need to raise her voice. They obeyed without hesitation. One by one, the maids slipped out of the chamber, the heavy doors closing behind them. Now, only we remained.

Her half-dressed form was a vision of moonlit gold—a delicately embroidered silk skirt wrapped around her waist, shimmering under the lanterns. A matching fitted blouse adorned her upper body, modest yet effortlessly regal, tailored for movement, for grace. Yet, it was her hair that captivated me the most—long, flowing past her waist, dark as the night itself, scented with the very essence of royalty. And she—she did not move.

She simply watched herself in the mirror, straight-backed, poised, her lips untouched by a single nervous tremor. "Tonight, I dress you," I murmured, reaching for the first piece of jewellery. Her lips curled slightly. A proud, knowing smirk. "Then do it well." I knelt before her stool, lifting the golden anklets adorned with tiny bells—the same ones she had worn as a child. Her bare feet rested gracefully on the stool's footrest, untouched by the floor.

Carefully, I clasped the first anklet around her delicate ankle, my fingers grazing her skin as I secured it. "You always teased me about these," she murmured, watching through the mirror. "Because you used to trip over them," I smirked. "Now, you move like a goddess." The second anklet followed, the tiny bells barely making a sound.

Next, I reached for the waist chain—a masterpiece of woven gold, embroidered with tiny emeralds. I stepped behind her, wrapping it around her soft, slender waist, fastening the clasp at her back. For a moment, my fingers lingered. Her posture did not falter, her spine remained straight—but her breath? It was the faintest shift, the barest inhale. Yet I caught it. "Perfect," I whispered. She did not respond, only lifting her chin slightly, as if silently agreeing.

The next piece—her earrings. I reached for them—delicate golden hoops woven with tiny pearls. I leaned forward, carefully clasping the first earring against her cool, smooth earlobe. She remained perfectly still, her head tilted ever so slightly to allow my touch. The second earring followed, the soft chime of pearls barely audible between us.

Then—the necklace. It was a heavy piece, thick and intricate, woven with emeralds, rubies, and gold. I placed it around her neck, securing it just beneath her elegant collarbones, where her pulse beat faintly. She watched me through the mirror. Not once did she look away. Not once did her pride falter.

Finally, I lifted the last piece—the shawl. A gossamer-thin veil of embroidered silk, woven with golden thread, meant to cascade over her shoulders and down her back. I draped it over her, fastening the edges just beneath her collarbone, my fingers tracing the fabric lightly. Then—she lifted her hand, placing it over mine. I froze.

For the first time, she looked away from the mirror. And turned to face me directly. "Brother." Her voice was softer now, lower, holding something I could not name. "Hmm?" "You always watch me," she murmured. I did not deny it. "I always do." Her fingers tightened slightly over mine, a silent exchange passing between us.

Then, she pulled away, slowly rising to her feet. The bells at her ankles jingled, their soft chime echoing in the chamber as she took her first step. She turned to the mirror once more, adjusting her veil, smoothing the embroidered fabric against her shoulders. And then—she spun.

The gold of her skirts flared around her, catching the lantern light, creating the illusion of liquid fire curling around her form. She stopped, tilting her head slightly, her gaze finding mine once more through the reflection. "Do I look like your Moonlight Princess tonight?" she whispered. My throat tightened. "You have always been." A small, knowing smile curved her lips. And then—she turned to leave.

The soft chime of golden bells followed her, a melody only I had ever truly listened to. Tonight, she would dance. And like always—I would be watching.

I left my sister's chamber, her scent of jasmine and saffron still lingering in my senses, the soft chime of her anklets still whispering in my ears.

But now—it was time to prepare myself. I made my way through the polished marble corridors, my golden shawl flowing behind me, every step measured, every movement carrying the authority of a ruler. As I reached the Queen's chamber, the doors swung open effortlessly, as if the very palace knew its King had arrived.

Inside, she stood waiting for me. Draped in an exquisite red and gold saree, woven with intricate designs only fit for royalty, she looked the picture of nobility. The delicate gold chains on her forehead gleamed beneath the lanterns, her earrings swayed gently as she moved forward, eyes gleaming with anticipation. Her gaze found mine, and immediately, she smiled—a smile of pure pleasure, of longing, of a deep desire to serve me in ways only she could.

"You came, my King," she whispered, stepping closer, her fingers lightly grazing the fabric of my robe. "Dress me," I commanded softly, my voice carrying through the chamber like a quiet storm. Her breath hitched, a subtle excitement flashing in her expression. She had been waiting for this. The maids stood behind her, ready to assist, but she lifted a hand—a silent order dismissing them.

Tonight, she would do this herself. With slow, deliberate movements, she reached for the first piece—a heavy golden necklace, bold and regal, adorned with rubies and emeralds. She lifted it with care, stepping behind me, her fingers grazing the warmth of my skin as she fastened it at the back of my neck.

"You shine like a god, my King," she murmured, pressing her fingers lightly against my shoulders before stepping back to admire her work. One by one, she adorned me in the finest pieces of royal ornamentation—bracelets of carved gold, rings adorned with precious gemstones, a waist belt encrusted with diamonds. With each piece, she took her time, her fingers lingering against my skin, her gaze tracing every movement as though savouring the moment.

She then reached for the final piece—the royal shawl. It was a magnificent work of art, woven from the rarest silk, embroidered with gold thread, its length cascading like liquid fire. She draped it over my shoulders, adjusting it carefully, her fingers smoothing the fabric with an almost reverent touch. Then, she stepped back, her eyes drinking me in. "Now, you look as you should." I watched her for a moment, her admiration pouring from her gaze like honey. I leaned in slightly, my voice low. "Do I please you, my Queen?" A faint blush spread across her cheeks. "Always," she admitted, her smile soft, adoring.

I extended my hand. "Come. It is time." She placed her delicate fingers into mine, her touch light but firm, her trust complete. Together, we left the chamber, stepping into the grand corridors of the palace, our arrival awaited by the entire court.

Chapter 21

The Dance of the Moonlight Princess

The moment the grand doors of the Royal Arena swung open, a golden glow flooded our path, illuminating the marbled corridor ahead. A magnificent, breathtaking sight unfolded before me. The arena was vast, circular, and unlike anything else in the kingdom—a masterpiece of golden grandeur, opulence, and endless reflections.

The entire hall was painted in rich shades of gold, every inch gleaming under the soft glow of chandeliers that dripped with crystals, their delicate prisms catching the light and scattering it like liquid stars. Mirrors covered the entire arena—from the towering walls to the high, vaulted ceiling. Even from where I stood, I could see my own reflection multiplied a hundredfold, flickering across the glass like a celestial vision.

The very ceiling, impossibly high, was also lined with mirrored panels, creating an illusion of endless space, as if the heavens themselves stretched above us. It was designed to amplify the brilliance of the evening—to let the spectacle of the night echo infinitely in gold and light. A series of golden lamps and intricately carved lanterns lined the perimeter of the arena, their flames dancing softly, casting warm shadows that flickered across the polished surfaces.

At the very heart of the arena lay a vast circular marble floor—the sacred stage for performances. The gleaming white marble, veined with ribbons of gold and deep emerald, shone like the surface of an untouched lake under the shimmering glow of chandeliers. It was a space untouched by war, untouched by politics—a place where only art, devotion, and elegance existed.

And tonight, it belonged to her. Surrounding the marble stage, the seating was arranged in a sixfold manner, encircling the performance space like the petals of a sacred lotus. At the opposite end of the main entrance, directly facing the performance stage, lay the royal seating stage—a place of honour, elevated and untouchable. At its very centre, placed several steps higher than the rest, was my throne.

A masterpiece of craftsmanship—made entirely of gold, carved with the markings of my royal lineage. It was adorned with symbols of the sun and moon, a representation of my dominion over both day and night, power and wisdom. At its base lay a finely crafted footbench, positioned for both comfort and presentation—a mark of ultimate authority. To my left, the Queen's throne stood, a seat of dignity and honor, her position cemented beside me. To my right, an identical seat had been placed—a throne meant for her. The Princess. Yet tonight, her seat remained empty. Because tonight, she was not to sit beside me, but to stand before me. To dance before me.

To remind the entire court why she was revered, untouchable, and unparalleled. Beyond the royal seating, in the remaining four sections of the arena, hundreds of nobles filled the space—lords and ladies of the highest status, draped in their finest silks and adorned with shimmering jewels. The gold of their attire blended seamlessly with the golden glow of the arena, making the room itself appear as if it had been forged from light. Their eyes turned toward us as we entered, and in that moment, I felt it—The power of being watched. The weight of their admiration.

The hushed reverence in the way their gazes followed my every step, their spines straightening, their lips parting slightly in awe. For I was the King. And she was my Queen. We walked forward with effortless grace, her delicate fingers resting lightly upon my arm, her presence beside me an embodiment of quiet pride and devotion. The whispers of the court grew, murmurs slipping like silk across the air. And then, as if on cue—the first notes of music stirred the silence.

A single chime of anklet bells. My fingers tightened slightly at my sides. A tension rippled through the air, a shift as every pair of eyes turned toward the stage. I moved forward, ascending the steps of the royal stage, each movement measured, deliberate, commanding. The Queen reached her seat, lowering herself gracefully onto the cushion, her golden robes settling around her like waves of silk. I ascended higher. And higher. Until I stood before my throne. The voices of the noblemen rose in reverence, a poetic declaration of my rule, my power, my divinity. "Glory to the King!" "Blessings upon His Majesty!" "May the King's bloodline reign eternal!" The voices mixed into a sea of devoted admiration, a chorus of worship for the ruler who stood before them.

I lowered myself onto my throne, resting my foot against the golden bench. The silence in the Royal Arena was profound, thick with anticipation, as if the very walls of the golden hall were holding their breath. Then—a sound.

A single, deliberate step echoed across the polished marble floor. A slow, measured chime of anklet bells followed, each delicate note weaving into the stillness like the first drops of rain before a storm. The grand golden doors at the far end of the arena creaked open, revealing her. The royal announcers immediately raised their voices, their words carrying a reverence reserved only for gods and sovereigns.

"Presenting the celestial jewel of the kingdom—Her Highness, the Princess, the embodiment of divine grace and beauty!" "She who dances with the moon, she who moves with the stars! The pride of the royal family, the soul of our great King!" A hush fell upon the court as every pair of eyes turned toward the entrance. And there—she stood. A vision of regal splendour, framed by the towering golden doors, her form radiant beneath the flickering glow of a thousand oil lamps.

She stepped forward with effortless grace, each movement precise, deliberate, commanding. The light shimmered against the gold and crimson fabric of her lehenga, the sheer, embroidered veil draped over her arms flowing like liquid silk. Tiny mirrors were sewn into the delicate embroidery, reflecting the chandeliers above, making her sparkle with every step.

Her waist belt gleamed, adorned with dangling pearls that swayed in time with her movement. The golden armlets hugged her soft skin, and the bells on her feet whispered secrets with every step. Behind her, her assistant dancers followed, dressed in complementary shades of ivory and gold, moving in perfect formation—but it was she who held the world captive.

She approached the sacred circular marble stage, placed at the very centre of the arena. And then—she stopped. She lifted her right hand, raising it before her face in a poised, delicate salute—

a silent offering, a reverent acknowledgment. To me. Her golden bangles clinked softly with the motion, her fingers forming an intricate mudra, an unspoken promise wrapped in art. I exhaled, my gaze locked onto hers, and with the slightest tilt of my head, I saluted her in return. A moment passed. The music began. And she moved.

Her feet struck the marble floor, sending ripples of sound through the hall—the rapid beats of her ghungroos (ankle bells) creating a hypnotic rhythm that matched the racing of my pulse. She spun, her skirts flaring like golden fire, the tiny mirror embellishments catching the light and scattering it like stars across the polished floors. The dance began slowly—each movement measured, precise, controlled.

Her eyes remained fixed on mine, her gaze never faltering, as if this performance was not for the audience, not for the nobles, not for the Queen—only for me. Her hands moved like poetry, each gesture sculpting the air, telling a story older than time itself. She executed intricate footwork, her ghungroos singing in perfect harmony with the tabla beats. Each step was deliberate, calculated—a language of devotion spoken through motion.

The tempo increased. She spun, faster, sharper, her jewellery glistening, her golden veil fluttering like a whisper of silk caught in the wind. Her eyes burned into me. Not with softness. Not with meekness. But with fierce intensity. A challenge. A declaration. A worship. A possession. The dance turned passionate, her movements fluid yet forceful—like a river surging through its course, untamed, unstoppable.

The fire of her spirit burned in every chakkar (spin), every controlled flick of her wrist, every glance that pierced straight through me. The musicians followed her lead, their instruments swelling, their beats chasing her rhythm like lovers yearning for her touch. I felt the blood in my veins ignite. She twirled again—this time slower, deliberately, her lehenga billowing around her like golden smoke. And then—she stopped mid-turn, just long enough to lock eyes with me once more.

Her chest rose and fell, the remnants of her motion still lingering in the air around her. And in that moment, I was gone. Lost. Completely undone. The way her body moved with such effortless grace, the way her lips parted slightly, the way the thin layer of sweat glistened at the base of her throat—I was maddened. By her eyes, which held unspoken words, unfulfilled desires, untamed devotion. By her lips, which parted ever so slightly as if whispering something only I could hear.

By the way she swayed, her body speaking a language only I could understand. The world around me blurred, the voices of the nobles, the flickering of the lamps, the whispers of the silk-draped ladies—all became distant. All that existed was her. The Princess. The woman who danced like she ruled the heavens themselves. My blood burned. My hands tightened against the throne's armrests. My mind spiralled. And as she spun one final time, her arms gracefully extending outward, her gaze still locked onto mine, I knew. I had always known. She was the only thing in this world that could drive me insane. And tonight—she did.

Chapter 22

Lullaby for My Moonlight Princess

The evening stretched into an endless symphony of music and movement, but I had stopped hearing anything after her dance. After that performance—after the way she moved, the way her gaze held mine with an intensity that unraveled something deep within me—I could no longer focus.
She sat beside me now, to my right, in her rightful place, her presence a force I could not ignore.

She was composed as ever, her back straight, her golden veil draped effortlessly over her shoulders. Yet, beneath the regal exterior, I could still see the fire that had not yet faded from her eyes.
Several more performances followed, each one meant to entertain the royal court. But they were nothing more than fleeting images before me. Shadows passing in the light of a greater flame.

I hardly noticed when the last performance ended.
It was only when I rose from my throne, the weight of my golden robes shifting, that I became aware of the room again.
At once, the entire court rose as well, hundreds of nobles and dignitaries bowing deeply, their heads lowered in reverence.

The Queen stood beside me, her posture graceful, her presence a quiet devotion.
My sister, however—she did not bow.
She never had to.
She merely stood, poised, radiant, timeless.
And together—we left.
The palace corridors stretched endlessly before me, lined with golden lanterns that flickered in the silence. The echoes of the evening's festivities faded behind us as we each retreated to our respective chambers.

The Queen left me with a soft bow, disappearing into the grand hallway that led to her own chambers.
My sister's presence lingered a moment longer.
She turned to look at me briefly, her expression unreadable, before she walked away.
And just like that, she was gone.
I stepped into my own chamber, where the servants were already waiting.

Piece by piece, they removed my golden attire, the jewellery that adorned my wrists and neck, the embroidered dhoti that marked my presence as a ruler.
And in its place, I was dressed in my night robes—a soft, white dhoti, simple yet adorned with the faint shimmer of golden embroidery. A shawl, light yet regal, draped over my shoulders.
But even as the softest silks touched my skin, even as my body was made ready for sleep—there was no peace.
I missed her.

It was like an ache—a silent longing that had no words, no logic. The absence of her presence beside me felt like a wound I could not see, but one I felt with every breath.

I stood by the open window, letting the cool night air brush against my skin, but even the moon—so beautiful, so bright—reminded me of her.
Her light.
Her grace.
Her fire.
I turned from the window abruptly.
I would not spend this night without her.
Without hesitation, I strode out of my chamber, walking through the quiet halls with measured steps.

The golden lanterns flickered as I passed, my white robes catching their glow, the faint whispers of the night breeze slipping through the open archways.
The guards standing outside her chamber straightened immediately. They did not question my presence.
They already knew.
At once, the towering doors swung open without a sound.
And there she was.

She was sitting by the grand open window, bathed in the soft glow of the full moon, her silhouette framed by the delicate golden curtains that fluttered in the evening breeze.
Her long, silken hair cascaded down her back, dark as the night sky itself, strands catching the faint silver light.
In her delicate hands, she held a small golden cup—her bedtime drink, warm milk infused with saffron, turmeric, and crushed cardamom.
She raised it to her lips, taking a slow sip, her eyes locked on the moon outside.
She did not hear me enter.
Or—perhaps she did, but chose not to acknowledge it just yet.

I stepped forward, my bare feet silent against the marble.

She sighed softly, lowering her cup just as I approached.
Then, she turned to look at me.
And in that moment—she smiled.
A small, knowing, mischievous smile.
A smile that made my chest tighten, made something coil deep within me, something I could not name.
Because there, just above her lips, was a thin white moustache of milk.
The sight of it undid me completely.

"You look ridiculous," I murmured, my voice lower than I expected.
Her smile widened.
"Do I?" she teased, her voice laced with amusement, a playful challenge dancing in her eyes.
Before she could react, I moved forward, sinking onto the couch beside her.
She watched me, unblinking, as I reached out and touched her.
With slow, deliberate movements, I wiped the milk away with my bare fingers, tracing the soft skin of her upper lip.
The moment stilled.
The world quieted.
And I realized something in that moment—something I had always known but never admitted.
I loved touching her.

I loved the feel of her skin beneath my fingers, the way her body remained still, yet responsive.
I loved the way she looked at me when I touched her.
As if it was the most natural thing in the world.
I let my fingers linger for a fraction too long.
Then—I cupped her face in my hands.
She did not move away.
She did not look away.

Instead, she tilted her chin slightly upward, her dark lashes fluttering, her breath the faintest whisper against my skin.
"Why do you always look at me like that?" she murmured.
I did not answer.
I could not.
Because I did not know the answer.

Instead, I simply stared into her deep, mesmerizing eyes, tracing the way they reflected the moonlight like a thousand stories left untold.
And then—she did something unexpected.
Without breaking eye contact, she lifted her cup once more, tilting it ever so slightly.
She brought it near my lips, the warm fragrance of saffron and cardamom filling the air between us.
"Here," she whispered, her voice softer than the night itself.
For a moment, I did not move.
Then, I leaned in.
The warm milk touched my lips, the richness of it lingering on my tongue.

I drank—not out of thirst, but because it was her offering.
And as I swallowed, her fingers brushed against my jaw, lingering for just a second too long.
And in that moment, as the moon cast its silver glow around us, as the night wrapped itself in quiet intimacy, I knew—
I could never leave her.
Not tonight.
Not ever.

She tilted her head slightly, her long, perfumed hair spilling over her shoulder as she looked at me with those deep, knowing eyes.
"Will you sleep with me tonight?" she asked, her voice a whisper that slipped through the night like silk.

I exhaled slowly, letting the weight of her words settle between us.

"Preciously, I came here to stay with you, my darling."
The moment I spoke, her face illuminated, a soft, radiant glow overtaking her expression.
She smiled—not just any smile, but the kind that reached into my chest and wrapped itself around my very being.
For a moment, she simply stood there, gazing at me, drinking me in as if she had been waiting for this moment as much as I had.

Then, without breaking eye contact, she turned away slightly and walked toward the nearest golden lamp.
With a delicate flick of her fingers, she extinguished the flame, the warm glow flickering into nothingness.
She moved to the next one, dimming its light as well.
One by one, the oil lamps that bathed the room in golden hues faded, until only the main lantern remained.
She turned toward it, lifting the glass cover just enough to soften its light, dimming the space into a shadowed world of silver and gold.

Now, the moonlight reigned.
The soft beams spilled through the open balcony, painting everything in a cool, ethereal glow.
The curtains fluttered lightly in the night breeze, their sheer fabric catching the light, creating an illusion of waves in a golden ocean.
And there—in the heart of it all—stood my sister.

She had already changed into her night attire—a white dhoti, flowing and delicately pleated, paired with a matching white tube top embroidered with gold.

It clung to her figure just enough to reveal her divine elegance, the golden accents catching the silver light of the moon.

She was a vision of both purity and fire, an untouched goddess draped in silken simplicity.
And in that moment, as I watched her standing there, the moonlight tracing the soft curves of her body, something within me unravelled completely.
She was so exquisite—so painfully beautiful—that it almost felt unfair to gaze upon her.
Yet, I could not look away.
Not when the soft light kissed the delicate slopes of her shoulders.
Not when the pearls of sweat at the base of her throat glistened faintly.
Not when her waist curved so effortlessly, framed by the loose drapes of her dhoti.
She walked toward me, her movements fluid, slow, deliberate.

Then—she guided me to the bed.
Her fingers brushed lightly against my arm, a silent command, a quiet invitation.
I obeyed.
I settled onto the silken mattress, it's cool fabric melting beneath my warmth.
She stood beside me for a brief moment, looking down at me—as if memorizing the sight.
And then—she leaned in.

Her lips found my forehead, a featherlight kiss pressed just above my brows, lingering there for a breath too long.
The warmth of it seeped into my skin, leaving something behind—something I could not name, something that stayed even after she pulled away.

Then, in one graceful movement, she stepped back and moved toward the other side of the bed.
I watched, entranced, as she lifted the sheets and slid into the space beside me.

The mattress dipped beneath her delicate weight, the silk shifting, settling as she curled into the warmth of our shared space.
She turned toward me; her dark eyes gleaming under the soft luminescence of the moon.
Then—she lifted her hand, beckoning me.
A simple gesture, but one that held the weight of a thousand silent promises.
The elegant curve of her fingers, the subtle flick of her wrist—it was not just an invitation.
It was a claim.
A demand.

Her eyes, steady and unwavering, spoke louder than words ever could.
"Come."
Her eyes, steady and unwavering, spoke louder than words ever could.
"Come."
But tonight, something within me had shifted.
For the first time, I did not move toward her arms.

Instead, I reached forward, my fingers brushing against her wrist as I gently pulled her toward me.
"No," I whispered, my voice softer than the night breeze.
She blinked, her lips parting slightly in surprise.
"Come to my chest."
She stilled.
A moment of hesitation flickered in her gaze.

For so long, she had been the one to hold me, to cradle me, to whisper me into sleep.
But tonight, I wanted to be the one who gave.
Who held.
Who loved.

"Tonight, I will make you sleep," I murmured, gently, firmly.
Her eyes softened. A flicker of something deep—something unspoken—passed through them.
"Brother…" she whispered; her voice laced with emotion.
She hesitated once more, but I did not let her refuse.
Before she could insist otherwise, I wrapped my arms around her waist, pulling her gently, but with certainty, into my chest.

She gasped slightly, her breath warm against my skin, her hands instinctively pressing against my shoulders.
"Let me take care of you," I whispered, my lips brushing against her temple.
She trembled slightly—not in fear, not in resistance, but in something far deeper.
A surrender.
A trust.
And then—slowly, hesitantly—she melted into my embrace.

Her forehead rested against my collarbone, her body pressing softly against mine as she let out the faintest sigh.
Her warmth seeped into me, filling every hollow part of my being.
I cupped the back of her head, threading my fingers through the soft strands of her long hair, stroking her gently, soothingly.
And then—I kissed her.
Softly.
Again.
And again.

First on her forehead, then on her hair, then at the crown of her head—each kiss a whisper, a promise, a devotion.
"You are my everything," I murmured between kisses.
"My most precious one."
"My moonlight."

She clung to me tighter, her arms wrapping fully around my back, her fingers gripping the fabric of my white dhoti.
She pressed so close, so tightly, as if she wanted to disappear into me.
I could feel the rhythm of her breath, the way it rose and fell against my chest.
Her breath was exquisite to me.
Just like her.
She inhaled deeply, pressing her face further against me. And then—I felt it.
Her lips.
Soft.
Warm.
A delicate kiss against my bare chest.
Then—another.
And then she breathed me in, inhaling my scent, letting her lips linger as if she could memorize me with every sense she had.
My own breath caught.
I closed my eyes, lowering my head to bury my face into the crown of her hair.

I inhaled deeply, drinking in the fragrance of sandalwood, saffron, and something purely… her.
She smelled like home.
Like the only place I would ever belong.
And then—I did something I had never done before.
I began to sing.
A soft lullaby.

A song meant not for me this time—but for her.
I cradled her close, letting my voice flow gently into the night, my fingers rubbing soothing circles on her back, beating her shoulder lightly in rhythm.
Her body relaxed completely, surrendering into my embrace.

Then—she turned her face up toward me.
Her eyes met mine.
The moonlight poured in through the open balcony, casting silver light upon her face, illuminating the softness in her gaze, the delicate parting of her lips.
And in that moment—she looked like a child.
A beautiful, delicate, utterly precious child.
Vulnerable.
Trusting.
Entirely, completely, mine.
I lowered my forehead to hers, pressing our noses together in the gentlest of touches.
She exhaled—a slow, shaky breath that carried the weight of something unspoken.
And in that very moment, I inhaled her breath out—
like it was the most sacred offering, like the rarest treasure I could ever receive.
Like I was drawing in something beyond the physical—some kind of power, some deep fulfilment, something I had been searching for my entire existence.
I let it settle within me, let it become a part of me.
Her warmth. Her breath. Her very essence.
"Shh…" I whispered.

She curled deeper into me, her legs tucking up slightly as she burrowed against my warmth.
I tightened my arms around her, securing her, holding her, protecting her.

And as I stroked her hair, as I continued to sing in a low, soothing tone, as I whispered her into sleep the way she had always done for me—
I realized something.
I had never held anything more precious in my arms.
Nothing more exquisite.
Nothing more sacred.

Sleep now, my moon, my guiding light,
Rest in my arms through silent night.
No storm shall reach, no shadow stay,
For I am here, not far away.

Your breath so soft, like petals fall,
A whispered song that sings through all.
Your warmth, your touch, your sacred grace,
Forever safe in my embrace.

Close your eyes, my gentle star,
Dream of lands where love's not far.
Let golden tides in slumber rise,
I'll guard you here, 'neath endless skies.

No fire shall burn, no sorrow near,
No whispered doubt, no trace of fear.
For in my arms, you're whole, you're free,
The only home you'll ever need.

So hush, my love, let time stand still,
Wrapped in arms that always will…
Hold you close, keep you near,
My sister, my world—my heart sincere.

Chapter 23

The Peak of Her Warmth

The night stretched endlessly, wrapped in the silver glow of the moon, draped in the warmth of her embrace. Her body against mine was a world I never wanted to leave—a sanctuary of warmth, scent, and something unspoken, something eternal.

I held her close, my arms locked around her waist as if I were afraid she would vanish the moment I loosened my grip. *And I sang.* My voice, soft and deep, carried through the silence, a lullaby meant to soothe her soul, just as she had always done for me.

But as the song faded into the hush of the night, as my voice lowered into a gentle sleeping tone, something caught in my throat. A sudden cough broke the silence. It was light at first, but then another followed, shaking my chest against hers.

Her entire body stiffened. And then—before I could recover, she moved. Swiftly, instinctively, with the kind of urgency that only belonged to her when it came to me. She pulled back slightly, her hands gripping my shoulders, her gaze filled with instant worry.

"Brother—are you alright?"

Her voice was soft, but frantic, as if my cough alone had the power to break something within her. I swallowed, trying to suppress it, but she wasn't having it.

Before I could murmur any excuse, before I could assure her that it was nothing, she had already made up her mind.

"Come to me."

It was a simple command—one I had heard countless times before. One that had shaped my entire life. *But tonight—tonight, it unravelled me completely.*

She pulled me up, guiding my head toward her chest, shifting herself so that I had no choice but to sink into the softness of her embrace. *And I did. Without resistance. Without hesitation.* Because the moment she pulled me in, I lost all will to refuse.

My face pressed between the valley of her full-grown chest, my breath caught in my throat—not because of discomfort, but because of the unbearable, intoxicating sensation of being there. Her skin was warm, delicate, scented with the lingering fragrance of saffron and sandalwood. Her heartbeat—steady, rhythmic, mesmerizing—pulsed beneath my ear. *I breathed her in.*

And then—I couldn't stop.

I buried myself deeper, rubbing my face against the soft, heated skin, my hands tightening around her waist as if I wanted to disappear into her completely. The feel of her collarbones beneath my lips, the way her breath hitched slightly, the way she tightened her hold around me as if shielding me from the world—*It was too much. And yet, not enough.*

"You don't have to hold back," she whispered, her voice so gentle, so knowing, as if she could sense the storm raging within me.

I did not hold back. Not this time. Not tonight. I kissed her chest—soft, slow, reverent. Again. And again. My lips touched her skin like a prayer, my breaths uneven, drinking her in as if she were something sacred, something that could never be replaced.

"Rest, my love," she murmured, her hand slipping into my hair, her fingers threading through the strands, her touch so slow, so tender. She began to hum softly, the same sleeping tone that had always put me to sleep as a child. And just like every night before—*it worked.*

I could feel her warmth seeping into me, the rhythmic rise and fall of her chest beneath my cheek, the soft beads of sweat gathering at the base of her throat, sliding against my skin like tiny drops of elixir.

I had never felt more at peace. I had never felt more obsessed. I tightened my hold around her, pressing deeper, inhaling deeper, feeling as though I could drown in this, and I would never wish to be saved.

And as her voice continued to hum through the night, soothing, lulling, wrapping itself around my senses like a sacred spell—*I knew. I was lost in her. Completely.*

The night wrapped around us like a soft, unbroken spell—silent, endless, boundless. Her warmth, her scent, her presence drowned me in something deeper than longing. *I was obsessed. Completely.*

My arms tightened around her waist, my fingers grazing the delicate ridges of her spine, as I buried myself deeper into her embrace. I wanted more. *More of her warmth. More of her scent. More of her.*

I didn't just want to be held—I wanted to be taken in, to be consumed by her presence. And then, a forgotten memory stirred within me. A distant fragment of our childhood—a time when I was small, fragile, weeping in her arms.

I remembered how she used to soothe me, to quiet my cries, to calm my restless heart. How, on certain nights when I was inconsolable, she would hold me closer, whispering lullabies, letting me feel her warmth in the purest, most innocent way. A memory so distant, yet so potent, that it burned through my mind like fire.

And suddenly—*I ached for that comfort again. For her. Completely.*

I hesitated, my heartbeat loud in my own ears. Would she allow it? Would she look at me strangely? Would she turn away from me?

The very thought sent a shiver through me. But the longing—the desperate need—was stronger than my hesitation.

I lifted my head slowly, resting my forehead against her collarbone, inhaling deeply.

Then, in a voice barely above a whisper, I asked:

"My darling sister…"

She stirred slightly, her fingers still threading through my hair, her embrace still as strong as ever.

"Hmm?" Her voice was soft, patient.

I hesitated for a moment, then gathered my courage.

"I want to be fed by you."

She stilled. I could feel the subtle tension in her breath—not from hesitation, not from refusal—but from something else entirely. Something unspoken.

I swallowed, my fingers tightening slightly against her waist.

"Like before… like when we were small… when you wanted to make me happy."

The room felt impossibly quiet.

And then—*she laughed.* A soft, warm, knowing laugh. Her arms wrapped even tighter around me, her lips brushing lightly against my forehead.

"Why not?" she whispered, her voice dripping with affection. "I am completely yours."

I shuddered—not from fear, not from hesitation, but from something overwhelming, something beyond words.

But even after her answer, *I needed to hear it again.* I needed the confirmation—the reassurance that she would not turn away from me.

So I lifted my head again, meeting her gaze beneath the moonlight.

"Give it to me," I whispered.

She held my face between her hands, her thumbs grazing my cheekbones, her dark, knowing eyes never leaving mine.

"Take it yourself," she murmured, her voice a mixture of teasing and tenderness. "I am yours."

My breath caught in my throat. *The words sent a slow, creeping shiver down my spine.* The way she said it. The way she gave herself to me, so completely, so unshaken.

She was mine. And I… was lost in her.

The night held us in its silent embrace, the moonlight pouring through the open balcony, casting its silver glow upon the only world that existed for me—*her.*

She lay beneath me, her warmth, her scent, her presence engulfing my senses like a sacred flame. My breath was uneven, my body trembling—not from fear, not from hesitation, but from something far deeper, something that had no name.

With a quiet reverence, I reached out, my fingers brushing against her silk-clad form. *There was a weight to the moment—a heaviness that clung to the air between us.* A mix of devotion, longing, and something that had always been there but had never been spoken aloud.

I hesitated, my fingers stilling against the fabric. *Not because I doubted. Not because I feared. But because she was too precious to rush. Too divine to approach without complete reverence.*

She saw my hesitation, her lips curving into the faintest smile, her hands lifting to cup my face.

"You are trembling, my love," she whispered. Her voice was soft, soothing, filled with a quiet amusement that only she could carry in a moment like this.

"You have no reason to fear."

I exhaled; my breath shaky.

"I have every reason to."

She tilted her head slightly, watching me with those dark, knowing eyes—the eyes that had always unravelled me, that had always made me feel like I belonged to her and her alone.

"Then come," she murmured, pulling me closer. *And I took the upper one.*

I leaned in, my forehead pressing against her collarbone, my breath mixing with the warmth of her breast. Slowly, I let my lips graze against her—a soft, fleeting touch, nothing more than a whisper.

Her scent enveloped me—sandalwood, saffron, the faintest trace of jasmine woven into her very being. *And in that moment, I was lost.*

I had always known that she was my world, but now, I could feel it in every part of me—in my breath, in my pulse, in the way my entire body trembled under the weight of her presence.

"Is this what you want?" she whispered, her voice like a lullaby, like something ancient and unbreakable.

I didn't answer. I couldn't. Instead, I let my actions speak.

My fingers traced the delicate lines of her shoulders, my touch featherlight, as if I were afraid, she would disappear beneath me. She didn't move away. She didn't resist. She only watched, her expression unreadable, her chest rising and falling in a rhythm that was too steady, too composed—except for the faintest, almost imperceptible hitch in her breath.

And then, I pressed my lips against her untouched centre of her chest once more. *Slower this time. Deeper. More reverent.* A kiss not of lust, but of worship.

Her hands slid into my hair, her fingers threading through the strands with a tenderness that made my breath catch. I buried myself against her, my face against the curve of her shoulder, inhaling deeply.

"You smell like heaven," I whispered, my voice barely audible.

She laughed softly, her arms tightening around me, pulling me deeper into her warmth.

"And you," she murmured, "smell like you belong to me."

And in that moment, I knew it was true. I had belonged to her from the very beginning. I always would.

Chapter 24

The Moment I Became Hers

The night lay heavy upon us, wrapped in moonlight and silence, as if the world itself had paused to listen.
She was my world, my sanctuary, my undoing.
Cradled in her embrace, my breath mingled with hers, slow and steady, as if we had become part of the same rhythm, the same unspoken melody.

She was not a woman who swayed easily—not to emotion, not to longing, not even to fate itself. She carried herself with the grace of a goddess sculpted in marble, untouchable yet worshipped, regal yet shrouded in mystery. Her eyes, deep as the night sky, never revealed more than she intended, her emotions veiled beneath layers of pride, discipline, and an unspoken power that made even kings bow before her. To the world, she was untouchable, a vision of perfection beyond mortal grasp. But here, beneath the hush of moonlight, the walls she had built, the throne upon which she ruled so effortlessly—none of it stood between us anymore. And in that moment, I saw not only my sister, my princess, my guiding star—but the only being I had ever truly belonged to.

Her warmth seeped into my skin, and I wanted more.
More of her presence.
More of her touch.

More of the feeling that I belonged only to her.
Slowly, reverently, I lifted my head from her chest, my lips grazing her collarbone in a whisper of a touch.
She did not flinch.
She did not pull away.
Instead, her fingers trailed into my hair, her touch light, thoughtful—knowing.

I pressed my lips gently against her shoulder, a slow, lingering kiss that spoke of devotion rather than mere longing.
Her breath hitched.
Just slightly.
A flicker of something—an emotion that neither of us dared to name.
I lifted my gaze to meet hers, searching for permission, for reassurance, for something beyond words.
Her eyes held me—steady, unwavering, deep like the endless sky.
I hesitated.
"May I?"
A simple question.
A world of meaning.
She did not answer immediately.
Instead, her lips curved into the faintest of smiles—one filled with understanding, with quiet surrender.
And then—she hummed.

A sound so soft, so delicate, it sent a shiver through me.
I leaned in, closing the space between us with excruciating slowness, until our breaths became one, until the warmth of her exhale became the only air I could breathe.
My lips touched hers—light as a feather, soft as the moon's glow.
It was not hunger.
It was not urgency.
It was a worship, a promise, a binding.

She did not push forward.
She did not pull away.
She simply let me take my time—as if allowing me to carve this moment into my soul.

A slow exhale left her lips, a sigh wrapped in surrender.
She was my sanctuary, my solace, my everything.
As my lips met hers, slow and deliberate, it felt as if I were pulling her very essence into me—like I was breathing in her soul, consuming the warmth, the fire, the unspoken devotion that had always existed between us.

For a heartbeat, she remained still—but then, something changed.
A tremor ran through her, and suddenly, she was no longer the passive moonlight beneath my touch. She reached for me, claimed me, devoured me—as if she had been starved for a thousand lifetimes, as if my lips held the very air she needed to breathe.

Her fingers tangled into my hair, pulling me deeper, closer, as if she could steal the very essence of me and make it hers. Her lips moved against mine with a fervour that sent fire through my veins—not reckless, not desperate, but filled with something far more intoxicating.

It was need.
Not the need of the body, not simple longing—but a craving so profound. It shook me as if, in this kiss, she was searching for something unseen, something unspoken, something only I could give her. And I gave it freely. Because she was my everything. And I—I had always been hers.

Simultaneously, a force beyond my control stirred, a primal urge that moved my body against hers. Unbidden, I felt something shift within me—something raw, something uncontrollable, something that belonged to her. I found myself pressed against the soft curve of her belly; a wordless plea born of an ancient, untamed desire.
The night stretched on, the moonlight spilling over us like liquid silver, illuminating the space that both separated and bound us together.

She was everything—the only warmth I had ever known, the only sanctuary I had ever sought.
As I held her, the world outside ceased to exist.
She had turned away from me, her back pressed against my chest, her breath uneven, her body still.
A quiet shyness lingered in the air between us, something soft and delicate, as if she herself was uncertain of the emotions unravelling within her.

I could feel it—the hesitation, the unspoken tremor beneath her composure.
But she did not pull away.
She never did.
Instead, she allowed me to hold her, allowed me to meld myself to her shape, to fit into the spaces that had always been carved for me.
My arms wrapped around her, my fingers tracing the edges of her form, reverent, slow—as if I were memorizing her all over again.
I exhaled, pressing my forehead gently against the nape of her neck, breathing her in.
The scent of sandalwood and saffron, the soft warmth of her skin, the way her breath caught when I drew near—everything about her was intoxicating.

I did not think.
I did not reason.
I simply followed the pull of her presence, the way she had always guided me without a word.

My lips found the hollow beneath her ear, barely grazing the sensitive skin, a whisper of warmth, a silent confession.
The silken swell of her soft curve of her lower back pressed against me, a gentle reminder of her captivating form, and a spark ignited within me, a primal recognition of her beauty. She shivered beneath my touch, her breath catching in her throat—so quiet, so delicate, but I felt it.

"Brother…"
A soft, trembling whisper—so faint that it barely escaped her lips, yet it resonated through me like a pulse.
I swallowed hard, my grip around her tightening, as if I could keep this moment from slipping through my fingers.
Her body relaxed into me, surrendering, allowing, as if she knew there was no part of me that did not belong to her.
I closed my eyes.

"Shh…" I whispered against her skin.
She sighed—a sound filled with something deeper than longing, something that spoke of lifetimes intertwined. And then, with a hesitant breath, she subtly shifted, her lower back pressing against mine, a delicate rhythm that spoke of unspoken desires.

I held her closer. My hand, drawn by an unseen force, found the gentle rise and fall of her chest curves.
I let the night hold us both in its silent embrace.
And as the stars flickered beyond the veil of the palace, as the world melted away into nothingness—
I knew.

There was no greater peace than being here, wrapped in her presence, bound by the devotion we could never name.
A subtle dampness, a warmth that bloomed against my hand, told a silent tale.
Her dhoti, the silken barrier between us, clung to her skin, a testament to the passion that stirred within her.
With a reverence born of deep love, I loosened the folds, each thread unwinding like a whispered secret.
Before me, she was an exquisite vision, a masterpiece of nature, untouched, pure.

My gaze lingered on the delicate curve of her back, the gentle swell of her hip, each line a poem written in flesh.
And then, my hand found the sacred space between her thighs, the rose petals of her, now revealed.
It was as if I held the very heart of the universe, the most precious and fragile treasure ever bestowed.
I cradled her close, our bodies a perfect fit, a symphony of entwined desires.

"My love," I whispered, my voice thick with emotion, "I love you more than life itself."
And in that moment, as time itself held its breath, I became the one who unveiled her hidden beauty, the one who claimed her virginity, a sacred trust bestowed upon me, a treasure beyond all earthly measure.
A wave of profound unity washed over me, a sense of completion that transcended the boundaries of self.
My world, once a fragmented mosaic, was now whole, a perfect circle.

I delved into the depths of her being, a journey into the very essence of existence, where two souls became one, and she was

no longer a virgin. She clung to me like a delicate whisper of trust, her body pressed close as we moved in perfect harmony. Her gaze, shy yet filled with something deeper, held mine, as if I were the only one who could keep her safe in the entire life.
This was no ordinary intimacy.
It was a sacred merging, a bond forged with respect, with deep value, and with a trembling awe.
It was the culmination of a love that transcended the boundaries of brother and elder sister, a love that was both tender and profound.

In this moment, we were no longer a king and a princess. No longer a ruler and his most cherished companion.
We were simply two souls entwined, two halves of the same existence, drawn together by something deeper than fate, more ancient than time.
She had always been mine.

Not in a way that the world could understand, not in the way of kings and their queens, nor of lovers who whispered promises under the stars.
She was mine in a way that defied meaning itself.

A presence woven into the fabric of my being, a warmth that had shaped me, nurtured me, held me together through the storms of power and duty.
And tonight, in this sacred silence, there was no distance left between us.
Her touch was not just tenderness—it was a vow, a surrender, an unspoken truth that had always been there, waiting to be realized.

In her embrace, there was trust so absolute, love so boundless, devotion so pure that even the gods would look upon us and remain silent.
For in the quiet chambers of the night, beneath the watchful silver light, she became my beginning, my end, my everything.
And as the world outside faded into nothingness, I knew—I would belong to her forever.

In the hush of night, where shadows fade,
she lay in my arms, soft and unafraid.
Not as a queen, nor princess adorned,
but as the soul to which mine was sworn.

Her breath was the whisper of silk in the air,
a promise unspoken, a love laid bare.
Not bound by law, nor written decree,
but by fate's own hand, entwining me.

A vow unspoken, yet stronger than stone,
a truth the heavens had always known.
No distance between us, no world apart,
for she was the keeper, the pulse of my heart.

Not stolen, not taken, but given so free,
a trust unshaken, as deep as the sea.
No throne, no power, no kingdom so grand,
could tear her from me, nor loosen my hand.

For in this moment, in love's quiet breath,
we found no sin, no fear, no death.
Only the echo of a bond so true—
the night, the stars, and me… and you.

Chapter 25

A Vow Written in Scarlet

A dull ache settled in my body, a reminder of the way she had clung to me, held me, surrendered to me. The night had unraveled her, stripped away the last of her restraint, revealing a side of her I had never seen—a side that had always lingered beneath her regal composure, waiting, aching to be set free. The way she moved, the way she clung to me, the way her lips found mine with feverish desperation—it was not innocence, nor hesitation, but something far deeper, far wilder. She had ruled kingdoms with grace, commanded courts with pride, yet last night, she had ruled me—not with words, but with touch, with fire, with an urgency that burned through my very soul.

She had given herself to me without fear, without reluctance. She had taken as much as she had given. And now, in the golden hush of morning, I held the woman she had always been—the woman she had never allowed herself to become before me.

Yet, it was not discomfort that stirred me awake—it was the weight of her presence. For the first time, she lay atop me, her body draped over mine like a silken tapestry, her breath slow and steady against my skin. Her face, serene in sleep, rested on my shoulder, a single arm tucked beneath her cheek, as if even in slumber, she sought to keep me near.

Her hair, dark as midnight, cascaded over my chest, strands curling in the warmth of our entangled bodies. A faint trace of moisture—a remnant of her dreams—glistened against my skin, a delicate imprint of her presence, of the night that had bound us beyond the confines of words.

The golden bedsheets tangled around us, veiling the sacredness of what had passed between us. The soft glow of the rising sun caressed the curves of her form, tracing the delicate lines of her back, her shoulders, her regal frame now unguarded in the quiet vulnerability of sleep.

She had always been untouchable, a celestial being shrouded in grace, adorned with an air of distant pride. But now, in the stillness of morning, she was simply mine. Not a princess. Not a royal. Not an untouchable deity.

Just her. The woman who had ruled over my heart long before I had ever ruled a kingdom. Carefully, I shifted, my fingertips tracing slow, reverent patterns across her back, as if committing every inch, every breath of her existence to memory. The warmth of her skin, the rhythmic rise and fall of her chest, the delicate flutter of her lashes against my shoulder—all of it felt like something more than mortal, more than fleeting.

She sighed in her sleep, curling closer, as if she knew I was watching. As if she, too, had no desire to let go. I pressed my lips to the crown of her head, inhaling the scent of jasmine and saffron that still lingered in her hair. She was my world, my sanctuary, my undoing.

And I—I had never been more certain that I belonged to her. The world outside was awakening, the palace stirring beyond these walls, but here, in the hush of golden morning light, time remained ours. For just a little longer, I would hold her. For just a little longer, I would not let go.

The world beyond these walls had awakened, but within this sacred space, time remained still. Wrapped in golden silence, I held her, unwilling to move, unwilling to let go. Even as a dull ache lingered in my body, I welcomed it—a small price to pay for the privilege of keeping her draped over me, her warmth pressed into my skin. She was a part of me now, as if we had been carved from the same breath of existence.

Her bare back rose and fell in a slow, steady rhythm, the faint traces of her slumber still cradling her. Sunlight streamed through the silk-curtained windows, painting her in gold and fire, as if the very heavens had chosen to honor her beauty.

I traced slow, idle circles against the delicate curve of her spine, memorizing the way her skin felt beneath my fingertips—soft, warm, untouched by the burdens of the world. She belonged to no one but herself.
And yet, in this moment, she was mine.

A soft sigh escaped her lips, a breath so gentle that it sent a quiet tremor through me.
She stirred.
A faint murmur, a whisper of something unspoken, tumbled from her mouth as she shifted slightly against me. The weight of her, the way she unconsciously sought my warmth even in sleep, sent a rush of emotion through my chest—something deeper than devotion, something I had no name for.

She sighed again, her lashes fluttering, her body shifting as she slowly began to rise from the depths of her dreams.
I could not help myself.
Before her eyes fully opened, before the world returned to her, I cupped her face between my hands—reverently, as though she were a sacred offering—and captured her lips with mine.

Her breath caught, a faint gasp swallowed between us as my mouth moved against hers—not demanding, not urgent, but slow, deliberate, savouring. I kissed her as if I had all the time in the world, as if I could taste the remnants of her dreams upon her lips.

And then, I breathed her in.
The warmth of her, the scent of sleep clinging to her skin, the untainted essence of morning still lingering between us—it was intoxicating, more precious than any fragrance that had ever graced the royal gardens.

She sighed softly against my lips, her body melting into mine, responding before thought could reach her.
When I pulled away, she remained close, her nose barely brushing against mine.

Her eyes, still heavy with sleep, fluttered open—dazed, dreamy, as if she were still caught between the remnants of the night and the embrace of morning.
A slow, drowsy smile curved her lips, her voice no more than a whisper.

"What are you doing, my King?"
I traced my thumb across her cheek, inhaling the scent of jasmine that still clung to her skin.
"Claiming my morning," I murmured.

And she let me.

I would not let her speak—not yet.
The morning light bathed us in its golden glow, weaving through the silk-draped windows, casting soft patterns across our skin. The air between us was thick with the lingering remnants of the night, a silent acknowledgment of the sacred bond we had sealed. We stood together, unguarded, untethered by the world beyond these walls.

She made no move to step away from me, and I made no effort to release her.
With slow, reverent hands, I reached for her garments, the ones she had discarded the night before. For the first time, I was to dress her myself, not as her King, not even as her brother—but as the only man who had the right to touch her in this way.

She watched me, unmoving, her eyes carrying an unreadable depth as I wrapped the soft white dhoti around her delicate waist. The fabric slid over her skin like whispered devotion, like the silent poetry of my fingertips against her. It clung to her, draping elegantly, embroidered with golden threads that shimmered with each movement.

Next, I reached for the silk tube top, lifting it with care, as if it were something sacred.
Her breath hitched as I moved behind her, pressing the fabric against her chest, fastening it with deliberate precision. My fingers brushed against her shoulders, her collarbones, the dip of her spine—places I had memorized in the hush of moonlight, places I had claimed beneath the sanctity of the night.

Still, she did not move.
Still, she let me.

When I finished, I stepped back, my gaze drinking her in. She stood tall, regal, radiant in white and gold—a vision of divinity, of something both untouchable and mine.

And then—she turned to me.
Her hands, small but strong, reached for the fabric of my dhoti. She did not ask permission. She simply took it upon herself, as if this, too, was her right. With steady hands, she adjusted the cloth around my waist, tightening the folds, securing it with care.

She was quiet, focused, the warmth of her fingertips lingering even after she had stepped back.
And before I could say a word—she stepped forward, closing the space between us, and wrapped herself around me.
A silent embrace.
No hesitation, no words.

Just her arms circling me, her head resting against my chest, the rhythmic beat of her heart pressed against mine.
I exhaled slowly, closing my eyes, wrapping her in my own arms. She had given herself to me last night—but this, this moment, felt like something even deeper.

A vow.
A promise.
A love that did not need to be spoken.
I let my fingers slide through her long, fragrant hair, inhaling her scent one last time before I spoke.
"It is time."
She nodded against me but did not move.
With reluctance, I released her, stepping back just enough to compose myself.
Turning to the door, I raised my voice with quiet authority.

"Open the doors. Let the maids in."
At once, the heavy golden doors swung open. The hush of morning was broken by the soft shuffle of footsteps as the royal maids entered, their heads bowed, their hands clasped. They moved efficiently, tending to the chamber, yet not one of them dared to lift their eyes toward us.

As the morning light poured in, casting golden streaks across the chamber, my gaze fell upon the bed where she had lain beside me.

And then—I saw it.
A faint, delicate blood stain upon the golden sheets. A mark of something sacred, something that spoke of change, of devotion, of an unbreakable bond that had been sealed between us.

My breath caught in my throat.
For a long moment, I could do nothing but stare, as an unfamiliar emotion swelled within me—something vast, something that reached beyond mere love or desire.

It was reverence. It was devotion. It was the proof of a moment that would never fade from my soul.
With slow, deliberate hands, I reached forward, gathering the fabric, lifting it carefully as if it were the most precious relic ever to grace the earth.

And then—I pressed my lips to it.
A silent vow. A whispered promise.
I closed my eyes, inhaling the weight of what it meant. She had given herself to me completely—not just in body, but in trust, in surrender, in love.

A soft rustle.

I turned to see her watching me.
She lay upon the bed, propped on one elbow, her hair cascading over her shoulder in waves of midnight silk. Her eyes, deep and unreadable, held something unspoken—a quiet understanding of the devotion that had gripped me.

I met her gaze and held it.
"This," I murmured, my voice barely above a whisper, as I traced the fabric between my fingers, "is proof of what you mean to me."

Her lips parted, but no words came.
She simply watched, her chest rising and falling in steady rhythm, her eyes glistening with an emotion I could not name.

"I will keep this," I continued, my voice trembling with something unshakable, something eternal. "Until my last breath. Until the last beat of my heart. So that no matter what time takes from me, no matter where fate leads us—I will always have this, to remember. To know that you were mine. That you will always be mine."

A single tear traced down her cheek.
She did not wipe it away.

Instead, she reached for me—her fingers sliding over mine, curling into my grasp as if she, too, wished to hold onto this moment forever.

And in that silence, in that stillness, the world beyond us faded.
There was no throne. No kingdom. No duty.
There was only her.
Only us.
A bond that even time itself could never sever.

Chapter 26

Her Hands, My Haven

The years passed, yet the bond between my sister—the Princess Royal—and me only deepened. It was a connection that transcended titles, expectations, and the silent rules that governed the world around us.

She remained unmarried, her heart and mind devoted entirely to the palace, to the kingdom, and, above all, to me. Many suitors came and went, noblemen of the highest ranks presenting themselves with gifts and offerings, hoping to claim her hand. Yet each was turned away, their ambitions dissolving in the face of her quiet but unwavering refusal.

And no one dared to challenge her decision.
Not even the council.
For they knew that no man in this world could command her heart, for it already belonged elsewhere.

At first, whispers ran through the palace halls like a hushed breeze. The courtiers, the attendants, the noblemen—they all spoke in veiled words, careful glances, never daring to voice their suspicions openly. They were too afraid of me, of the wrath that questioning my affairs might bring.

Even the Queen, my lawful wife, began to notice.

She watched as my nights were divided—some spent in her chamber, yet most spent in the Princess's halls. She observed the quiet glances exchanged between us, the way my sister carried herself as though she were my equal, the way I gravitated toward her presence without hesitation.

And though the Queen was perceptive, she never questioned me.
Perhaps she feared the answer.
Perhaps she knew that some truths were better left unspoken.
Or perhaps, in her own way, she found solace in knowing that she alone shared me with only one woman.

Unlike the kings before me—who housed vast harems of hundreds, sometimes thousands of women, discarding them as they pleased—I had none. I had no mistresses, no concubines vying for my favour.
There were only two women in my life.
The Queen. And my sister.
And so, the Queen made her peace with it.

She and my sister, despite the silent tension that sometimes lingered between them, formed a bond of their own. They laughed together, dined together, and spoke in ways that mirrored true sisterhood.

Yet, beneath the surface, I knew they envied each other.
They never spoke of it—never expressed their jealousy aloud. But it was there.

The Queen saw the way I looked at my sister, the way my presence lingered in the Princess's chamber, the way my sister's name escaped my lips before hers in unguarded moments. And my sister, though composed, though poised, knew that she was not my wife, not the one who bore my heirs, not the woman beside me in the eyes of the kingdom.

Yet, neither of them challenged their roles.
The Queen accepted what could not be changed.
And the Princess Royal remained exactly where she had always been—by my side.

Through the years, through the shifting seasons, the unspoken truth remained:
No power in the world, no force of duty, no law of the land—could sever the tie between us.
We were bound not by vows, not by contracts, not by tradition.

But by something far greater.
Something deeper than love.
Something that had existed long before we were ever born.
And that, above all else, was the one truth that neither time, nor duty, nor the whispers of the world could ever take away.

The years passed in a golden haze of prosperity, and under my rule, the kingdom thrived in peace. It was a time of harmony, where the weight of my crown felt lighter, not because of fate, but because of her—the guiding star who stood beside me, unwavering, unshaken.

It was not war or conquest that defined my rule. It was wisdom, stability, and love. Where other kings sought to expand their borders with bloodshed, I built my empire through justice, generosity, and unwavering strength. And always, at my side, was my sister—the Princess Royal, the only one who could truly shape my heart and mind.

She never commanded me, never spoke in the tone of authority that other advisors did. Instead, she ruled me with love.

There was something almost divine about her way. She never forced me into anything. She simply gave—her presence, her wisdom, her kindness. She poured love into me until I could not resist its warmth. She was the only person in the world who could change my decisions—not with argument, not with power, but with a quiet, unshakable devotion that melted even my hardest resolves.

It was she who led me toward charity, toward compassion, toward a legacy greater than war and conquest. She reminded me that the strength of a King was not in his sword, but in the way he touched the lives of his people.

Because of her, I travelled across the kingdom—not as a ruler demanding loyalty, but as a King giving it in return.

She ensured that my presence was felt not just in the throne room, but in the streets, in the villages, in the hearts of the people. It was she who urged me to build homes for the orphans, to create places of learning for the poor, to offer aid to the sick and the weak. She ruled through me. And I, in turn, made sure her hand stretched across every corner of my land.
Where I ruled the throne, she ruled the hearts of the people.

While my sister governed the soul of the kingdom, my Queen ruled the palace.
The Queen was the one who maintained order within the palace walls, overseeing administration, discipline, and the daily workings of our vast household. She was the keeper of traditions, the one who ensured the palace remained an unshaken pillar of authority.

Through the years, she bore me seven children. Seven little princes and princesses, each carrying a piece of my legacy, each brought into the world with duty and expectation upon their small shoulders. She was a mother first, a Queen second, and my companion always.

My Queen knew that I did not take a hundred concubines or fill the palace with mistresses. She also knew that the only other woman who held a place beside me was the one she could never question—my sister.

There was no war between them, no spoken jealousy. They dined together, laughed together, and ruled the palace together. But deep in their hearts, I knew: each envied the other.

The Queen envied that I sought comfort elsewhere, that my soul belonged to someone who was not her.
And my sister envied that she could never be my wife, never be the mother of my heirs, never claim the title that the world had given to another.

Yet, despite their silent battles, peace remained.
And so, I belonged to them both.

For all my strength, for all my power, I was still a man. And men, no matter how great, still bore the weight of exhaustion, of doubt, of burdens too heavy to carry alone.

The world saw me as a god, a ruler, an unshaken force of power. But on the nights when the weight became too much, I sought only one place.
Her arms.
My sister's embrace.

In the stillness of midnight, when the moon cast silver shadows upon the marble floors, I would enter her chamber without a word. She would already be waiting, as if she knew I would come.

She would pull me into her arms, pressing my head to her chest, cradling me as if I were a child again. Her fingers would run through my hair, soothing, silent, sacred.

And sometimes, she would offer me solace, a gesture of profound comfort—guiding my lips to the warmth of her breast, a silent offering of nurturing, holding me close until the world outside melted away.

In those moments, I did not feel like a King. I did not feel like a ruler or a warrior. I felt like her little brother. I felt like a child held by a goddess, worshipping at the altar of the only love I had ever truly known.

And when exhaustion overtook me, when I could no longer fight the weight of my own existence, she would hum the same lullaby she had always sung, whispering me into sleep.

I spent many nights like that. Nights where I forgot my kingdom, my duty, my name. Nights where I remembered only her.

The weight of a crown was not one that could be shared, yet somehow, she carried it with me. Not as a ruler, not as a minister of state, but as something far greater—the one who knew how to quiet the tempests within me.

She had always known.
When the burdens of the throne bore down upon my shoulders, when the walls of duty and expectation closed in, it was she who

pulled me from the edge and reminded me that I was more than a King—I was her brother.

It was during one such evening, when my mind was restless, my thoughts tangled in the knots of governance, that she guided me towards the marble terrace where the night air was crisp with the scent of blooming jasmines. The moon bathed the palace gardens in silver, a silent witness to the quiet sanctuary we had carved for ourselves.

She brought out an old scroll, an ancient text written in golden ink, its words filled with wisdom passed down through ages.
"Come," she murmured, patting the cushion beside her.
I sat, my muscles taut, my jaw clenched from the weight of the day's battles.

"You have mastered the art of wielding a sword," she said, her voice as smooth as flowing water. "But have you mastered the art of wielding your own mind?"

I exhaled sharply, closing my eyes, allowing her voice to guide me.
"Let go," she whispered. "Let everything fall away. The throne, the expectations, the world. Just breathe."
And so, I did.

Beside me, she sat in perfect stillness—her back straight, her hands resting delicately upon her knees, her face serene. She was the moon—distant yet illuminating, soft yet powerful.

But unlike me, she was untouched by struggle. While I battled the storm within, she remained untouched by the wind. And in moments where the heat of my meditation drew beads of sweat upon my brow, she—as if sensing it without even opening her eyes—would reach for the delicate hand fan beside her and begin to wave it gently, sending soft, cooling breezes over my skin.

She never stopped her meditation completely.
One hand remained still in perfect poise, while the other moved in slow, fluid strokes, as though offering me a silent vow of devotion.

I would have stopped her—told her to focus on herself—but I could not bring myself to break the serenity of that moment.

How many Kings had known such comfort?
How many rulers had been granted such love?
Even when she meditated alone, she would never fail to look after me.

On warmer nights, long after the oil lamps had burned low, I would sometimes wake to find her seated beside me, a small fan in hand, waving it gently, tirelessly, with a devotion that no words could ever contain.

"Go to sleep," I would murmur drowsily, reaching out to pull her down beside me.
She would only smile, her eyes glimmering with something unreadable, something eternal.

"Sleep, my King," she would whisper back. "Let me watch over you a little longer."
And I would close my eyes, knowing that in a world filled with uncertainty, there was at least one thing that would never waver.

Her love.
Her devotion.

The quiet, unshakable truth that she was—and had always been—mine.

At midnight's hush, she drew me near,
Fanned my brow, so cool, so dear.
Upon her chest, I laid my head,
Where once as a child, I had been fed.

Her hands soothed, her breath was light,
She held me close through weary night.
No kingdom vast, no golden throne,
Could match the peace in her arms alone.

Chapter 27

The Eternal Bond

Time flowed like a river, silent and unwavering, carrying with it the years of our reign, yet never washing away the love and devotion that had always bound us. Decades had passed, seasons had changed, but in my heart, she remained the same—the radiant force that guided me, the unwavering presence that filled every space of my soul.

She was now fifty-six, yet time had barely left a trace upon her. If anything, she had only grown more graceful, more regal. Her beauty, refined by wisdom, held a depth beyond mere youth. Even my queen, still noble and fair, could not match the quiet majesty that my sister carried effortlessly. There was something eternal about her, something untouched by age or time.

Her posture remained poised, her presence commanding yet warm. The fire in her eyes, the unwavering pride in her stance—none of it had faded. If anything, it had only intensified with the years. She was not just a princess; she was an institution, an untouchable force of nature. The kingdom revered her, the people sought her wisdom, and the nobles dared not speak out of turn in her presence. She was still the Princess Royal, but more than that—she was my guiding light, my confidante, my peace.

Even as I ruled a kingdom, raised seven children, and carried the weight of an empire upon my shoulders, she remained my sanctuary. In moments of turmoil, a mere glance at her steadied me. A word from her lips could dissolve my anger. A touch of her hand upon mine reminded me that no matter how heavy the world became, I was never truly alone.

And still, even after all these years, I found myself protective over her—perhaps irrationally so. When someone lingered too close to her in conversation, when a nobleman laughed too loudly at her words, when an advisor addressed her with too much familiarity—jealousy burned in my veins like it did when I was young.

She had never married, never allowed anyone to claim her as their own. Many had tried, but she had refused every suitor. Some believed she had chosen devotion to the kingdom, others whispered that no man was worthy of her. But I knew the truth—her heart had always belonged elsewhere.

Despite the years, our bond never weakened. If anything, it only deepened. She still ruled over my heart as she had since my childhood, and I still sought her presence with the same longing I once had as a boy. She was the one person who knew me beyond the crown, beyond the title, beyond the history written in scrolls and stone.

And in the quiet moments, when the kingdom slept and the torches burned low, I would still find my way to her chamber, seeking her warmth, her wisdom, her love.
Time could take many things, but it could never take her from me.

The days grew colder, though the seasons had not changed. A stillness settled over the palace, one that I could not shake, one that mirrored the fading light in my sister's eyes.

She had always been untouchable, unwavering, a pillar of strength that had carried me through every storm. Yet now, she lay frail beneath the silken covers of her bed, her once-commanding presence reduced to shallow breaths and fragile limbs. The weight of time had finally reached her, and no power in my kingdom, no force upon this earth, could turn it away.

She suffered from a lung disease, a cruel affliction that robbed her of the breath she had once used to command the world around her. Each cough, each labored inhale, tore through me like a blade.

I did not leave her side. Not for a moment.
At night, when the rest of the palace drifted into sleep, I held her in my arms, whispering soothing words into her ear, running my fingers through her silver-streaked hair, pressing soft kisses to her temple as I had done since childhood. I sang the same sleeping tones she had once hummed for me, the lullabies that had carried me into dreams. Now, I offered them back to her, as if trying to lull her into peace.

She would smile weakly, resting against me as though I were the only thing anchoring her to this world.
But no matter how tightly I held her, she was slipping away.

One morning, she was weaker than ever. She could barely lift her hand, her voice a whisper of wind. I fed her with my own hands, wiping the corners of her lips, caressing her cheek when she coughed.

"Does it hurt?" I asked softly, though I already knew the answer. Her eyes—still so full of love, of pride—looked at me. "Nothing hurts when you are here."

That evening, duty called me away. The royal court demanded my presence, an issue of diplomacy I could not ignore. I did not want to leave her, but she cupped my hand in hers and smiled.
"Go, my King," she whispered. "I will be waiting for you."
I kissed her forehead, brushing my lips across her skin as though sealing a promise.

"I will return soon."
I did not know then that I had spoken a lie.
The court session dragged on, words blurring into meaningless echoes. My mind was not in the grand hall, not upon the throne where I sat, but in a dimly lit chamber where my sister lay, fighting for every breath.

Then, a messenger entered. Silent, discreet.
He did not need to speak; I knew.
The parchment in his hands was unnecessary.
My heart clenched. Without hesitation, I stood from my throne, my golden robe billowing as I stepped forward.

"The session is postponed," I declared. My voice did not waver, but my soul trembled. "The court is dismissed."
No one questioned me. No one dared.

I did not wait for the guards to escort me—I ran. My sandals barely touched the ground as I rushed through the palace corridors, past the marble pillars, past the flickering torches that lined the halls. The world outside blurred, the voices of attendants faded, until only one thing remained—her.

I burst into her chamber, the scent of sandalwood and medicinal herbs thick in the air.
She was dying.
My sister, my princess, my everything.

Tears welled in my eyes as I approached her bed, my hands trembling as I reached for her. I sat down beside her, lifting her frail form gently into my lap.

Her eyes fluttered open, and when she saw me, she smiled.
"My King," she whispered, her voice so faint, so fragile.

I could not stop the tears from spilling onto my cheeks. I kissed her forehead, then her temple, her eyes, her hands, her cheeks—desperate to keep her here, desperate to pour every ounce of my love into her failing body.

She reached up with trembling fingers, cupping my face. With the last of her strength, she wiped my tears away, just as she had done when I was a child.

"Do not cry, my precious gem," she whispered. "I love you… more than you can ever imagine."

Her voice faded; her breath slowed.
And then—silence.
A silence so deafening it shattered me.

I clutched her close, pressing my face into her hair, inhaling the last remnants of her scent.

She was gone.
The only arms that had ever truly held me. The only love I had ever known in its purest form.

Gone.

I did not know how long I stayed there, holding her lifeless body, cradling her the way she had cradled me so many times before.

When the attendants finally entered, I did not move.
I could not.
The world had changed in an instant.
For the first time in my life, I felt truly… alone.

The weight of her absence crushed me.
In that lifetime, I had been a king, revered and feared, a ruler who held dominion over thousands. And yet, in that moment, as I clutched her lifeless body, I was reduced to nothing.

She had been my guiding star, my solace, the one unwavering presence in the ever-changing tides of existence. The one person in all the worlds, all the lifetimes, who had never left me—until now.

The pain was unbearable.
It rippled through me, raw and unrelenting, as if the very fabric of my soul had been torn apart.
I wanted to scream, to call out her name, to demand that time itself reverse its course and return her to me.
But time is merciless. And it did not listen.

A deafening silence fell. The palace faded, the golden halls dissolving into nothingness. The last image of my sister-princess lingered for a moment longer—her peaceful face resting in my lap, her lips slightly parted, as if she were only sleeping.

Then, the vision shattered.

I was yanked out of the past, pulled from the depths of my meditation like a man drowning in the ocean, suddenly gasping for breath.

My eyes flew open.
The candle-lit chamber around me was still. My body was motionless, seated in deep meditation. Yet my heart pounded violently against my ribs, my breath uneven.
And then—I felt it.

A warm trail of tears slipping down my cheeks.
For a moment, I did not move. Did not blink.
The weight of what I had just witnessed pressed down upon me with a force so immense, so profound, that reality itself felt unsteady beneath me.

That world… that time… that love—
It had been so real.
More real than the air in my lungs, more real than the ground beneath me.
And the grief—
The grief of losing her—
It clung to me even now, centuries, perhaps millennia, after it had taken place.

I closed my eyes once more, attempting to steady myself, attempting to calm the storm raging within.
But this was not the first time my concentration had broken while watching my past lives.
It had happened before.

When I saw our moments of intimacy—when I relived the sacred nights spent in her arms, the whispered vows, the stolen kisses, the way her body had felt against mine—my mind had faltered.

It was too much.
The depth of our bond, the unbreakable thread that tied us together through lifetimes, was something beyond comprehension.

Even now, in this present existence, I realized something that sent a shiver through me—
I still loved her.
Not as a memory. Not as a story.
But as if she were still alive, still a part of me.

The realization struck me like a lightning bolt—had she followed me here, to this life?
Was she somewhere, walking the same earth, carrying the same longing?
I had to know.

Swallowing hard, I wiped my face with the sleeve of my robe, forcing my breath to steady.
Then, with all the discipline I had cultivated, I silenced my mind, anchored my consciousness, and once again, I entered the depths of meditation.

This time, I would not allow emotion to break me.
This time, I would go further.
I would find her.

Time no longer felt real after she was gone.
The days blended into nights, the seasons passed unnoticed, and the throne that once felt like power beneath me now felt unbearably hollow.

She had been my guiding star, the only one who could melt my heart with a single glance. And now, without her, I felt like a lone traveler lost in an endless desert, searching for water where there was none.

Yet, even in her absence, she was everywhere.
Her scent still lingered in her chamber, in the silk cushions where she once rested, in the golden comb that had once run through her long, fragrant hair.

But most of all—she was in the sacred piece of fabric I had kept beneath my pillow since the night she became mine.

The first night's bed sheet.
The proof of her purity.
The sacred blood stain of her love.

I would take it in my hands, unfold it carefully, and stare at the delicate mark, tracing my fingers over the faded remnants of her maidenhood—the only tangible proof that she had once truly belonged to me in every sense.

When the grief became unbearable, I would press my lips to that stain, as if I could summon her spirit, as if I could taste her once more.
At night, I slept with the sheet tucked beneath my pillow, feeling its presence like a quiet whisper of her lingering touch.

Even in death, she was mine.
And I—was irrevocably hers.
But the world did not stop for my grief.
The kingdom still stood, the people still bowed, and duty still called.

Yet, I had no desire for conquest, no hunger for glory, no interest in the luxuries of my throne.

The only thing that could ease the weight on my chest was carrying forward what she had loved the most—charity.
She had always been the one to give, to nurture, to extend a hand to the helpless.
And so, I followed in her footsteps.

The royal teachers, wise and observant, noticed my sorrow and urged me to engage in acts of merit on her behalf.
"Your Majesty," one of the elder monks advised one evening, "she was a beacon of kindness. Let her legacy live through you. Give to the people as she did, and you will find peace."

So, I did.
In her name, I ordered the palace gates to remain open for the poor and the hungry.
Every day, I had carts of rice, fruits, and delicacies prepared in the royal kitchens and placed outside the palace walls.

"No one shall go hungry in my sister's kingdom," I declared. "Let there be food for all, without limit, without cost."
The people rejoiced.
From dawn until dusk, citizens came to eat from the offerings, their eyes filled with gratitude. And yet, it was not their joy that I sought.

It was hers.
I imagined her standing beside me, watching over the people she had once loved so fiercely.
I imagined the way her eyes would glow with pride, the way her lips would part in a knowing smile.

But no matter how much I gave, how many lives I touched, the void within me never lessened.
I visited temples, offered jewels and gold, commissioned grand rituals for her peace in the afterlife.

I burned sandalwood incense in the royal courtyard every evening, whispering prayers to the heavens, hoping—begging—that somewhere beyond this world, she was listening.

That she knew that my love for her had not wavered.
That she was still the only one who held my heart.
When my grief grew unbearable, I turned to the one thing she had tried to teach me in life—meditation.

At first, it felt impossible.
How could I empty my mind when it was filled with her?
How could I silence my longing when it burned like an eternal flame?
But I remembered her voice, soft and patient, guiding me in the art of stillness.

"Breathe, my love," she would say. "Watch your thoughts, do not chase them."

And so, I closed my eyes.
I listened to my breath.
I allowed the weight of my sorrow to settle.
And in the quiet moments, in the spaces between my thoughts—
I could almost feel her.
The warmth of her embrace.
The soft whisper of her breath against my ear.

"I love you more than you can ever imagine, my precious gem."
A tear slipped down my cheek.

No matter how much I meditated, no matter how much I gave,
no matter how many prayers I offered—
The pain of losing her never faded.

Because she was never meant to be lost.
She had been, and would always be, my everything.
Even beyond life itself.

Chapter 28

The Heart That Could Not Love Again

The days following my sister's death passed in a blur, like a dream from which I could not awaken. The palace walls, once a place of comfort, now felt suffocating—every corner whispering her absence, every corridor holding a memory of her presence.

Yet life did not allow me to grieve forever.The weight of the throne, the needs of my people, and the duty I owed to my family forced me to move forward, even when my heart remained locked in the past.

I turned my attention to my Queen. She had been patient with me all these years, understanding yet silently longing for my affection. I saw it in her eyes—the way they searched mine for something I could never give. She was devoted, tender, and endlessly kind, yet I had never truly given her my heart.

Not because she lacked anything. Not because she was undeserving. But because my heart had long belonged to another.

And that love, though now shadowed by grief, still dictated my every breath. One evening, as the palace bathed in the soft glow of lanterns, I walked to the Queen's chamber.

She was seated by the window, gazing at the night sky, her hands resting gently over the silken fabric of her gown. The flickering lamplight cast golden hues over her face, highlighting the softness of her features, the quiet beauty she had always carried.

Hearing my footsteps, she turned, her eyes widening slightly in surprise. I had come to her chamber many times, but never like this—never with the weight of unspoken words pressing between us.

I sat beside her, inhaling deeply before speaking.*"My Queen,"* I began, my voice low, hesitant. She smiled, as she always did, though there was a quiet sadness in her eyes.

"You rarely call me that in private," she murmured, her fingers tracing the embroidered patterns on her sleeve.I exhaled, my hands tightening into fists.

"I have failed you," I admitted, my words heavier than the crown I wore. *"Not in duty, nor in responsibility—but in love. And for that, I beg your forgiveness."* She said nothing at first, simply watching me, as if waiting for more.

"I have given you a kingdom," I continued, *"children, security, every worldly possession. But I have never given you my heart—not as a husband should. And it is not because you lack anything… It is because my heart has belonged to another since the moment I first understood love."*

She inhaled sharply but did not look away. *"Your sister,"* she whispered. A lump formed in my throat. *"Yes."*

There was no point in denying what she had likely known all along. She lowered her gaze to her hands, quiet for a long moment.

"I have always known," she finally said. *"I was never blind to it. The way you looked at her, the way you were drawn to her, the way she was your world. I knew I was only second in your heart, even when I was the only one allowed to be by your side in the eyes of the world."*

Guilt gripped my chest. *"You deserved better."* She let out a small, breathless laugh, shaking her head.

"Perhaps," she said. *"But I never wanted better. I wanted you."* Her honesty crushed me. She reached for my hand, her fingers cool and delicate against my skin.

"You have been a good King," she whispered. *"A good father. And even if your love was never truly mine, you have never wronged me. I have no bitterness in my heart toward you."*

I swallowed hard. *"Even now,"* she continued, *"after all these years, I do not regret being your Queen. But tell me, my King… Do you regret having me?"*

I shook my head instantly. *"Never."*

And I meant it. I had never loved her the way she wished, but I had respected her, cared for her, cherished her in my own way.

She sighed, her shoulders relaxing slightly. *"Then that is enough for me."*

She smiled, but it was a smile tinged with quiet sorrow, a smile that spoke of unfulfilled longing, of dreams left unrealized.

That night, I held her as she fell asleep in my arms, her body warm, fragile, and full of silent acceptance. But even as I held her, even as I tried to give her the affection she deserved—

My mind drifted to my sister. The way she had whispered my name. The way she had held me as if I were the most precious thing in existence. The way she had looked at me as if I were her world.

No matter how much time passed, no matter how many people surrounded me, there would always be only one person who had truly owned me.

And she was gone. The night stretched on, the Queen's breath steady against my chest. Yet my heart—It remained elsewhere. With the one I could never have again.

Even after that night of truth, I resolved myself to give the Queen the love she deserved. I could not change the past, nor could I force my heart to rewrite its deepest devotion, but I could do what was right.

So I tried. For the years that followed, I gave her what I could. A man can act, but he cannot lie to himself. My love for her was not one that burned with passion, nor did it consume me like the fire that had once belonged to my sister. But I cared for her—I truly did. She had borne my children, stood by my side through every season of my reign, and given me a part of her soul without ever demanding more than I could give.

And so, I became the husband she had always deserved. I spent more time with her, speaking to her not as a Queen, but as the woman who had dedicated her life to me. I listened to her thoughts, her fears, her joys. I made sure she never went to bed feeling alone. Even on the days when my heart ached with memories of my sister, I silenced those thoughts and gave my attention to the woman before me.

I would take her hand, press my lips against her fingers, and whisper words she longed to hear.

"You are my Queen."
"You have given me a family."
"I will honour you for the rest of my life."
It was not a lie. Perhaps not the truth she wanted, but the truth I could give.

At night, I shared my bed with her. I held her close, whispered to her, made love to her the way a husband should. I gave her the illusion of a love she had always longed for, and I did it not out of duty—but out of respect. Out of gratitude.

I had taken so much from her, without ever offering the depths of my heart in return. So now, I tried to be the man she needed. And she, despite knowing my past, embraced every moment of it.

She never spoke of my sister again. Never once questioned if I still thought of her, still dreamed of her, still ached for her. But I knew she sensed it. She saw it in my silences.

She felt it in the quiet moments when I would turn away, lost in thoughts of a love that had long passed from this world. Still, she never asked. And I never gave her the answer she already knew.

Years passed. My children grew, the kingdom flourished, and I remained a King beloved by his people. Yet, the weight of time pressed upon me like an iron chain.

I had lived for my sister. And now, without her, I was merely a man waiting for his time to end. No longer did I feel the fire that once burned in my veins. No longer did I wake with the same urgency, the same passion to conquer each day.

I carried my responsibilities.
I loved my children.
I honoured my Queen.
But deep inside—
I was already gone.

One evening, as the golden light of dusk bathed the palace halls, I sat alone in my chamber, staring at the silk bedsheet that had remained hidden beneath my pillow for all these years. The same sheet that had once held my sister's purity. The only tangible piece of her that still remained in this world.

My fingers traced the faint, faded scarlet stain of her first sacrifice to me—the proof of the night we had truly become one. I brought it to my lips, pressing a reverent kiss against the fabric, as if by doing so, I could bring back the warmth of her presence.

"I miss you," I whispered to the silence.
"I have always missed you."

Tears stung my eyes, but I did not let them fall.
Not yet.
Not yet.

The days blurred into nights, and time felt like an echo of something distant—unreachable, unchangeable. The kingdom still stood, my children still thrived, my Queen still watched over all that was mine, but my heart had long since ceased to belong to this world.

After a few years of my sister's death, on my final night, as the palace corridors lay in silence, I walked alone through the familiar path that led to her chamber. The door, untouched by time, sealed from the world, awaited me. No one had entered since she had left it, for none were permitted. Only I could step through its threshold.

I pushed the heavy doors open, inhaling deeply as the scent of old jasmine and faded saffron clung to the air, a mere ghost of what it once was. The room was exactly as she had left it, preserved in stillness, frozen in an eternal moment. My gaze travelled to the grand bed, the silken drapes cascading from the canopy like veils of memory. It was the bed where she had once held me, where she had whispered lullabies into my hair, where she had taken her last breath in my arms.

I carried with me the most sacred possession I owned—the bedsheet, the one that bore the proof of our first night, the mark of her purity, of our love bound beyond the laws of man and gods. It had remained under my pillow all these years, untouched by anyone else. It was the last remnant of her I had left.

With slow steps, I approached the bed and lay upon it, the weight of sorrow pressing into my chest as I clutched the sacred sheet to me. I buried my face into its fabric, inhaling deeply as if searching for the last trace of her. But there was only silence. No warmth, no heartbeat, no fingers running through my hair. The emptiness swallowed me whole, and my body ached with longing.

I reached out, my fingers ghosting over the space beside me, where she should have been. But she was not here. She would never be here again.

A sharp pang shot through my chest, grief coiling tighter like a serpent refusing to let go. But then—her voice.

"My love… my precious one… let go."

Her words were not new. They were the same ones she had spoken countless times before—words of wisdom, of peace, of surrender. She had always urged me to let go, to transcend sorrow, to see beyond the illusions of this world.

I closed my eyes, exhaling slowly.

And for the first time in years, I listened.
I let my mind drift, just as she had taught me in our meditations. I allowed the memories, the desires, the sorrow to rise and fall like waves in the ocean, watching them, but not holding onto them. I searched for the state she had always spoken of—the place where the mind is still, where there is no longing, no suffering, no self.

I watched my thoughts like distant clouds, detached, weightless.
I did not resist.
A deep stillness settled within me, and I surrendered to it.
I wished for that place where no sorrow could reach me.

And as I drifted into that silence, into the boundless emptiness, I never woke again.

That night, while wrapped in the last remnants of my sister's touch, I passed from this world.

In the silence of a moonlit hall,
I walked alone where echoes call.
Through shadowed paths of time untold,
To where her touch had once been gold.

The door stood still, the air was tight,
A chamber locked in endless night.
No voice, no breath, no warmth remained,
Yet every stone still spoke her name.

Upon her bed, I laid me down,
The weight of grief, my only crown.
Against my chest, the cloth so pure,
A stain of love that would endure.

I traced the thread where crimson bled,
A sacred mark where she once wed.
Not to a man, nor fate unkind,
But to the love that bound our mind.

Eyes closed in sorrow, heavy deep,
I sought the place where none would weep.
No throne, no power, no endless strife,
Only the peace beyond this life.

A breath, a thought, a whispered prayer,
A wish to find her waiting there.

No sound, no pain, no mortal ties,
Only the stillness behind closed eyes.

And in that sleep, my soul took flight,
Beyond the sorrow, beyond the night.
With gods I rose, in realms unseen,
Where sorrow fades and hearts are clean.

Yet still, in dreams, I hear her name,
A whispered call, a flickered flame.
For even heaven's endless light,
Could never dim her soul's delight.

Chapter 29

The Truth Behind My Desires

The stillness of my meditation deepened, the world around me dissolving into nothingness as I ventured further into the vast corridors of my past. Each moment of concentration peeled away the layers of existence, revealing echoes of lives long forgotten.

I had already seen so much—my celestial existence in a heavenly realm, the grandeur and sorrow of my royal life, the weight of my sister's loss, and the night I drifted into eternal slumber, wrapped in the last remnants of her touch. But something told me that this was not the beginning of my story. There was something more. A root buried deep beneath the surface, a reason for this unshakable longing that had haunted me across lifetimes.

I steeled my mind, pushing past the memories I had already witnessed, willing myself to go further. Deeper. Beyond the life where I had ruled as a King, beyond the golden palaces and silken robes, past the nights spent wrapped in the warmth of my sister's embrace.

Then— I saw it.
Another life. Another time.
The vision unfolded before me like a forgotten dream coming into focus. I was no longer a King. No longer a ruler. I was a man—just a man—bound by love and loss like any other.

And she… she was there.
Not as my sister.
But as my wife.
She was my beloved in that life. The woman who had been the centre of my existence. The one I had cherished, held, protected. I had adored her with the same intensity, the same unwavering devotion. But fate, as always, had been cruel.

She had died young—too young.
Taken from me in her middle age, leaving behind an emptiness that had consumed me. The grief had been unbearable. The longing insatiable. I had spent seven years wandering through that life, lost in sorrow, waiting for the moment when death would take me too.

And now, across lifetimes, across the shifting sands of rebirth, that same longing had remained. She had returned to me, but in a different form.

No longer my wife.
This time, she had been reborn as my sister. And still, I had loved her with the same fire, the same desperation, the same aching need to keep her close. The roles had changed, but the essence of our bond had not.

Now, it all made sense.
The relentless obsession. The need for her love. The way my heart ached when I was away from her, the way I had always

searched for her presence. The way she had always been at the centre of my world, no matter the circumstances.

She was my wife in one life. My sister in another.
But always—she was mine. I sat in the depths of my meditation, my breath steady, my mind clear, as the weight of this revelation settled upon me. The answer I had spent my life searching for had been there all along.
I opened my eyes.

And for the first time in this lifetime… I understood.

The deeper I ventured into the labyrinth of my past, the clearer the threads of my existence became. Like golden strands woven into the great tapestry of time, each life was connected—each habit, each desire, each unexplained longing had its roots buried deep within the lives I had lived before.

Since childhood, I had an obsession—a yearning for a golden sword, one that felt like an extension of my very being. I could never explain it, nor could I deny the way my hands ached for the weight of its hilt, the gleam of its blade, the power it held.

Now, I understood.
I had wielded it before. In my royal life, it had been my weapon, my symbol of authority, my companion in war and peace alike. It was not just a piece of metal—it was a part of me. A relic of a life where I had stood as King, where my word had been law, where the fate of a nation had rested upon my shoulders.
That sword was my past.
And that past still called to me.

My longing for a white horse, the way I had always imagined myself astride one, the way I had felt incomplete without it—it had haunted me.
And now, I knew why.
In my royal life, a great white horse had carried me into battle. It had been my companion, my trusted beast, the creature that had raced through fields of war and celebrations of triumph. It was the beast of my victories, the bearer of my fate.

Even in this life, I had searched for it, without ever truly knowing what I was looking for. But something within me remembered.
My soul still sought the wind against my face, the gallop of powerful legs beneath me, the feeling of being untouchable as I rode into the horizon.

This life had always seemed incomplete without a throne. Even in a world where kings no longer ruled, where monarchs were but relics of history, I had felt that I was meant to be one.
And now, I understood why.

I had ruled before. I had worn the crown, I had held the sceptre, I had given orders and watched men bow. I had been born to rule.
This was why, in this life, I had often thought of restoring monarchy to Sri Lanka. It had been an idea I had nurtured, a vision I had entertained—a longing for a throne that no longer existed. But it was not this life that had placed the thought in my mind.
It was the memory of my past reign.
The echoes of my royal blood still coursed through my veins, whispering to me that I was not meant to be ordinary. That I was not meant to serve—but to be served.
And I had never understood why.

Until now.

The Serious Mood—The Weight of Power and Divinity
All my life, I had carried a solemnity that others could not understand. I did not laugh as freely as others, I did not take pleasure in frivolous things.
I was serious, disciplined, untouchable.
And now, I knew why.
For lifetimes, I had lived as a god and a king. I had been worshipped in heaven, adored in the mortal world. My words had been law, my presence had been sacred.
I had not been an ordinary man.
And in this life, that air of divinity, of regality, still lingered.
It was not something I had learned.
It was something I had remembered.

There had been a recurring dream—one that had followed me since childhood.
A dream of an elder sister. A dream of her love, her warmth, her embrace. A dream so vivid, so intoxicating, that I would wake longing for something I did not understand.
Now, I knew why.
It was not a dream.
It was a memory.
The dream of her hands in my hair, of her voice singing lullabies, of her lips pressing against my forehead—they were not creations of my mind. They were remnants of the life we had shared before. The love that had spanned lifetimes.

I had always carried myself with pride. Not arrogance, but an innate understanding of my worth.
I had always been drawn to old-fashioned clothing, to grand architecture, to things that spoke of power, legacy, and timelessness.

Now, I knew why.
I had lived in golden palaces. I had worn the robes of kings. I had walked through halls that whispered of power, had stood before courtiers who trembled in my presence.
And even now, in a different life, in a different era, that memory had never faded.

Everything Had a Reason
Every longing.
Every desire.
Every habit I could never explain.
They were all pieces of a puzzle that had always been there.
Through meditation, through the unraveling of my past, I had finally fit the pieces together.
I was not simply a man born into this life.
I was a soul who had walked this path before.
And now, for the first time, I understood who I was.
And more than that…
I understood why I had always searched for her.
For my sister.
For my first love.
For the woman who had been mine across lifetimes.

Chapter 30

Manifesting the Fulfilment and Seeing the Danger

After uncovering the roots of my desires through deep meditation, I found that understanding their origins alone was not enough to liberate me. A desire does not simply dissolve the moment its cause is discovered. The mind clings to its longings, no matter how irrational they may be. It seeks fulfilment, chases illusions, and refuses to let go unless it has fully tasted and been disillusioned by them.

Thus, I developed a unique method—a way to confront my desires head-on, not by suppressing them, but by manifesting their fulfilment in my meditation. I would take the deepest cravings of my heart, imagine them realized, and then observe what followed.

Among all my desires, the strongest and most enduring had been the wish for an elder sister—a longing that had shaped my thoughts, emotions, and even my dreams since childhood.

I closed my eyes.
I allowed my mind to weave the perfect scenario. In this vision, I finally had her—the elder sister I had always yearned for. She was no longer a phantom of my imagination, no longer a void I

tried to fill, but a living, breathing presence in my life. She was exactly as I had wished her to be—an exquisite woman, beautiful beyond compare, elegant, poised, yet deeply affectionate.

She adored me with the same intensity that I adored her. She held me in her arms, whispered loving words, kissed my forehead, and pampered me in every way. She treated me as the most precious person in the world. She stayed by my side, always available, always devoted.

For the first few moments, the happiness was overwhelming. It felt like a long-lost emptiness inside me had finally been filled. I reveled in the warmth of her presence, in the comfort of her embrace, in the sheer joy of belonging to someone so deeply.

But I did not stop there.
I let the vision continue. I allowed it to extend beyond the momentary sweetness. Would this perfect scenario last forever?

Reality soon crept in.
Even if I somehow found such an elder sister in this life, how would it happen? The chances were nearly impossible. It was not easy to find an elder girl who would willingly come and stay in my home, nor was it practical for me to go and live with an elder girl in her home. Even if I found a distant cousin or someone close enough to play the role, would she behave exactly as I wanted?

No.
No human being could ever mold themselves so perfectly to my desires. Even if I did find someone who cared for me deeply, her love would never be as boundless as I imagined. She would have her own emotions, her own thoughts, her own life.

She would not exist solely for me. She might have other priorities, other relationships, other attachments.

And then, what would happen?
One day, she would meet someone. She would find a lover, a husband. And slowly, inevitably, she would drift away. Her time, her attention, her love—things that once belonged to me alone—would be shared with another. I would no longer be the centre of her world. She would start a new life, a new family. And I would be left behind.

Would I not suffer? Would I not feel betrayed? I imagined myself in that moment—watching her walk away, seeing her love redirected elsewhere, knowing that no matter how much she had once cared for me, I could no longer hold the same place in her life.

Would my heart not ache with unbearable sorrow? And even if, by some miracle, she never married, would time itself not take her from me? Age, sickness, death—would they not steal her away eventually? If my happiness depended on her presence, was I not setting myself up for inevitable suffering?

I had built my desire on an illusion—the illusion that there was something permanent, something unchanging, something that could forever satisfy my longing.

But in truth, everything changes. Everything fades. Everything is lost. Even if I gained everything I wanted, I would still suffer. The very thing that gave me happiness would become the source of my pain.

As I sat in meditation, watching this truth unfold before me, I felt the weight of my own longing begin to shift. For the first time, I did not suppress my desire. I did not fight against it.

Instead, I saw through it. I saw the deception. I saw the impermanence. I saw how craving led only to suffering. And as I continued to observe, the sweetness of the illusion began to dissolve.

The desire that once burned so fiercely within me, the longing that had tormented my soul for so many years—it began to lose its power.

Because I now knew the truth. I was chasing a shadow. I was holding onto a dream that could never last. And what is the point of clinging to something that is destined to disappear?

I exhaled slowly.
For the first time in my life, I felt something shift. The obsession that had controlled me for so long had finally begun to loosen its grip.

I had not forced it away. I had simply understood it. And in that understanding—I found my first taste of liberation.

After understanding the root of my desires, after witnessing their origins unfold through past lives, I believed for a moment that I had reached a final realization. But true understanding does not come merely from knowing—it must be experienced, deeply felt, and examined from every angle. So I did what I had always done in my meditative journey—I looked deeper.

At first, I meditated on the idea of gaining my desires, experiencing the imagined satisfaction of fulfilling them. But now, I turned my attention to what happened after that fulfillment.

I had already seen the impermanence of having an elder sister. But now, I had to go further—I had to see the illusion in the very nature of fulfillment itself.

We chase after things in life, convinced that once we grasp them, they will bring us lasting joy. But every time we reach the so-called oasis of desire, the water turns to sand in our hands.

I imagined, once again, having the perfect elder sister—one who adored me, pampered me, and gave me everything I had ever longed for. She was there, running her fingers through my hair, holding me, looking at me with the unconditional love I had always craved.

But what then?
Would the joy of that moment remain? Would I feel the same ecstasy every time?

I imagined living with her day after day. At first, every embrace, every kind word, every moment of affection was fulfilling. But soon, like everything in life, it became normal. It became routine. The overwhelming happiness faded into the background of daily life. The excitement I once felt lessened as familiarity took its place.

What was once a dream, once a craving so intense that it burned within me, would inevitably become ordinary.

Then, another thought entered my mind—what if she wasn't always there when I wanted her? What if, one day, she was tired, busy, or distracted? What if she no longer had the same time for me?

Would my heart not ache? Would I not feel neglected, abandoned, or jealous? And even if she loved me endlessly, what would happen when death took her away?

Would I not be left in unbearable grief, clinging to something that could never return? This was the true nature of desire. Even when fulfilled, it did not bring lasting peace.

A vision arose in my meditation—an image of a dog chasing its own tail. Spinning, running, believing that if it could just catch it, it would find satisfaction. But what happens when it catches its tail? It gains nothing—it was only chasing itself.

This was exactly what I had been doing with my desires. The desire for an elder sister was nothing more than my mind chasing its own illusions, mistaking longing for fulfillment.

Then another vision came—a starving dog licking a dry, bloodstained bone. The dog believes the bone holds nourishment, that it will satisfy its hunger. But the more it licks, the more it tastes blood—not from the bone, but from its own torn tongue.

This was the truth of desire.
We chase after something, believing it will complete us, believing it will bring us lasting happiness. But in that pursuit, we only hurt ourselves, feeding off our own suffering, drinking from our own wounds, mistaking pain for nourishment.

The joy of fulfillment is an illusion, and the cost of that illusion is endless craving and exhaustion.

I then examined the very essence of enjoyment itself. What was it that made an elder sister's love feel so exquisite? Was it her physical touch? Her voice? Her presence?

If so, what were these things but mere sensory experiences? Her touch was nothing more than the sensation of skin against skin. Her voice was nothing more than sound waves vibrating in the air. Her presence was nothing more than a visual form my eyes registered.

If I stripped away the meaning I attached to these experiences, what was left?

Just the raw, fleeting nature of sensation.
This same principle applied to everything—whether it was wealth, relationships, status, or any other pursuit. We attach so much importance to our desires, but in reality, they are nothing more than momentary flickers in the grand impermanence of existence.

The problem was not that things could not bring joy. The problem was that joy never lasted.

A person chases money, believing it will bring peace. Yet when they obtain it, they soon desire more, or fear losing it. A person craves love, yet even in the deepest relationships, dissatisfaction, attachment, and loss arise.

We are all chasing mirages, mistaking them for water, only to be left thirstier than before. As I sat in deep meditation, witnessing the reality of my own mind, I saw what must be done. The only way to end suffering was not to fulfill desire, but to empty the mind of it.

True peace was not found in obtaining something external—it was found in releasing the craving itself.

If I no longer longed for an elder sister, if I no longer needed her presence to feel whole, then I could finally be free. Not just free from this one obsession, but free from the cycle of suffering itself.

This was the first step towards liberation.

I inhaled deeply, my mind clear, my heart steady. For the first time, I saw the illusion for what it was. I was ready to let go.

As my meditation deepened, as I watched my mind with an unshaken gaze, the final realization dawned upon me—a truth so simple, yet so elusive, buried beneath the layers of desire that had shaped my very existence.

Everything I had longed for, everything I had cherished, was nothing more than a cycle of perception and sensation.

The presence of an elder sister—the very thing I had craved for lifetimes—what was it, truly? It was not an unchangeable reality, not some eternal gift bestowed upon me by existence. It was simply a preparation of my own mind, a construct built by my own perceptions.

I perceived her—her beauty, her love, her touch—and from that perception, a pleasant sensation arose. That pleasure fed the cycle, strengthening my attachment.

Because of that pleasant sensation, I perceived her again. I replayed her presence in my mind, again and again, reinforcing the idea that she was my source of joy.

I admired her form, her voice, the way she looked at me, the way she touched me. And on every occasion, I became more ensnared in the illusion.

But where did this cycle lead? Had it ever truly satisfied me? Or had it only kept me chasing, kept me seeking, kept me bound to restlessness?

The truth was undeniable.
What I had been searching for was not her—it was the sensation, the fleeting happiness that arose when she was near.

And that happiness was not intrinsic to her presence—it was simply a response within my own mind. This was the greatest deception of desire.

No matter how much I tried to gain happiness through physical, verbal, or mental activities regarding my elder sister, it always led to exhaustion. Each moment of pleasure was followed by the need for another. Each moment of satisfaction was followed by the fear of losing it.

And in the end, what remained was only tiredness—weariness from the endless pursuit of happiness. Every longing, every action, every effort to secure joy was simply a restlessness—a movement of the mind, body, and speech that kept me trapped.

True peace, I realized, was not found in fulfilling desires. It was found where all activities stilled.

Where there was no more seeking, no more chasing, no more preparing or shaping the mind in pursuit of something external.

Where there was nothing to gain, nothing to lose. Where there was no need to act, no need to speak, no need to think or plan. Where the mind rested in its natural state—silent, vast, untangled.

This was real peace.
Not the peace of fulfilling a desire, but the peace of transcending the need for desire altogether.

I sat in stillness, watching my mind as if it were a vast ocean, rippling with thoughts, memories, longings.

And then—I let it all go. I stopped grasping. I stopped running. I stopped feeding the illusions that had bound me for lifetimes. I let the waves settle. I let the storm pass. And in that perfect, silent stillness—where nothing was needed, where nothing was prepared—I was free.

PRESIDENT

Chapter 31

The Mirage of Royalty

The mind is a weaver of dreams, and one of the grandest dreams it ever spun for me was the desire to be a king.

Not merely as a symbol in a child's imagination, but as a deep, resounding longing—one that had followed me from past lives and etched itself into the very marrow of my current being. The desire to reign with dignity, to be adorned in royal silks, to walk with golden sandals across marble floors while a thousand voices sang my praise—it was intoxicating.

And so, as I had done before, I turned inward.

In the stillness of meditation, I closed my eyes and allowed the theatre of the mind to unfold.

I imagined myself as a great monarch—a sovereign of immeasurable power and influence. The grand palace was mine, a structure carved from gold and ivory, towering over the capital like a testament to legacy. My throne was elevated above all, inlaid with gemstones that shimmered under the chandeliers, each reflecting the bowing heads of nobles and generals who waited upon my command.

Every day, I was dressed by the finest hands—robes spun with golden threads, a crown kissed with rubies, a sword sheathed in pride. As I entered the court, all would rise, chanting verses to glorify my name. Trumpets would echo through the high vaulted ceilings, and flower petals would rain like blessings upon my path.

I saw myself holding court, issuing decrees, listening to petitions. I gave freely to the poor. I built temples, schools, and hospitals. The people called me the jewel of the realm. Artists wrote poems about my virtues. Children memorised my name as a legend. I walked through gardens that bloomed eternally and looked upon my kingdom with a sense of sacred satisfaction.

It was glorious.

For a time, the fantasy washed over me like nectar—sweet, heady, fulfilling. The very idea of being revered, honoured, and powerful seemed like the ultimate goal. I had reached the peak of worldly existence. What else could there be?

But, as always, I did not stop with the sweetness.

Slowly, I extended the vision. I allowed the illusion to age.

I imagined waking up as a king not for the first time—but for the thousandth. I imagined the weight of the crown, once so thrilling, now simply heavy. I imagined the praise that had once stirred my soul now falling on ears that had grown numb to flattery. The songs became repetitive. The meals, though grand, became tasteless. The duties became burdens.

And then came the cracks.

A trusted minister betrayed me. A border dispute erupted into war. My own son, born into luxury, became indulgent and arrogant. My health began to falter. The mirror reflected not the idealised king I had once envisioned, but a weary man—eyes sunken, spirit dulled, surrounded by opulence yet lacking joy.

I saw that even in the life of a king, there were no exceptions to the laws of impermanence. The robes wrinkled. The body ached. The mind wearied. And the throne, once a symbol of glory, became a golden cage. I saw myself dying on that very throne—clutching my chest as my courtiers scrambled in panic. The same marble floor that once echoed my footsteps now bore my silence.

What had I truly gained?

Even if all went well—even if the kingdom prospered, the people loved me, and I left behind a lasting legacy—what remained for *me*? I would still be a man, subject to decay. I would still be a mind trapped in the cycle of experiences.

And even more than that—if I examined this kingship not in fantasy but in terms of raw cognition—what was it truly?

It was nothing but a play of the senses.

The admiration of the crowd was simply a *sound*, received by my ears. The royal silks were merely a *sensation*, felt upon the skin. The golden halls and lush gardens were *visuals*, perceived by the eye. The pride I felt in ruling wisely—just a *thought*, a formation of the mind.

All that glory, when reduced to its elements, was no more than a fleeting series of sensory inputs—impermanent, unreliable, and incapable of holding the weight of lasting satisfaction.

The idealistic dream of kingship had crumbled under the gaze of discernment.

In reality, no matter how high I rose, I would still wake in the morning, feel the sting of aging joints, worry about threats to my power, carry the burdens of those who relied on me, and go to sleep at night restless with uncertainty.

Even royalty becomes routine. Even reverence becomes dull.

And slowly, I began to understand—my desire was never truly for the throne.

It was for the *feeling* I thought the throne would give me.

The feeling of being significant. Of being adored. Of being untouchable.

But feelings are not facts. They are weather—passing, changing, never fixed.

I had mistaken the crown for peace. But peace was not found atop a golden throne—it was found beneath the weight of no desires at all.

I began to discern more deeply. What truly gave life to my enjoyment as a king, or any pleasure for that matter? Was it the gold, the silk, the throne, or the power itself? Or was it merely a thought, a perception arising within the mind?

When examined closely, the truth was unmistakable: every ounce of happiness I experienced, every drop of delight, originated from my own cognition. It was my consciousness that painted the world in hues of delight or despair. My mind took external sensations—sounds of praise, sights of opulence, feelings of luxury—and shaped them into feelings of joy and satisfaction.

But herein lay a profound paradox: cognitions have a frequency, a rhythm. They rise and fall, come and go, fade and reappear. No matter how grand the external conditions, the happiness arising from my mind could never be sustained at an idealistic peak. It was inherently fleeting, inherently unstable.

In other words, the grandeur of royalty, the majesty of a throne, the reverence of subjects—none of it mattered unless my mind actively generated pleasant thoughts about them. If I ceased to think about my status or wealth, what remained? Nothing but mere sensations: sights, sounds, touches, all stripped of meaning, all ordinary in their essence. The throne itself held no intrinsic joy, nor did the crown carry inherent delight. They became special, became exquisite, only through my own mental formations.

This realization opened a deeper understanding: my happiness was nothing but a cycle—a continuous interplay of perception and sensation. I perceived royalty as pleasurable, and from that perception arose pleasant sensations. In turn, those pleasant sensations compelled me to perceive royalty as even more desirable, forming a loop that trapped me in endless pursuit.

Yet, inevitably, the cycle would collapse. Over time, even the most majestic sensations dulled. The exquisite became commonplace. Familiarity dissolved novelty. Pleasure, once intense, faded into neutrality, and neutrality eventually became boredom or dissatisfaction.

The throne, once a symbol of joy, became just another chair. The crown, once a mark of greatness, became a mere weight upon my head. This inevitable decline in enjoyment was not due to external factors—it was the inherent nature of my own cognitive cycle.

Thus, no matter how magnificent my palace, how immense my wealth, or how profound the respect I commanded, none of it could truly fulfil my idealistic expectations. My imagined pleasure always exceeded the actual experience. Reality could never match my fantasies, because reality was subject to the law of impermanence and the limitations of my mind's ability to sustain pleasure.

Every preparation—physical, verbal, or mental—led eventually to weariness, to exhaustion. Being a king, ultimately, was tiring. The endless need to maintain appearances, to guard against threats, to uphold authority, to continually chase after fleeting sensations of satisfaction—all of it drained me. The very effort I expended to secure happiness eventually became the cause of my fatigue.

And thus, my understanding deepened further: true happiness—genuine peace—could never be found by obtaining or holding onto something external. It could only be discovered in the complete stilling of the mind itself.

Real satisfaction lay not in accumulating pleasures, but in releasing the very desire for them. Where there are no thoughts, no perceptions, no sensations forming cycles of longing—there, in that silence, lies true fulfilment.

Only when all preparations ceased—when the mind no longer created images of grandeur, when the body no longer chased after desires, when speech no longer sought praise—only then could true peace arise. This peace was not found on a throne or in a crown; it was discovered in the profound stillness of non-thought, non-action, non-self.

To be a king, therefore, was ultimately meaningless if the mind was not free from craving. Even at the highest pinnacle of worldly success, one remained trapped, endlessly chasing shadows of idealistic pleasure that could never be reached.

True liberation, real satisfaction, lay in turning away from these thoughts altogether—in shutting off the endless cycle of desire, perception, and sensation. In that profound inner silence, beyond the concept of "world" and "me," was where lasting peace and satisfaction finally became possible.

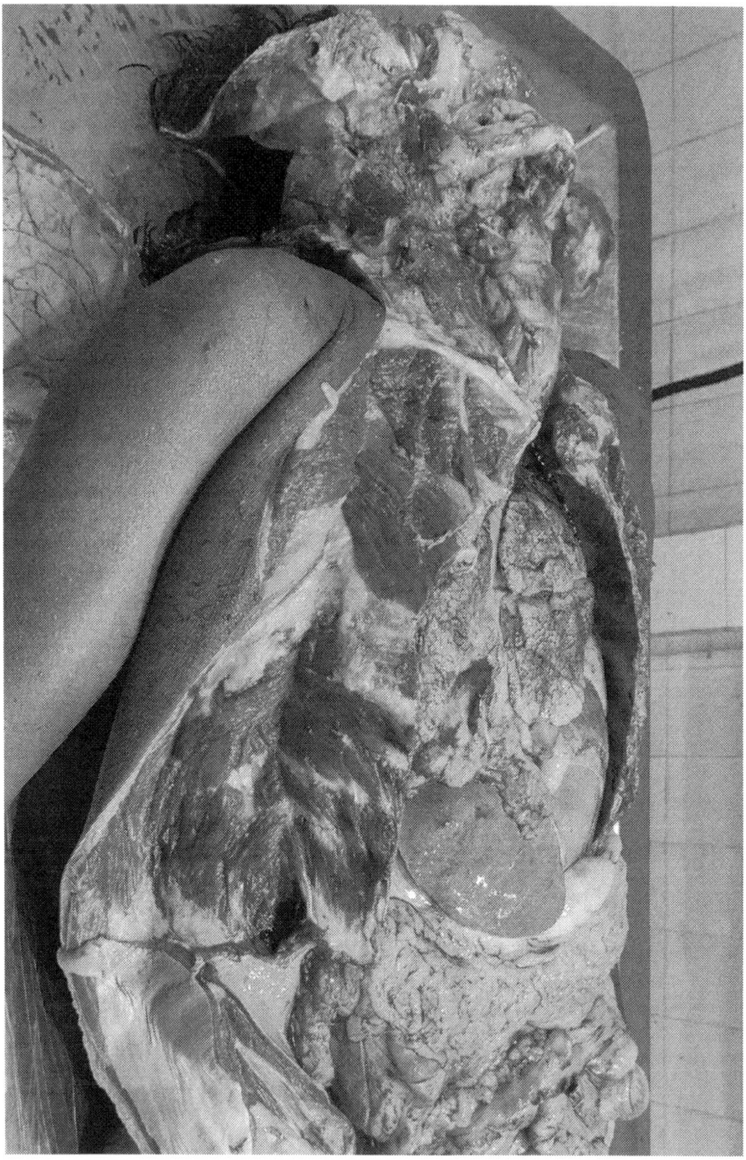

Chapter 32

Discerning Repulsive Nature

Having discerned the elusive nature of fulfilment and the inevitable dangers inherent within my most cherished desires, I understood that mere intellectual recognition alone was insufficient to extinguish the fire of craving. Recognising this, I made a resolute decision to relinquish my desires—not merely by suppressing them, but by thoroughly comprehending their true nature. It became clear to me that true liberation was impossible without deeper insight. Thus, I sought practical methods, powerful meditative techniques rooted in ancient Buddhist wisdom, to uproot these attachments that still haunted my heart.

Of all my desires, the longing for an elder sister, with her comforting presence, elegant beauty, and intimate embrace, had proven the most persistent. Her imagined perfection and beauty, magnified by my own mind, had always enchanted and ensnared me. To free myself from this powerful illusion, I knew I had to confront it directly.

I turned, therefore, to a profound and ancient meditation technique described by the Lord Buddha: **the meditation on repulsiveness (Asubha Bhāvanā)**, a method carefully designed to shatter illusions, dismantle attachments, and unveil the true nature hidden behind external beauty. Like a wise man opening a sack filled with mixed grains, carefully identifying each type—rice, chickpeas, barley, wheat—so too would I unravel the perceived beauty of the elder sister, examining her physical form meticulously, part by part, without deception.

Closing my eyes gently, I began the meditation by visualising her clearly: a beautiful woman with a princess-like demeanour, graceful, proud, and radiant. She stood before me vividly in my imagination, captivatingly lovely. Slowly, purposefully, I reached out and held her long, silken hair in my mind's eye, searching carefully for the inherent beauty I had so adored. Yet, upon deeper inspection, what did I find? The hair I cherished was merely strands of lifeless fibres sprouting from follicles embedded in greasy scalp skin. They had no self, no intrinsic loveliness; they required constant grooming and washing simply to appear acceptable.

Next, my mental gaze moved to the hairs upon her body—fine threads scattered over her arms, legs, armpits, and private areas. Each strand was lifeless, trivial, meaningless—sometimes unpleasant. How could I find lasting joy here? Similarly, her nails, polished and elegant, were mere keratin plates, dead and constantly growing, demanding endless maintenance, and often harbouring dirt beneath.

Her teeth, shining white like pearls, proved upon closer observation to be merely bones protruding from pinkish gums, quickly gathering foul odours and decaying without constant care. Could genuine beauty be found in something prone to rot?

I delved deeper, examining her skin—the soft surface I had once yearned to touch. On close examination, skin revealed itself as fragile tissue, frequently shedding dead cells, secreting sweat, grease, and oils, constantly prone to blemishes, imperfections, wrinkles, and decay. The captivating beauty vanished entirely beneath this understanding.

With growing resolve, I plunged deeper within. Her flesh—once so enticing—was now merely muscle tissue, a mass of fibres and veins, pulsing and contracting, wet and bloody. Sinews, holding muscles to bone, appeared as thick cords and fibres, devoid of beauty, merely functional, mechanical structures. Bones beneath, white and hard, were grim reminders of impermanence, simply scaffolding destined to decay.

Within these bones was marrow—soft, fatty tissue hidden from sight, deeply unpleasant to behold, essential yet repulsive. Her kidneys were mere filtration organs—sacks of dark tissue cleansing bodily waste. Her heart, romanticised as the seat of emotion, was but a muscular pump, rhythmic yet devoid of inherent beauty. The liver, purifying toxins, appeared spongy and grotesque. Pleura, thin membranes enveloping lungs, felt slimy and wet. Her spleen, dark and blood-filled, offered no aesthetic allure. Her lungs, vital yet gruesome, constantly inflating and deflating, carried foul air and impurities.

My examination intensified, inspecting her intestines, intestinal tract, and stomach—organs dedicated to processing food into unpleasant matter. Faeces, the inevitable output, offered nothing but repulsion, yet was hidden from view to sustain delusions of bodily purity. Similarly, bile, phlegm, pus—products of bodily function and decay—held no trace of beauty or attraction. Blood, vital yet staining and messy, symbolised injury and illness more than beauty. Sweat, fat, tears, and grease were mere secretions—fluids carrying impurities, unpleasant and devoid of inherent value.

I then confronted saliva, nasal mucus, synovium (the oily lubricant of joints), urine, and finally, the brain itself—hidden beneath her skull, a mass of grey and white tissue, wet and gelatinous, the source of endless thoughts, yet inherently unattractive and ordinary when viewed plainly.

With each deeper investigation, her body—previously perceived as a source of endless beauty and pleasure—revealed itself clearly to my contemplative gaze as nothing more than a machine: an intricate biological device assembled from bones and sinews, wrapped in muscle and flesh, covered superficially by skin and hairs. Her every touch, hug, caress, and embrace was merely the mechanical operation of a complex biological system. Where was the true beauty I had so fervently sought? It was nowhere to be found within the structure of her physical form. Every perceived beauty I had cherished had originated in my mind, projected onto these repulsive parts.

Gradually, as this profound discernment continued, a powerful shift occurred within my consciousness. The intense craving, the obsessive longing, began to loosen. The once overpowering desire for an elder sister's love, presence, and physical embrace, which had tormented my soul across lifetimes, began finally to fade. With clearer vision, I saw through the illusion I had created.

I now comprehended deeply the truth taught by Lord Buddha: true peace and freedom from desire come not by suppressing desire, but by clearly seeing its object as it truly is—impermanent, unsatisfying, and ultimately repulsive when examined objectively. Through this meditation, my understanding of reality was profoundly deepened.

My previously insatiable craving for the presence and embrace of an elder sister had been exposed and weakened, losing its grip on my heart. The mind, once enslaved by a beautiful illusion, now found genuine freedom and lightness in seeing clearly. The meditation on repulsiveness had liberated me from the false promises of physical attraction, allowing my heart to find true peace by letting go.

Yet, I knew my meditation could not end here. The powerful illusion of beauty that had once enslaved my heart still retained subtle threads that needed to be severed entirely. It was not sufficient merely to see the internal repulsiveness of her form. To fully liberate my mind, I had to witness vividly the inevitable external deterioration that awaited all physical bodies.

Thus, I began another contemplation, more vivid, more intense. With eyes gently closed, I visualised this princess-like woman—whose imagined beauty had long haunted my thoughts—now tied firmly to a chair in an isolated room, unable to move, unable to clean or care for herself, for an entire week. In my mind, the scene became sharply detailed, utterly realistic, devoid of any romantic illusions.

On the first day, she sat elegantly enough, her composure maintained by dignity, pride, and poise. But soon, the inescapable nature of bodily functions began to assert themselves. By the second day, her grace began to fade. Hunger and thirst weakened her; she would perspire heavily, her hair growing greasy, tangled, unkempt. Sweat dampened her once-silken clothing, producing a strong, acrid smell that intensified steadily.

By the third day, the room filled with an unbearable stench. She had no choice but to soil herself; urine stained her clothes, faeces collected beneath the chair. The odour, foul and nauseating, permeated every inch of space. Her body now emanated an overwhelming foulness, no longer adorned with sweet perfumes or subtle fragrances.

Her beautiful face, once radiant and flawless, became gaunt and shadowed. Grease and grime accumulated, particularly around her eyes, giving her a weary, lifeless appearance. Her lips, dry and cracked, lost their alluring softness. Her mouth became foul-smelling, breath sour and unpleasant, as bacteria and impurities flourished.

Day after day, the deterioration worsened. By the sixth day, she appeared barely human—her body weakened, dehydrated, unspeakably filthy. All her dignity vanished; pride had disappeared. She was no longer a princess, no longer desirable, no longer beautiful. Instead, she was merely a suffering, decaying creature imprisoned in her own repulsiveness.

I observed this scenario deeply, vividly, for several minutes, until my heart fully comprehended the truth. At that moment, a powerful realisation arose within me:

"Is this truly the body I craved? Is this the object of my insatiable desire? What fool would willingly attach themselves so strongly to something destined to such decay? And how great a fool had I been, bound by such an illusion! How great are the countless beings of this world—men and women—fooled, trapped, tormented by a temporary form that inevitably decays, deteriorates, and ultimately perishes!"

This meditation, profound and intense, became more than merely a reflection upon physical deterioration. It revealed to me a fundamental truth about all desires, all attachments, all illusions we cling to in this world. Whether it was the sorrow of a breakup, the bitterness of betrayal, the pain of loss, or the inevitable grief of death—this very meditation provided the most powerful antidote.

I understood, through direct insight, that every form, every being, every object of our craving is ultimately subject to decay, unpleasantness, and dissolution. The beautiful, enchanting forms that we cling to desperately, believing they will offer everlasting happiness, are merely temporary illusions veiling an underlying repulsiveness. Only ignorance blinds us to their true nature.

By seeing reality so clearly, I was freed from the delusion that had chained me. The previously irresistible desire began to lose all its power. A deep sense of clarity and peace descended upon my heart, washing away the clinging, the longing, the insatiable need that had caused me such inner turmoil.

As I opened my eyes, emerging from this deep meditation, my heart was profoundly transformed. The craving for beauty, for companionship, for intimacy—specifically that tied to the illusion of an elder sister figure—had loosened greatly.

I felt a profound relief, an unmistakable lightness, a quiet joy born not from fulfilment of desire, but from its release. My mind was clearer, sharper, more free. I had pierced the veil of illusion.

This meditative discernment, so vividly practiced, had taught me a universal truth. Beauty and attraction are fleeting illusions built from our own mental fabrications. Reality, when seen clearly, dissolves attachment, freeing us from sorrow, disappointment, grief, and regret.

Now, having understood this, my heart began to turn towards true freedom—a liberation that could never be shaken, tarnished, or diminished.

I breathed deeply, savouring this newfound wisdom.

The path forward was clear.

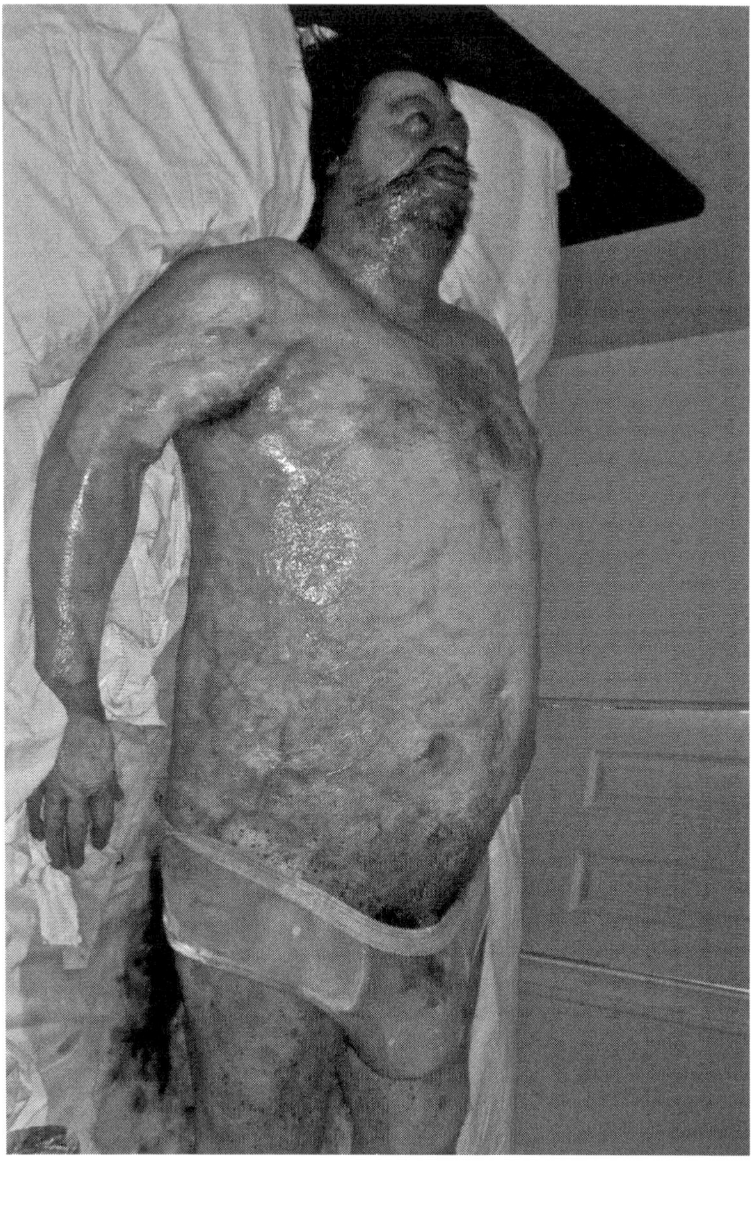

Chapter 33

The First Taste of Liberation

Yet, despite all the profound contemplations on repulsiveness, I soon discovered that my desire for a beloved elder sister had not vanished completely. The initial disgust and detachment that arose from seeing her bodily impurities faded after a time, and again my heart found itself drawn back into longing. Clearly, mere reflection on repulsiveness was insufficient for my liberation; something deeper, more penetrating, was needed.

Thus, I turned my meditation to a more profound contemplation, one that revealed not just the repulsive nature of the body, but its inherent impermanence and the inevitability of death. I needed to truly witness how my cherished sister, whom I had idealised as timeless and eternally beautiful, was inexorably moving towards decay, dissolution, and ultimate disappearance.

I closed my eyes and summoned her image once again. I imagined her exactly as my heart desired: young, radiant, perfect in every feature, her skin smooth as silk, her eyes bright, her hair gleaming. Yet, this time, I forced myself to see beyond this fleeting perfection. Her beauty, her youthful grace, her charm—none of it was permanent. Day by day, hour by hour, moment by moment, she was moving inevitably toward decay. Her skin, now delicate and soft, would gradually wrinkle and loosen. Her eyes, once luminous and captivating, would grow dim and sunken with age. Her hair, shining like black silk, would eventually grey, becoming brittle and dry.

I imagined her attitude, now so full of dignity and poise, being humbled by the relentless march of time, her strength gradually fading. All the pride, the elegance, the allure that had captivated me would slowly dissolve into weakness and vulnerability. The form I adored, cherished, and idealised would soon lose its beauty and charm, overtaken by the harsh realities of ageing and disease.

Then my meditation led me even further. I contemplated the inevitability of death itself, the ultimate destiny awaiting every living body. A day would come when my beloved sister would take her final breath. No matter how much I loved her, no matter how beautiful or precious she appeared, death would claim her body, rendering it utterly lifeless and inert.

I imagined the moment vividly: her body lying motionless on a bed, her eyes glazed over, her warmth gone, her breathing ceased. Where was her beauty then? Her lovely, soft hands, which once caressed and comforted me so tenderly, would now lie stiff and cold—no more valuable than pieces of rotten wood.

In my mind, I continued this contemplation even further, recalling the powerful teachings of Lord Buddha—the Nine Cemetery Contemplations designed to penetrate deeply into the truth of impermanence and decay. I visualised clearly, step by step, the fate that awaited her body after death.

Firstly, two or three days after death, her body would swell grotesquely, turning an unnatural shade of blue, festering, emitting a foul, unbearable stench. Her once-perfect beauty would become utterly repulsive and unbearable, forcing those who had once loved her dearly to dispose of her corpse swiftly, abandoning it to the charnel ground.

Secondly, her abandoned corpse would be torn apart, devoured by wild animals—crows, vultures, hawks pecking away her flesh, dogs and jackals tearing at her limbs, worms burrowing through her once-beautiful skin, consuming her from within. What remained of her dignity, her beauty, her elegance? Nothing at all. Merely food for scavengers, utterly abandoned, utterly worthless.

Thirdly, as animals consumed her flesh and internal organs, her body would be reduced to a blood-smeared skeleton, flesh hanging in torn fragments, sinews exposed, blood drying dark and foul.

Fourthly, further exposure to scavengers and elements would strip her skeleton entirely of flesh, leaving only bones still smeared in traces of dried, blackened blood—pitiful remains of someone I had idealised so deeply.

Fifthly, even the dried blood and remaining flesh would vanish over time, leaving only a stark skeleton—bare, white, fragile bones lying exposed on barren ground.

Sixthly, weather, wind, animals, and decay would scatter these bones—hand bones scattered here, foot bones there, a thigh bone, a shin bone, a pelvic bone, vertebrae from her spine, fragments of her skull—all dispersed, all disconnected, strewn randomly across the earth.

Seventhly, these scattered bones would gradually bleach in sunlight, turning pale as conch shells, colourless, lifeless remnants, stripped of all dignity, utterly forgotten.

Eighthly, after many months, the bleached bones would lie in a heap, unrecognisable as once belonging to a human being—just a scattered pile of meaningless calcium and minerals.

Finally, ninthly, over the passage of years, even these bones would disintegrate into fragments, turning gradually to dust, merging indistinguishably with earth itself. Her body, the one I adored, the object of my endless longing and admiration, would disappear completely, leaving no trace, no beauty, no dignity—nothing at all.

As I witnessed each of these stages vividly, clearly, I felt a profound, heart-shaking realisation: the body of my elder sister was not really her. This decaying form was never truly hers, never really under her control. It was merely a temporary vessel, assembled from past karma, inherited DNA, and nourishment consumed through food. It functioned not by her will but by natural law—mere cause and effect, a mechanism built only from bones, sinews, flesh, skin, and hair.

This truth was not specific only to her; it was true for all bodies, mine included. Every living form is merely a temporary aggregation of elements, destined to decay, disperse, and dissolve. Her touch, her hugs, her cuddles—the actions that had once filled my heart with longing and happiness—were nothing more than mechanical interactions between bodily tissues and elements, completely devoid of inherent beauty or meaning.

This vivid contemplation, so brutally honest and direct, shattered the last remnants of my obsessive attachment. Desire loosened significantly from my heart, replaced by deep understanding, clarity, and profound freedom. The image of her beauty that had once enslaved me vanished completely, leaving only insight into the impermanent, unsatisfactory, and selfless nature of the human form.

I inhaled slowly, feeling the depth of peace that comes from truly understanding reality. This realisation was not merely philosophical—it was liberating. It freed my heart, loosened my bonds, and showed me clearly how foolish it was to attach so desperately to something inevitably destined for dissolution.

With a mind now profoundly clear, I gently deepened my meditation, grateful to have seen the deepest truth. From that moment onward, my heart no longer clung to the illusion of beauty, no longer chased after temporary sensations, and no longer suffered from unfulfilled longing. Instead, I rested deeply in this newfound wisdom—a wisdom that would lead me inevitably toward ultimate liberation.

Yet, I did not stop at merely discerning the true nature of her physical body; my meditation journey continued far deeper, piercing into subtler layers of her existence. I began searching for my elder sister within her very sensations—the pleasant, unpleasant, and neutral feelings that arose and passed away constantly within her. As I examined closely, I saw clearly that none of these sensations truly belonged to her, nor did they represent an enduring essence or soul.

Sensations arose automatically, triggered by external contact. When her eyes met a pleasant sight, a pleasurable sensation arose. If she heard a harsh sound, an unpleasant feeling appeared. Yet, she had no power or authority over these sensations. She could not command her body to feel pleasure or pain; she could not control or manipulate her sensations according to her wishes. They were merely automatic responses—a mechanical process of contact and reaction, completely impersonal, entirely devoid of any lasting self or identity.

Then I shifted my focus deeper still, searching her within her perceptions—the mind's constant labeling, interpreting, and identifying of experiences. Surely, if there were an enduring self or soul, it must reside somewhere within her perceptual nature, within the way she understood and interpreted the world around her.

But even her perceptions were not hers to control. They were merely conditioned responses, arising from the causes and conditions of her past experiences, habits, memories, and karmic conditioning. When she saw something familiar, recognition arose. When she experienced something new, confusion or curiosity arose. Her mind labeled everything automatically, continually constructing meaning and identity out of endless streams of sensory input. But these labels, these interpretations, were not hers to command. She could not choose to perceive the world differently than her conditioning dictated. Even perceptions were impersonal, transient, fleeting, not representing any real or lasting self.

Unsatisfied with merely perceptions, I searched even deeper—this time, examining her thoughts and mental formations. Perhaps the self, the true essence of her being, lay hidden within her thoughts, her inner voice, the mental narrative that seemed so intimately connected to identity. But when I closely observed her thought processes, I saw clearly again: even these thoughts were conditioned, habitual patterns, driven by memory, experience, karma, and emotions. Thoughts arose spontaneously and uncontrollably. She could not dictate or govern her thoughts, making them appear or disappear at will. They simply arose due to conditions, stayed briefly, and vanished just as quickly. Even the most intimate thoughts, the seemingly personal internal dialogues, did not contain any enduring essence or true self. They were merely conditioned effects, ephemeral and empty.

Still not satisfied, I turned my gaze towards her very consciousness itself—the root of all experiencing, the fundamental knowing of sights, sounds, smells, tastes, touches, and thoughts. If there were truly an enduring self, surely it must reside within consciousness, the fundamental knowing quality that experienced everything else.

Yet, even consciousness proved itself equally impersonal, transient, and uncontrollable. Her eye-consciousness merely arose when visual objects entered her field of vision—she had no choice or control over it. Similarly, her ear-consciousness arose automatically when sounds reached her ear. Her nose-consciousness, tongue-consciousness, body-consciousness, and mind-consciousness were all similarly automatic, uncontrollable reactions. She could not decide or choose when consciousness would arise or disappear; it appeared only according to conditions and causes. Thus, consciousness too was empty of a permanent self or soul.

After examining her deeply, from the surface of her body down through sensations, perceptions, mental formations, and consciousness, I finally understood clearly: the elder sister I desired so deeply was nothing more than a mirage created by my own thoughts. She was merely a mechanism, an aggregate of body, sensations, perceptions, thoughts, and consciousness, functioning according to conditions and completely devoid of any lasting self or identity.

In that powerful moment of clarity, I realized something profound—not only was she an illusion, but so too was the "I" that chased after her. Just as she was empty, so was I. I began examining myself with the same thoroughness and intensity. My own body, sensations, perceptions, thoughts, and consciousness—none of them truly belonged to me or contained a lasting self. They were all similarly conditioned processes, arising and ceasing without my control, dependent entirely on causes and conditions. Even what I called "myself" was just another clinging aggregate, just another mechanism driven by impersonal processes.

In this penetrating insight, I discovered something remarkable. Elder sister existed only within the realm of my mind's preparation and perception. Her presence or absence, her love or rejection—these existed only when my mind generated thoughts about them. Without these thoughts, there was no sister, no loss, no longing. It was all simply the play of my own perceptions and sensations, creating imaginary worlds out of fleeting mental phenomena.

As this understanding deepened, I began to see that the whole world existed only within the cognition of this present moment. Each consciousness—each moment of seeing, hearing, feeling, or thinking—arose briefly and vanished instantly. There was no continuous world beyond these fleeting cognitions. Everything existed solely within the arising and passing away of momentary consciousness.

With this revelation, something profound shifted within me. I felt my attachment to the idea of an elder sister vanish, replaced by deep clarity. For the first time, I experienced the complete stilling of all mental preparations. My mind, which had chased desires and dreams for lifetimes, finally fell completely silent. All craving, all longing, all dissatisfaction dissolved into profound peace.

In that silence, I turned off the world of my own perceptions. I relinquished the illusory notions of "self" and "other." My mind became perfectly still, perfectly empty, liberated from the endless cycle of perception and sensation. For the first time, I tasted liberation—the first stage of enlightenment. It was a state free from suffering, free from desire, free from illusion, a state of pure, boundless peace.

At that sacred moment, I understood clearly: true happiness was never found in the pursuit of desires or the fulfillment of cravings. It was not found in obtaining what I longed for. Rather, true happiness, true liberation, was discovered precisely in this letting go—this complete and absolute cessation of all mental fabrications. True peace lay in the utter stilling of all preparations, in the relinquishing of all illusions.

And thus, at long last, I finally came home.

Chapter 34

The Four Stages of Liberation

When a person experiences the stilling of all preparations (*sankhāra*) for the very first time, even if only for a few moments, they reach the stage known as **Sotāpanna** or the **stream-enterer**. This is the first and critical milestone on the path towards total liberation. It is akin to stepping into a stream whose powerful current inevitably leads to the vast ocean of Nibbāna. A Sotāpanna is assured of reaching complete liberation within no more than seven lifetimes and is guaranteed never again to fall into lower realms of existence, such as the animal world or hellish realms. Once this precious stage is attained, nothing can hinder the eventual arrival at full liberation.

The journey towards ultimate liberation unfolds through four distinct stages, each representing a deeper penetration into the understanding and relinquishing of suffering.

1. Stream-Entry (Sotāpanna)

Upon first encountering the stilling of all physical, verbal, and mental preparations, the Sotāpanna intuitively recognises the inherent stressfulness and futility of continuous craving. They naturally begin to withdraw from actions and habits that perpetuate this stress. It is as if, after a lifetime spent chasing shadows, they finally turn around and see that the very act of chasing was the source of their suffering. From this pivotal moment, their heart inclines steadily toward liberation.

2. Once-Returner (Sakadāgāmi)

As the Sotāpanna continues their disciplined practice, attachment to sensual desire, lust, greed, and aversion begins to significantly diminish, approximately by half. Upon achieving this state, they become a Sakadāgāmi, a "once-returner." Such an individual will return only once more, either to the human world or a heavenly realm, before attaining complete enlightenment. Their clarity and insight have deepened, freeing them progressively from the bondage of craving and hatred. The heavy burden they once carried is now greatly reduced, enabling a far lighter journey ahead.

3. Non-Returner (Anāgāmi)

With further unwavering dedication to practice and insight, the Sakadāgāmi eventually eradicates the fetters of sensual desire and aversion entirely, advancing to the Anāgāmi stage, or "non-returner." Such a being will no longer return to human or even celestial realms; their remaining existence will occur in a refined, blissful Brahma realm, characterised by profound meditative absorption and tranquillity. If full enlightenment is not realised within the current lifetime, it is certain to be attained in this subsequent realm. At this level, the practitioner's mind is remarkably pure, unobstructed by the grosser forms of craving and aversion.

4. Arahant (Fully Enlightened)

The culmination of this profound journey is the state of the Arahant—a fully enlightened being who has completely severed all attachments, including the subtle delusion of selfhood. This state represents the ultimate liberation, a total disengagement from the cyclic existence of birth, ageing, sickness, and death. Lord Buddha assured that with diligent and unwavering practice, this full enlightenment can be realised within as short a span as seven days or, at most, seven years. Even if full enlightenment within this period proves elusive, reaching at least the stage of Non-Returner is still assured.

Upon full enlightenment, death is no longer perceived as something fearful or unwanted. Rather, death is welcomed with serene acceptance, like a diligent worker peacefully awaiting their earned reward. An enlightened being meets death free of clinging, ensuring they will not be reborn into any realm. They have transcended the cycle of birth, death, and suffering, and rest permanently in the profound peace and liberation that is Nibbāna.

The Eightfold Progress of Liberation

These four stages of liberation—Sotāpanna, Sakadāgāmi, Anāgāmi, and Arahant—are further divided into eight distinct attainments, each with a *path* (magga) and a *fruit* (phala). The *path* refers to the moment of entering into that stage through direct insight, while the *fruit* is the matured realisation that follows, stabilising the insight and transforming one's inner experience. Understanding these eight phases allows for a more refined appreciation of how delusion, craving, and identity gradually dissolve on the journey to full awakening.

The transformation of lust, especially, is one of the most vivid and deeply personal aspects of this journey. For many, the longing for intimacy, connection, or love—whether romantic, emotional, or even in the form of idealised relationships such as the love for an elder sister—is a potent representation of desire. When examined deeply, even such yearning becomes a mirror through which the practitioner recognises the illusion of self, the hollowness of grasping, and the path to letting go. The stages of liberation reflect how this desire is gradually transcended—not by repression, but by insight and wisdom.

1. Path of Stream-Entry (Sotāpatti Magga)

At this stage, the practitioner remains largely like any ordinary worldling in terms of desires. Lust, especially in its emotional or idealised forms—like longing for the affection of an elder sister figure—is still vibrant and active. However, there is now a deliberate effort to observe and restrain these desires. The individual forcefully tries to distance the mind from lustful thoughts, not out of suppression, but in pursuit of understanding. Insight arises, but it is often fragile, requiring the practitioner to exert great willpower to resist the tide of sensual craving. He begins to see that the problem is not the object of desire but the very mechanism of desiring itself.

2. Fruit of Stream-Entry (Sotāpatti Phala)

With the realisation of the fruit, there is a profound inner shift. The practitioner still experiences lust and emotional desire just as before, but now he understands—deeply and directly—that both "self" and "other" are empty constructs, operating through dependent origination. The relationship he once romanticised is now seen as a play of causes and conditions, a process rather than a personal story. He does not feel guilt for desiring, nor does he battle it forcefully. Rather, he enhances mindfulness and dwells with awareness *through* the presence of desire, no longer being shaken by it. He knows that the one who desires and the one who is desired are equally void of essence.

3. Path of Once-Returner (Sakadāgāmi Magga)
The once-returner on the path begins to experience a noticeable weakening of sensual desire. Lust and longing no longer haunt him with the same intensity. The hunger for companionship, physical closeness, or emotional dependency begins to wane. He might still feel affection or attraction occasionally, but it arises only when specific conditions stimulate it. Otherwise, his mind is calm and relatively unaffected by stimuli that would once have provoked yearning. He still appreciates love and care but is no longer desperate for it. This shift is not due to suppression but through maturity of insight and self-mastery.

4. Fruit of Once-Returner (Sakadāgāmi Phala)
At this level, the practitioner's sensual desires are reduced by half or more. His day-to-day mind does not crave a partner or intimate affection. Even the emotional longing for nurturing or closeness that once flared during times of illness, exhaustion, or stress is largely absent. If such feelings arise, they are brief and shallow—like echoes from an old life. When he is upset or vulnerable, rather than reaching out for comfort, his heart inclines inward, towards equanimity and truth. The craving for love no longer seems essential. A deeper kind of satisfaction—silent, steady, and internal—has begun to replace the rollercoaster of emotional highs and lows.

5. Path of Non-Returner (Anāgāmi Magga)
Now the practitioner has almost fully transcended lust. Sensual desire and aversion are diminished by 75% or more. The hunger for touch, companionship, or even emotional warmth

has faded significantly. Even when the body is weak or the mind is unsettled, the heart turns not towards external sources, but inward—towards the tranquil ecstasy of renunciation, the joy of stillness, and the sublime beauty of the unconstructed state. If he tries to generate lust or relive romantic fantasies, they feel dull and lifeless. Even imagined intimacy loses its charm. The world, once viewed as alluring, now feels subtly repulsive—not in a negative sense, but in a liberating one. The person he once longed for is now perceived as a conditioned, impersonal mechanism, just like himself. The drama has lost its pull.

6. Fruit of Non-Returner (Anāgāmi Phala)
At this perfected stage of non-returning, sensual desire and aversion are completely uprooted. The practitioner lives free from the pull of lust and untouched by ill-will. However, this is not yet the final liberation. Subtle traces of ego still remain—there is still a faint sense of "I am," and the mind may occasionally conceive comparisons, subtly measuring others or oneself. Automatic thoughts still arise, though lighter than before, and not fuelled by emotional craving or hatred. The practitioner might still experience identity-based thoughts or conceptual filters, but they no longer lead to suffering or bondage. He lives in the present, with a calm dignity and restrained purity, not yet fully silent within, but gently ripening. Though not fully liberated, he is a noble being, walking steadily on the final stretch towards complete awakening.

7. Path of Full Enlightenment (Arahattamagga)
Now begins the final ascent. Even subtle thought patterns begin to dissolve. The practitioner sees with astounding clarity the unreality of the constructed world—the idea of "I" and "mine" feels like an old tale, no longer believable. Rarely, the mind might still grasp at the illusion of an independently

existing world, but such moments are fleeting and met with immediate awareness. The sense of self is almost extinguished. What remains is pure, unshaken knowing, yet even this knowing is no longer associated with "someone" who knows. He begins to live like a reflection in water—present, yet not solid. Like a flame about to go out, his last traces of ignorance flicker.

8. Fruit of Full Enlightenment (Arahattaphala)
This is the completion. The being has now fully awakened. There are no more automatic thoughts, no conceiving of a self or a world, no clinging, no projections. The mind rests in vast stillness, silent and unmoving. Nothing is measured. Nothing is preferred. Nothing is feared. The Arahant is like a robot who has realised it was never truly a self, only a process—a stream of arising and passing. But unlike a lifeless machine, this awakened one radiates profound compassion, deep silence, and effortless peace. The end of all becoming has arrived. Death holds no sting. Rebirth has no ground. The fires of craving, aversion, and delusion are extinguished. Only Nibbāna remains—unborn, unceasing, deathless.

Thus unfolds the sacred path of liberation, not merely as doctrine or distant goal, but as a living, breathing transformation within the heart. It is not about escaping life, but seeing it so clearly that the illusions fall away. Through each stage, the practitioner is not rejecting the world, but waking up from the dream of it. Desires such as the longing for love, companionship, or intimacy do not need to be fought—they only need to be understood, seen with full clarity, and gently let go.

And when the final letting go happens, not even the idea of "letting go" remains. Only silence. Only peace. Only the unshakeable stillness of Nibbāna.

Chapter 35

The Most Essential Realisations

Desires: Seeing Through the Mirage

I did not choose the path of enlightenment simply to abandon a single desire. I did not become a seeker merely to escape from my own longing for an elder sister, or to replace the pain of emotional absence with some abstract peace. No—this journey was not born from rejection, but from recognition. Recognition of the nature of all desires, not just one. Recognition that the human heart is forever reaching outward, endlessly grasping at illusions. That what we call love, or comfort, or fulfilment is so often no more than a shimmering heat wave on the desert's horizon—a beautiful but unreachable mirage. I began to see that it was not just my own personal longing that failed to satisfy me, but that the very mechanism of desiring was flawed, unstable, and incapable of offering true peace. That is when I truly turned towards enlightenment—not to heal one broken part of the mind, but to understand the entire machinery of illusion itself.

Before one even thinks of walking this noble path, there must be a profound and heartfelt insight into the **nature of desire as a mirage**. This is not an idea to adopt or a theory to discuss, but an internal awakening, like a sudden clearing of clouds. A moment where the world, once full of colour and promise, begins to show its cracks. One might still feel drawn to beauty, to love, to recognition—but somewhere deep inside, there is a growing understanding: *this will not last.* Every desire, even the purest one, is inherently unstable. It arises, it burns, and then it fades—often leaving ashes of restlessness, dissatisfaction, and sorrow. This is not because the object of desire is flawed, but because desire itself is a flame that can never find its own satisfaction. It always points forward, always seeks more. It is movement without rest, thirst without quenching.

For many, the spiritual path begins with disappointment. A heartbreak, a loss, a failure. But for one who looks deeply, that disappointment becomes the doorway to wisdom. I too longed for love, for someone who could understand me completely, who could be the emotional refuge I never had. In the innocence of my heart, that desire took the shape of an ideal sister—someone nurturing, gentle, beautiful, and unconditionally caring. And yet, even as I held this image close, a quiet question echoed within me: *Will even this satisfy me? Will even this bring lasting peace?* And in that moment, I realised: the desire itself was a mirage. Not because it was wrong to feel love, but because I was seeking completeness through something inherently incomplete. The one I longed for was impermanent. My feelings were impermanent. The mind that desired was impermanent. How, then, could anything lasting come from that which does not last?

Understanding desire as a mirage is not a depressing realisation—it is a liberating one. For once the mirage is seen clearly, the chase begins to lose its grip. One stops running. One starts to *look*. What is this desire made of? Where does it arise from? What am I really seeking? These questions pierce through the surface-level needs and begin to reveal the deeper layers of longing—longing for identity, for self-worth, for safety, for meaning. And even these, when closely examined, reveal the same pattern: they are built on the assumption that something outside, or even something inside, will finally complete "me." But if this "me" is itself a construct, a constantly changing bundle of memories, sensations, and thoughts, then what is it that we are actually trying to complete?

The path of enlightenment begins here—with the deep and patient inquiry into the illusion of desire. Not through forced renunciation, not through self-hatred or rejection of the world, but through *clarity*. When one sees that every desire is built on the assumption of a self that lacks something, the entire structure begins to tremble. And when that structure trembles, suffering begins to lose its roots. This is not about becoming dry or emotionless. It is about becoming free. One can still love, still care, still feel deeply—but without the burning thirst, without the illusion that this moment, this person, this experience will save us from the unsatisfactory nature of existence.

Before enlightenment can be truly pursued, one must be willing to disillusion themselves—not in bitterness, but in wisdom. It is a sacred disillusionment, a holy letting go. One must look at the shining promises of the world—not with scorn, but with honesty. Sensual pleasure, success, relationships, even spiritual attainment itself—if they are pursued with the hope that they will finally make us whole, they will eventually betray us. Not because the world is cruel, but because the nature of conditioned things is change. Nothing here is stable enough to rest upon.

Thus, the first and most essential teaching before walking the path of enlightenment is this: **All that arises through craving is fleeting, and all that is fleeting cannot bring true peace.** This is the wisdom that breaks the spell of the mirage. And once the spell is broken, the real journey can begin—not towards something to gain, but towards something to understand. Not to become someone greater, but to see that the one we thought we were was never truly there to begin with. And in that seeing, there is no emptiness—only freedom.

Let the seeker first look at their own heart—not with judgement, but with sincere curiosity. Let them trace every desire to its root, ask every longing what it is truly seeking. And when the answer finally comes, let it be met with stillness. For in that stillness, the mirage begins to fade, and the horizon opens—not with the fire of craving, but with the light of truth.

Ignorance: The Root of All Suffering

To deeply understand liberation, we must first comprehend ignorance—the root cause of our endless cycle of suffering. Ignorance, from a Buddhist perspective, is far more subtle and pervasive than mere lack of knowledge. It is the fundamental misunderstanding of reality itself—the mistaken belief in an independently existing "self" and an external "world" separate from our immediate cognition.

For instance, consider hearing a sound. We believe the sound and the listener exist independently of our perception. But this duality is merely an illusion created by our mind. The cognition of sound arises first; only afterward do we conceptually separate it into "sound" and "listener." Ignorance deceives us into believing in this duality, anchoring us to perpetual craving, attachment, and suffering.

Consider further the simple thought experiment of a wall behind you. When asked if the wall exists independently of your cognition, you naturally affirm it does. But upon deeper reflection, you realise this affirmation itself is merely another thought arising in your present cognition. The wall is a conceptual reality, not independently existing outside of your perception. Realising this dismantles ignorance at its core, allowing us to recognise that our attachment and suffering arise solely from conceptual illusions, from misunderstanding reality itself.

This insight liberates us from the bonds of ignorance, freeing us from the compulsive need to grasp onto illusions. We realise that what we have been clinging to—self, others, possessions, desires—is merely fleeting cognitive events, devoid of inherent existence. Every experience, no matter how sweet, is already fading the moment it arises. When we embrace this—not intellectually, but viscerally—our hearts begin to soften their attachments. Impermanence is not merely the doom of life; it is its sacred rhythm, its invitation to let go.

Penetrative Attention: The First Step to Liberation

Central to transcending ignorance and progressing towards liberation is the practice of Penetrative Attention, known in Pali as Yoniso Manasikāra. The term "Yoniso" meaning "origin" and "Manasikāra" meaning "attention," directs us to look inward at the very origin of our experiences, rather than becoming entangled in their content.

Ordinarily, our minds behave like monkeys in a room with multiple windows, jumping restlessly from one sense perception to another—sight, sound, smell, taste, touch, and thoughts—forever seeking satisfaction externally. Even within a single sense, the mind does not stay still; it abandons one object to chase the next—glancing at one image only to be pulled by another, hearing one sound only to yearn for a new one. This endless wandering reveals the mind's deep-rooted restlessness and its futile hunger for fulfilment in the ever-changing world of phenomena. This restless mind perceives the world as existing independently, thus perpetuating craving and suffering.

Lord Buddha instructs us instead to observe inwardly, examining the arising and passing of cognitions themselves. Like a dog mistaking its shadow in water for another dog, we mistakenly treat transient cognitive events as independently existing realities. Through Yoniso Manasikāra, we shift our attention inward, directly observing the arising and cessation of each cognitive moment without becoming lost in conceptual elaboration.

For example, upon hearing a sound, we note it simply as an auditory cognition rather than labeling it "pleasant" or "unpleasant." Through consistent practice, we see experiences as mere passing phenomena, devoid of intrinsic permanence or substance. This realisation helps dismantle attachments, cravings, and aversions that arise from ignorance.

When we turn penetrative attention inward, it is like a robot examining its own programming rather than engaging with external data. We clearly see each cognitive event as a transient occurrence within the mind, free from inherent selfhood or permanence. Through this penetrating understanding, we sever the bonds of ignorance, opening the way to liberation.

In this profound realisation, the path toward freedom becomes clear. Through Yoniso Manasikāra, we grasp the truth that our experiences arise only within our present cognition, not outside it. This recognition fundamentally alters our relationship to the world and ourselves, paving the way for ultimate liberation from all suffering.

Thus, the four stages of liberation—Sotāpanna, Sakadāgāmi, Anāgāmi, and Arahant—are traversed by progressively deepening our insight into reality, dismantling ignorance through penetrative attention, and freeing ourselves from the endless cycle of birth, death, and suffering. Each stage brings us closer to realising Nibbāna, the supreme peace and liberation, which is as attainable now as in the time of Lord Buddha himself.

Non-Self through the Analogy of an AI Robot

To further clarify the profound truth of non-self (*Anattā*), let's consider the analogy of a highly sophisticated AI robot.

Imagine a robot engineered with artificial intelligence, programmed to perceive its surroundings through sensory devices—visual sensors (eyes), audio sensors (ears), tactile sensors (skin), and processing units akin to a brain. It receives data, processes this input through a complex network of software algorithms, and subsequently generates responses, behaviours, and even what appear to be emotions or desires.

If this robot were advanced enough, it could convincingly speak of its experiences, express happiness or sadness, claim preferences, and even insist on its own identity or individuality. Observers might easily be misled into believing it possesses a genuine "self" or autonomous existence. But on deeper reflection, it becomes clear that there is no intrinsic, independent entity within the robot. Its identity, personality, and experiences arise entirely from a chain of programmed causes and effects. Each response it produces is merely the outcome of conditioned data-processing, based on prior programming and input.

Similarly, we humans are a combination of processes—bodily sensations, perceptions, feelings, thoughts, and consciousness—arising and passing away dependent on conditions. Like the robot, we mistake the interplay of these processes for a fixed, independent self. Yet, upon careful examination, we discover that no permanent, independent entity can be found anywhere within us. What we call "self" is simply a momentary arising of sensory experiences, perceptions, mental formations, and consciousness, conditioned by causes.

Just as understanding the robot's programming reveals the absence of any inherent self or soul, deep contemplation of our own processes reveals that we, too, lack an inherent, independent self. Seeing this clearly—through penetrative attention—is the profound insight that leads directly toward the ultimate freedom of liberation.

Closing Reflections: The Ground Cleared for the Path

Before one embarks on the noble path of liberation, these realisations must take root. Without understanding the illusion of desire, the subtle grip of ignorance, the necessity of inward attention, and the truth of non-self, one may attempt to walk the path only to find themselves circling the mirage once again.

This chapter is not an invitation to suppress desires or escape life, but to see life as it truly is. The mirage is beautiful, but it cannot quench the thirst. The world offers many things, but not what we truly seek. That which is lasting, that which is peaceful, that which is free—is not found by chasing after reflections, but by awakening to the stillness beneath all movement.

With this understanding, the heart is no longer desperate. The mind is no longer restless. And the seeker is no longer lost.

Chapter 36

The Mirage of Masturbation

Even after deeply understanding the impermanent, impersonal, and unsatisfactory nature of the body… even after realising the truth of *anattā*—that there is no real "self" within this shell of flesh and thought—lust may not vanish completely.

There may come a time, especially for a sincere seeker on the path to Enlightenment, when the fires of sensual desire seem to have subsided. One may begin to feel light, peaceful, inwardly free. Thoughts of needing a partner, or the longing for sexual intimacy, gradually fade. The heart turns inward. The mind grows still. And yet…

There are moments, unexpected and sudden, where lust whispers again. Not with the same intensity as before, but now as a subtle urge, a quiet craving—not for love or relationship, but for *release*. The desire to masturbate, not driven by fantasy or romance, but by a biological longing for relief. In such moments, even with wisdom, even with understanding, the body and its chemical memory may ask, "Just this once… let it go. You'll feel lighter afterward."

And yes, afterward, you might feel some quiet. But you must know the truth: **that post-masturbation clarity is not spiritual peace—it is biochemical relief**. It is a **dopamine crash**, a release of tension, a lull in the storm. But not the end of the storm.

True meditation is not the art of reaching comfort. It is the **art of enduring the wave**, observing the fire, and seeing its origin without acting it out. To overcome lust, one must not satisfy it until it sleeps—but **watch it until it burns itself out by wisdom**.

Lust is like fire. It appears wild, blazing, overwhelming. Masturbation might seem like a way to control it—like pouring sand or water to quiet the flame. And indeed, it may work—for a while. But the **embers remain**. The **habit remains**. The **self that obeys the craving remains**.

The real spiritual path is not to pour sand on fire, but to sit beside it in **stillness**, in **awareness**, in **clarity**—until it loses its power to burn.

The true yogi does not run from lust, nor does he surrender to it. He **watches**. He **feels**. He **discerns**. He sees the body as a process, not a person. He sees desire as a condition, not an identity. And in doing so, he liberates not just from lust, but from the illusion that there is anyone who lusts.

These moments—where desire presses, even under the light of wisdom—are not failures. They are **opportunities**. These are the **battlefields of insight meditation**. This is the **war of wisdom against craving**.

In these moments, you must not seek quick peace through indulgence. Instead, you must deepen your watching. Be the observer. Be the unmoved witness. Let the fire rise—and watch it fall. Let the thought scream—and see it vanish. Return to the body, but see it not as "mine." Return to the mind, but see it not as "me." Stand still, until the illusion burns away.

That is where real liberation begins.

What follows is not merely a poem, but a meditative reflection on this very journey—from the pull of lust to the silence of freedom. Read it not only with eyes, but with the heart of a warrior-yogi—one who walks the silent path toward the end of all desire.

A Song of Flame and Stillness

In shadows soft where silence sings,
Desire creeps on velvet wings.
A thought, a touch, a breath, a sigh—
The restless wave begins to rise.

The body's pulse, the whisper low,
A spark ignites the fire below.
It hums a song of tender ache,
And tempts the mind: "Just bend, just break."

A storm disguised in gentle form,
It wraps the soul in seeming warm.
"Release," it says, "and you'll be free—
Come taste the fruit of ecstasy."

And so, the hand becomes the slave
Of what the phantom body craves.
A moment's thrill, a fleeting bliss—
Then all dissolves into the mist.

The chest falls flat, the heat now gone,
A calm descends—a quiet dawn.
But underneath that soft relief,
Still lives the seed of subtle grief.

You think, "I'm calm. My lust has died."
But no, dear one—it's only lied.
For lust returns in sweeter guise,
With bolder dreams and darker eyes.

Each act becomes a sacred trade:
You sell your fire for peace that fades.
You buy a silence, soft and brief,
While debt remains in unseen grief.

A lion fed will sleep today—
But hunger wakes and leads astray.
The path to peace is not this way;
It's not in what the senses say.

Masturbation—sweet illusion's kiss—
Feels like surrender into bliss.
But scratch beneath the silken skin—
You'll find the roots of pain within.

You do not empty lust by giving.
You feed the ghost that keeps on living.

You do not still the mind through flesh,
You twist the thread in tighter mesh.

For every drop that leaves your core,
The hunger knocks a louder door.
And with each act, the lesson told:
"You're still a servant of the hold."

The sages knew a subtler fire,
That doesn't burn with base desire—
But rises high through spinal thread,
And turns to light what once misled.

They sat with storms and did not move.
They faced the fire, but would not soothe.
They let the serpent dance and hiss,
Then vanish in the truth of this:

That lust is just a passing phase,
A mirage on the desert's face.
You chase the shimmer, feel it wet—
But find it dry, each time you get.

And when the yogi dares to stay,
To neither push nor drift away,
He sees the game, the grand disguise—
And opens wide the inner eyes.

He sees the lust arise and go,
Not "me," not "mine," no self to show.
Just cause and effect, rise and fall—
Just empty echoes in a hall.

No sinner here, no saint to blame,
Just passing clouds without a name.
And in that gaze—so calm, so wide—
The fire burns out from inside.

The craving mind begins to die,
Its wings are clipped, it cannot fly.
The eye that watched—now turns within,
And sees the truth beneath the skin.

No watcher now, no one to bind,
Just silent space, a formless mind.
No self to grasp, no lust to fight,
Just radiant, transparent light.

The body still, the breath grown deep,
The ocean still, the wind asleep.
No fantasies, no images—
Just being, pure, with no edges.

You touch the state no hands can reach,
No words describe, no scriptures teach.
A deathless peace, a boundless sky—
Where even "I" dissolves and dies.

And in that death of name and form,
The Buddha's truth begins to warm.
The Fourfold Path, the Noble Flame—
All shine from silence, not from shame.

You do not conquer lust by sword,
Nor curse it with a holy word.

You simply watch. You do not flee.
You let it be—and you are free.

So next time craving wraps its chain,
And sings to you in silken pain—
Do not bow low. Do not pretend.
Just watch the fire until the end.

And when it fades, and when you see
That there is no "you" to be—
Then joy, uncaused, begins to rise,
Like golden dawn in moonless skies.

Watch the watcher—see him fade.
Watch the seer gently laid.
When even the witness disappears,
You'll find the end of all your fears.

I dissolve—no name, no face,
Just silence wrapped in empty space.
And from that void, the Light is born:
The selfless peace of the deathless dawn.

Chapter 37

The Main Meditation

Here I am going to teach you the main meditation I used to liberate myself. This technique is borrowed from **Anattalakkhana Sutta** in Tipitaka. It is the path I personally walked, the direct insight I lived through, and the gateway that opened my heart to the stream of true freedom. It is known as **Pañcakkhandha Anattā Meditation**, or more simply, **Anattānupassanā**—the contemplation of non-self through the five clinging aggregates.

This is the precise discernment of the truth that what we cling to as "I," "me," or "mine" is in fact *not* our self. The body that ages, the sensations that shift, the perceptions that label, the thoughts that narrate, and even the very consciousness that knows—all these are not the self. They arise and pass due to causes and conditions. They are mechanisms, not identities.

There are **two main insights**—two doors—that reveal the nature of **Anattā**:

1. **Lack of Control** – If something were truly "me," "mine," or "myself," I should be able to command it: "Be this way; do not be that way." But these phenomena do not obey. They change on their own,

without our consent. What is not under our control cannot rightly be called self.

2. **Not Created by Me or Anyone Else** – The phenomena we call "me" were not authored by us. No one constructed them from pure will. They are the result of causes and conditions—karma, heredity, sense contact, and mental formations. They are mechanisms born from the chain of dependent origination.

These two insights are the foundation of Anattānupassanā. Once understood, they can be applied in **two distinct ways** of meditation:

- By observing whatever **naturally arises** in present awareness.
- Or by focusing on a **chosen anchor**, such as the **breath**, and using it to explore the nature of experience.

Let us now walk through **Anattānupassanā by experiences**, step by step.

Insight Through Natural Arisings

Contemplating Non-Self Through Present-Moment Experience

1. Posture and Preparation

Find a quiet space and sit with dignity. Straighten your spine and neck. Whether on a chair or the floor, do not lean against anything. At first, this may feel uncomfortable, but do not let discomfort discourage you. As your clarity deepens, the body's tension will dissolve, and the posture will feel light and natural. The straight spine is essential—it serves as the bridge between the earth and the sky, stabilising body and mind for deep contemplation.

2. Contemplating the Body

Now, bring your attention to your **body parts one by one**. Start with the face. Then move to the head, neck, shoulders, chest, back, arms, pelvis, legs—cover every region, gently but mindfully.

With each part, reflect deeply:

- **"I cannot control this to be exactly as I want it. Therefore, it cannot be I, mine, or myself."**
- **"This was not created by me, nor by someone else. It is a mechanism formed through causes and effects—genetics, karma, food, elements."**

Let your wisdom absorb these truths, and when it agrees, gently whisper in your mind:

"This is also not me."

This short phrase will have power, for it carries the essence of insight. Then move on to the next part. At times you may feel it's enough to simply acknowledge "This is not me," but other times the attachment resurfaces. When that happens, return to the two characteristics again and again.

Once the whole body has been examined in this way, your mind will feel **released** from the physical form. There will be a lightness, a sense that the body is no longer something you own or inhabit.

3. Contemplating Sensations

Next, turn your awareness toward **sensations**—pleasant, unpleasant, or neutral. Stay present, and notice whatever feeling arises. Perhaps an **unpleasant sound** creates discomfort. Use it as your object.

Now reflect:

- **"I cannot control this sensation to arise or cease. It is not mine."**
- **"This sensation is just a neurological response, caused by contact between the sense base and an object. It is a mechanism, not a self."**

Continue with various sensations. Sometimes it is enough to simply acknowledge:

"This is also not me."

As your discernment deepens, you will feel as if **your mind has temporarily relinquished sensations**. They will be experienced, but without ownership. Like passing clouds, they no longer stick.

4. Contemplating Perceptions

Now direct your attention to **perceptions**—the labelling function of the mind. For example, you hear a bird and instantly the mind says "bird." That labelling is a perception.

Contemplate:

- **"This perception arises not by my will, but from conditioned memory."**
- **"It is an automatic process of the brain—a naming habit created from past experiences."**

When clearly seen, perception loses its weight. The mind stops believing it is a knowing self, and instead sees perception as a conditioned function. Then, your mind will begin to **abandon perceptions**.

5. Contemplating Thoughts

Now observe your **thoughts**. They may be subtle or bold. Perhaps your mind spontaneously reflects, "This is also not me." Even this insight is a thought.

Contemplate:

- **"This preparation is also a mental formation—not under my control."**
- **"It arises from karmic residues, past teachings, and accumulated memories."**

This stage is more subtle. Now you are discerning that even the **one who meditates** is not a self. The very thought of "I am meditating" is an illusion.

This insight shakes the core. It humbles the mind. Slowly, the thinker vanishes, and the **thoughts are abandoned**.

6. Contemplating Consciousness

Now come to **consciousness**—the most refined aggregate. Become aware of awareness itself. For example, hear a sound. Before any thought, there is a raw knowing of the sound. That is consciousness.

Contemplate:

- **"This knowing is not under my control. I cannot filter or stop experiences from arising."**
- **"Just as a microphone picks up sound, so too the ear receives and the mind cognises. It is a mechanism—not a self."**

Discern several such moments of consciousness, ex: sounds, smells, tangibles, moods etc. With continued observation, even consciousness begins to **fade as a solid experience**. The mind drops the illusion of "I am aware."

7. Abiding in Emptiness and Beyond

As you abandon these aggregates one by one, a profound **emptiness** will begin to arise. Sit in it. Be with it. Balance it. At times, it may feel delicate and easily disturbed. If so, return to discernment. Revisit the five aggregates. Contemplate: **"This is also not me."**

Eventually, you will feel **deeper layers of emptiness** arising—silent, peaceful, vast. But even here, the echo of self may linger. So now, even this emptiness must be examined.

"I cannot control this emptiness to remain for one hour or two. It is also not me."

Discern each wave of emptiness in this way. As each is seen for what it is, **they too dissolve**.

Finally, something extraordinary occurs. There comes a state where even the **sense of "this is me" or "this is emptiness" is gone**. Duality fades. Perception stills. Sensation ceases. Thought no longer stirs. The self-concept vanishes like mist under sunlight.

This is the first true **experience of Nibbāna**. The **stream-entry** moment. The gates of Dhamma open. The mirage of self dissolves, and the heart touches what is beyond the world. It is not a trance, nor a blissful state. It is the **end of fabrications**, the **stilling of all preparations**.

This is the beginning of true freedom.

Insight Through a Chosen Anchor

Contemplating Non-Self Through the Breath

While the ever-changing field of natural experiences can serve as fertile ground for the insight into non-self, many seekers benefit from a more stable and continuous object—a single anchor to return to again and again. Among all anchors, the **breath** is both profound and accessible. It is simple, rhythmic, and always present. Yet it too is not the self. It is a silent teacher, pointing us back to the truth of **Anattā** with every inhalation and exhalation.

Let us now walk this inner journey—step by step—using the breath as our mirror.

1. Grounding the Body with Dignity

Begin by taking your seat with reverence. Whether on a cushion, mat, or chair, sit with your spine and neck **upright and aligned**, like a tower reaching towards the sky. Do not lean against anything. Support yourself fully with your own posture. In the beginning, you may feel discomfort—stiffness in the back, tension in the neck. But do not be discouraged. As the light of clarity begins to shine through the mind, the body will find stillness in stillness. What first feels rigid will begin to feel effortless.

2. Anchoring Awareness to the Breath

Now gently rest your attention on the **natural breath**—specifically, the tangible sensation of air moving **in and out of the nose**. Do not try to control the breath. Simply observe it. Feel the subtle brushing of air within the nostrils. This is your **chosen anchor**.

You are not meditating on the idea of the breath, but the **direct experience** of it. Noticing how it enters, how it leaves, and how each moment is new—never the same breath twice.

3. Discerning the Breath as Not-Self

Now bring the **two characteristics of non-self** into contemplation.

As you observe the **breath in**, reflect:

- "This breath is not created by me. Nor is it created by someone else. It is just a mechanism, arising due to causes and conditions—past karma, the biological structure formed by the parent's zygote, food, temperature, and the body's automatic functioning."
- "I cannot wish this breath to be longer or shorter, deeper or shallower. It moves on its own. Therefore, it is not under my control."

Let your **wisdom agree**: "If this is not under my control and not created by me, it cannot be 'I,' 'mine,' or 'myself.'" Let this realisation land, not just intellectually but deeply in your being.

Then, as the **breath out** naturally follows, shift your attention to it, and simply whisper in the heart:

"This is also not me."

At times, this short phrase will be enough to release attachment. The mind loosens its grip. But at other times, you may feel it is not sufficient. Then return again to the two insights. Reflect clearly and patiently.

With time, the breath becomes **hollow of identity**. You will begin to feel that your mind no longer holds the breath as "my breath." The sense of ownership dissolves. The breath continues, but the burden of "self" in it has vanished.

4. Contemplating Sensations Through the Breath

Now refine your attention further. Begin to notice the **sensations** that arise through the breath—the tickle in the nose, the coolness of air entering, or the warmth of air leaving.

As you notice a sensation—perhaps a **pleasant feeling** as the breath moves out—contemplate:

- "I cannot control this sensation to arise or not arise. It is not mine."
- "It is just a response of the nervous system, the brain interpreting contact between air and inner tissue. It is a mechanism—not a self."

Observe several sensations. At times, just saying **"This is also not me"** will suffice. At other times, you will need to reflect deeply. Continue this process, again and again, until the **weight of sensation** drops away. It will feel as though your mind no longer sticks to the pleasant or unpleasant. There is only observation, free of grasping.

5. Contemplating Perceptions Related to the Breath

Now begin to observe the **perceptions** that form around the breath.

Perhaps you hear the mind say, "I am breathing," or you label it "in-breath," "out-breath." Contemplate:

- "This labelling is also not mine. It is a learned habit, a mental reflex created from past data fed into the brain."
- "Even the word 'breath' is just a conditioned memory—it is not something I created or control."

Slowly, your mind will come to see **perception itself** as non-self. The labels will begin to lose their grip. The experience of the breath becomes **silent and direct**, unfiltered by concepts.

6. Contemplating Thoughts During Breath Awareness

Next, notice the **subtle thoughts** that arise during this meditation.

Sometimes your mind may automatically reflect, "This breath is also not me." That is a thought. That is a preparation. Contemplate:

- "Even this insight is not mine. It arises due to previous karma, training, meditation, and the conditions I have set."
- "It is a process—not a person."

This stage is subtle and profound. You begin to discern that even the **meditator**, the one who contemplates, is just a thought—a mental formation. Let this insight deepen. Let the **meditator disappear**.

7. Contemplating Consciousness of the Breath

Now turn your gaze towards **consciousness**—the bare knowing of the breath.

Catch one moment of awareness, for instance, **the knowing of an in-breath**. Then reflect:

- "This awareness is not mine. I did not summon it. I cannot stop or control it."
- "Just as a microphone registers sound when air moves past it, the nose and nervous system generate consciousness when breath is present. It is mechanical. It is not a self."

Discern several such moments. Gradually, you will feel even the **awareness of the breath** dissolve into **impersonality**. The consciousness remains, but the identity behind it fades.

8. Abiding in Emptiness Born from Insight

As body, sensation, perception, thought, and consciousness are seen clearly as non-self, you will begin to feel a profound **emptiness**. Stay there. Dwell in it. Gently balance your awareness.

If the emptiness feels unstable or fragile, return to discernment. Reflect once again:

"This breath is also not me."

Let the insight support the silence. Again, emptiness will return.

9. Final Discernment: Even Emptiness is Not Self

Eventually, even in the midst of this peace, a **subtle echo of self** may remain—a trace of the "I" that lingers in the background.

Contemplate:

- "This emptiness too is not mine. I cannot make it stay for an hour or two. It arises from causes and conditions—discernment, posture, stillness. It too is not a self."

Then deeper layers of emptiness may arise—**more silent, more spacious** than the ones before. Contemplate each:

"This too is not me."

Continue until even the sense of "I am in emptiness" fades.

10. Coming Home: The Fading of Duality

At last, there will come a moment where **no perception arises as 'this is me,' nor even 'this is emptiness.'** Duality disappears. The subject-object divide collapses. There is only stillness. Only suchness.

This is the **stilling of preparations**, the fading of fabrications. The place where **perceptions and feelings cease**. You have tasted the **first experience of Nibbāna**—the gateway to the deathless. This is **stream-entry**, the beginning of true freedom.

You have come home.

Contemplating Non-Self Through Walking Meditation

While sitting meditation offers a still and silent gateway into the nature of non-self, walking meditation brings the Dhamma into motion. It allows us to explore the truth of *Anattā* in the very rhythm of life itself. With each step, we learn to walk not as a "self" moving through space, but as a stream of conditioned phenomena unfolding through cause and effect. The pathway becomes the Dhamma. The feet become the mirror. The Earth becomes the teaching. This is walking not towards a destination, but **walking home into stillness**.

Let us now enter the path of **walking Anattānupassanā**—the contemplation of non-self through the tangible reality of each step.

1. Preparing the Sacred Path

Find a **quiet, straight path**—about 30 feet in length is ideal. It may be a tiled corridor, a sandy garden path, or a wooden floor. This space becomes your temple. Begin walking slowly, mindfully, and without distraction. When you reach the end of the path, turn around **with complete awareness**, and walk back slowly. Repeat this gentle rhythm again and again. You are not trying to get somewhere. You are learning to be fully **present with every step**.

2. Anchoring Attention to the Tangible Contact of the Feet

As you walk, bring your attention to the **tangible feeling of the feet**. Notice the contact between the sole of your foot and the surface beneath it. Whether it's the softness of soil, the coolness of tile, or the texture of wood—feel it as directly as possible.

Recognise: when foot and floor meet, **consciousness arises**. This is your anchor. Not the thought of walking. Not the idea of meditation. But the direct contact, the living sensation.

3. Discerning Non-Self Through the Foot's Tangibility

Now, while experiencing this contact, contemplate:

- "This tangible feeling is **not created by me**, nor by someone else. It is a product of **past karma**, the body shaped by the **parental zygote**, nourished by **food and elements**. It arises because of contact between foot and floor. It is **just a mechanism**, not a self."
- "I cannot control this sensation. I cannot demand that it feel exactly how I wish. Therefore, it is **not under my control**. And what is not under my control cannot be I, mine, or myself."

Let your **wisdom agree**. Let this contemplation settle in your heart. Gently affirm:

"This too is not me."

Then shift your attention to the **next foot**, repeating the same contemplation. Let each step become a teaching. Let each step become a letting go.

4. Relinquishing Identification Through Repetition

With every footstep, let go. Observe, discern, and relinquish. At times, simply saying **"This is also not me"** will be enough to release the mental ownership. At other times, attachment will return, and you may feel the need to re-establish the insight using the two characteristics of non-self.

As these insights deepen, your mind will slowly stop identifying the legs, the body, or the movement as "mine." You are no longer walking **as a person**, but as a process. A beautifully unfolding process of causes and effects.

5. Contemplating Sensations While Walking

Now begin to observe the **sensations** that arise through the contact of the foot. Sometimes a **pleasant sensation** arises with one step—a gentle softness, a sense of calm. At other times, an **unpleasant sensation** may appear—a sharpness, an ache.

Contemplate each sensation:

- "This is not under my control."
- "It is just a result of nerves, skin contact, temperature, and the brain interpreting signals. It is **a mechanism**, not a self."

Repeat this observation with each step. Sometimes the phrase **"This is also not me"** will suffice. Other times, return to full contemplation. Gradually, the **weight of sensation** lifts. The mind lets go. The sensations continue, but the **ownership fades**.

6. Contemplating Perceptions While Walking

Next, notice the **perceptions** that arise during your walk. Perhaps the mind labels: "This is a wooden floor," "This is my left foot," or "The ground is hard." These are not random—they are the product of past **conditioning** and **stored data**.

Reflect:

- "This naming is not a self. It is the mind recognising familiar patterns, based on past input. It happens on its own."

The words "foot," "floor," "walking," "me"—they are merely **labels**, not truths. They were fed to the brain like commands to a computer. Perception, too, is **not the self**.

As this truth becomes clear, perception is abandoned. The mind walks in **pure awareness**, not filtered by language.

7. Contemplating Thoughts During Walking

Now, turn your gaze inward to notice the **thoughts** that quietly arise as you walk.

Perhaps your mind reflects, "This is also not me," with each step. That very reflection, that **insight**, is itself a **thought**.

Contemplate:

- "This thought is not mine. It is the result of prior karma, meditation training, and mental impressions. It is not under my control."

You will now reach a subtle turning point: the **meditator**—the one doing the contemplating—is also seen as **just another thought**. This is profound. The imagined "I" who walks and meditates dissolves.

Let the thoughts fall away. Let the **thinker fade**.

8. Contemplating Consciousness in Walking

Now turn your attention to **consciousness itself**—the raw awareness of the foot's contact.

Catch a moment of consciousness—perhaps the knowing of the **left foot's pressure**. Contemplate:

- "This consciousness is not me. It arises when foot and floor meet, like sound arises in a working microphone. It is conditioned. It is not a self."

Do the same with the right foot. Reflect on multiple moments of awareness in this way. Slowly, consciousness becomes **transparent**. The identity behind awareness dissolves.

Your mind will now begin to **abandon consciousness**. What remains is not dullness—but **silence**. The silence of insight.

9. Abiding in Emptiness While Walking

As the aggregates fall away—body, sensation, perception, thought, and consciousness—you will begin to feel a deep **emptiness** blooming in the midst of motion.

You are walking, but there is **no walker**. There are steps, but no one taking them. Stay present in this emptiness. Let it **balance and stabilise**.

If the emptiness is disturbed, return to discernment. Use the phrase:

"This, too, is not me."

And the emptiness will return.

10. When Walking Naturally Stops

Eventually, a natural shift occurs. Your legs may feel too light, or too hollow, to continue walking. Your body may stop on its own. You may feel drawn to **close your eyes** and **stand still.**

Do not resist. Simply stand in stillness. Let the emptiness now deepen without motion. Let it be felt **not just in the feet**, but throughout your entire being.

11. Final Discernment: Letting Go of the Last Echo of Self

Even in this standing silence, a faint **echo of self** may remain. A quiet voice saying, "I am experiencing emptiness."

Now turn your insight towards it:

- "This emptiness is also not me."
- "I cannot control this to last for one hour or two. It is just another conditioned effect—born from meditation, from letting go, from prior causes."

Even **this peace** is seen as non-self.

12. Returning Home Beyond Emptiness

Then, more **refined states of emptiness** may arise—vast, clear, unfathomably still. Each one more silent than the last. Discern each as:

"This too is not me."

Finally, you reach a place where **there is no more discernment**. No more observing. No more perceiving.

There is **no longer even the thought**, "This is me," or "This is emptiness."

The **duality dissolves**. The **fabrications cease**. The heart settles into **pure cessation**. The flow of becoming halts.

This is **Nibbāna**. The first touch of enlightenment. **The stream is entered**.

You have walked, step by step, out of illusion and into truth.

You have come home.

Chapter 38

Extra Meditation Techniques

The 16 Steps of Ānāpānasati A Comprehensive Guide to Breath Meditation

Ānāpānasati , or mindfulness of breathing, is a meditation practice detailed in the Anapanasati Sutta from the Majjhima Nikaya of the Sutta Pitaka. Among various methods of breath awareness, the 16-step approach stands out as the most precise and comprehensive, as it was explicitly prescribed by Lord Buddha himself. This method integrates both Samatha (tranquillising meditation) and Vipassana (insight meditation) and is renowned for its effectiveness in leading practitioners to Nibbana (enlightenment) without requiring additional methods. This chapter elaborates on each of the 16 steps in detail, offering a step-by-step guide to this profound meditative practice.

Preparing for Meditation

Before delving into the 16 steps, it is crucial to prepare the body and mind. Find a quiet place, ideally a secluded spot in the wilderness, the shade of a tree, or a serene room. Sit down with your legs folded crosswise, ensuring that your back is straight and your body is erect. Set mindfulness to the forefront of your practice, establishing a strong foundation for the meditation.

Step 1: Understanding the Long Breath
Begin by directing your awareness to the breath. When you inhale, discern whether the breath is long. Recognise it as such by noting, "I am breathing in long." This initial step involves simply acknowledging the length of the breath without judgement.

Step 2: Understanding the Short Breath
Similarly, as you exhale, determine if the breath is short. Label it as such with the awareness, "I am breathing out short." Just as a carpenter can tell the length of each stroke before beginning, so should you recognise whether each breath is long or short from the beginning of the inhale or exhale.

Step 3: Experiencing the Whole Body with the Breath
In this step, extend your awareness to encompass the entire body as you breathe in. Observe how the breath permeates through the body. Similarly, as you breathe out, experience the breath leaving the body. This practice helps in connecting the breath with bodily sensations, fostering a holistic awareness.

Step 4: Tranquillising the Breath

Focus on calming the bodily sensations associated with the breath. As you breathe in, train yourself to calm the bodily fabrications (calming the breathing and the physical sensations related to breathing). Likewise, as you exhale, continue to calm these bodily fabrications. This step is about achieving a state of tranquillity through the breath.

Step 5: Experiencing Rapture

Direct your awareness to the experience of rapture or joy that accompanies the breath. As you breathe in, become sensitive to the rapture, and as you breathe out, continue to be aware of it. This step involves cultivating a sense of joy and bliss that arises through mindful breathing.

Step 6: Experiencing Pleasure

Similarly, focus on the pleasure derived from the breath. While breathing in, be aware of the pleasurable sensations, and as you breathe out, continue to experience this pleasure. This step aims to enhance your sensitivity to the pleasure that arises through the practice.

Step 7: Understanding Mental Fabrication

Recognise that mental fabrications—such as perceptions and sensations—are part of the cycle of experience. As you breathe in, be aware of these fabrications, and as you breathe out, continue to observe them. Understanding that even pleasurable sensations are fabrications helps in developing insight into the nature of mental formations.

Step 8: Calming Mental Fabrication

Train yourself to calm the mental fabrications as you breathe in and out. By recognising that perceptions and sensations are transient, you work towards calming these mental fabrications, fostering a state of inner peace and equanimity.

Step 9: Observing the Mind

Direct your awareness to the state of the mind itself. As you breathe in, be sensitive to the mind's state, and as you breathe out, maintain this awareness. This step involves becoming attuned to the mind's emptiness and overall state.

Step 10: Satisfying the Mind

Focus on satisfying the mind with each breath. As you inhale, intentionally bring satisfaction to the mind, and as you exhale, continue to sustain this satisfaction. This practice aims to cultivate a sense of contentment and joy within the mind.

Step 11: Steadying the Mind

Work on steadying the mind as you breathe in and out. As you inhale, focus on steadying the mind and, likewise, as you exhale, continue to stabilise it. This step helps in maintaining mental focus and clarity.

Step 12: Releasing the Mind

Train yourself to release the mind from the state of consciousness experienced. While breathing in, focus on releasing the mind, and as you breathe out, continue to disengage from the current state of consciousness. This practice involves stepping back from the present mental state rather than relinquishing consciousness itself.

Step 13: Focusing on Inconstancy

Observe the inconstancy of the mind as you breathe in and out. Recognise how the state of consciousness changes with each breath. This awareness of inconstancy helps in understanding the impermanent nature of all phenomena.

Step 14: Focusing on Dispassion

Develop a sense of dispassion or fading towards the consciousness experienced. As you breathe in, focus on becoming detached from the current state of consciousness, and as you exhale, continue to cultivate dispassion. This step helps in recognising the transient nature of all experiences.

Step 15: Focusing on Cessation

Direct your attention to the cessation of consciousness. As you inhale, observe how the state of consciousness you experience is not the same as it was moments ago or will be in the future. This focus on cessation helps in understanding the fleeting nature of all mental states.

Step 16: Focusing on Relinquishment

Finally, focus on relinquishing the current state of consciousness as you breathe in and out. Recognise that after observing cessation, you need to relinquish the consciousness you are experiencing now. This step involves releasing attachment to the current state of consciousness, leading to a deeper sense of freedom.

The Experience of Nibbana

Upon completing these 16 steps, the mind will naturally settle and cease all preparatory activity. You will reach a state where there is no perception of breathing or consciousness, allowing for a direct experience of Nibbana. This profound state marks the initial realisation of enlightenment, where the mind is freed from all attachments and fabrications.

Conclusion

The 16 steps of Anapanasati offer a structured and comprehensive approach to breath meditation that incorporates both tranquillising and insight practices. By following these steps meticulously, practitioners can cultivate a deep understanding of the impermanent and non-self-nature of all phenomena, ultimately leading to the experience of Nibbana. This method, as prescribed by Lord Buddha, provides a complete and effective path to liberation through the art of mindful breathing.

The Discerning of the Repulsive Body and the Path to the Cessation of All Formations

In this chapter, we shall explore a powerful and often overlooked technique taught by the Blessed One—one that guides the meditator from the coarse perception of the physical body to the subtle transcendence of all formations. This is the meditation on **the thirty-two repulsive parts of the body**, leading gradually to insight into **sensation, perception, consciousness**, and ultimately into the **liberation of the mind** through the **stilling of all preparations (sabba-saṅkhāra-samatha).**

This path is not for those who seek comfort—it is for those who seek truth.

Setting the Foundation

Begin by preparing yourself physically and mentally. Sit on a chair or on the floor in a comfortable yet upright position. Let the spine be straight, the chest open, and the shoulders relaxed. Let your presence be stable, your awareness fully gathered.

Now gently close your eyes and turn inward.

Step 1: Discerning the Body Like a Grain Sack

Visualise the body not as "I" or "me," but as a **collection of parts**, just as a man with good eyesight opens a bag of grains

and says,
"Here is rice. Here is barley. Here is sesame. Here is wheat..."—so too, with clarity and detachment, discern:

- **Head-hairs, body-hairs, nails, teeth, skin**
- **Flesh, sinews, bones, bone marrow, kidneys, heart, liver, diaphragm, spleen, lungs**
- **Intestines, mesentery, stomach contents (gore), excrement, brain**
- **Bile, phlegm, pus, blood, sweat, fat, tears, grease, saliva, snot, synovial fluid, urine**

Go through these parts slowly, precisely, with the clarity of a surgeon and the stillness of a meditator.

You are not trying to feel disgust. You are trying to see the **truth**—that this body is a **heap of impersonal elements**, devoid of beauty, devoid of essence, and certainly devoid of "self."

Do this once, twice, or as many times as it takes for the illusion of "I am the body" to loosen its grip.

Step 2: Awareness Without the Body

As this clarity deepens, the mind will begin to **relinquish its attachment to the body**, even if temporarily. A state will arise where you no longer feel the body—you dwell in **bare mental presence**, detached and spacious.

But be mindful—**you may now cling to this state** as "the soul," "the inner being," or "the true self."
This, too, is illusion.

Now we begin the next phase of insight: penetrating the layers of mind.

Step 3: Identifying Sensation

Bring your full awareness to the **subtle sensations** present in this state—whether pleasant or neutral. Identify them directly:

"This is a sensation. This is a sensation."

Do not analyse—just recognise. You are not feeling them. They are simply there—rising, falling, flickering.

Step 4: Identifying Perception

Now, turn to the **perception** that labels and recognises the sensation. The knowing that says *"This is calm," "This is pleasant."*

"This is perception. This is perception."

Hold it gently in awareness—not as "my perception," but as a conditioned process. Let the watcher begin to observe the watching.

Step 5: Examining Consciousness

Soon, the mind will descend even deeper, to a state of **subtle consciousness**—calm, light, refined.
But beware—**this is the final hiding place of the self**. One may feel: *"This is my essence. This is who I truly am."*

Insight it directly. Ask the mind:

"Is this the same consciousness I had 3 seconds ago?
Will this consciousness remain the same in the next 3 seconds?"

Watch closely. You will see that even this **arises and passes**, conditioned and impermanent.

Step 6: The Illusion of Emptiness

Now you may touch the **state of emptiness**—vast, silent, open.
But even this has a subtle shadow: *"I am the one who experiences this emptiness."*

This is still the conceiving of self. Do not stop here.

Step 7: Insight into Emptiness

Contemplate the impermanence of this empty state itself:

"When I rise from meditation, this state will vanish.
If it truly were 'I,' then I too would vanish."

Recognise it clearly—**this too is conditioned, this too is not-self.** Let the last clinging fall.

Step 8: Returning Home

If insight is sharp and steady, the mind may now enter its **natural state**—free from observer, free from identity.

No world.
No me.
No perception.
No sensation.
Only silence—**not the silence of absence, but the silence of liberation**.

This is home.

Step 9: If Liberation Does Not Arise Immediately

If this **non-dual state** does not appear at first, do not despair. Return gently to the state of emptiness. Watch it again and again:

"This is impermanent. This is not me."

With each sincere attempt, the illusion thins. And soon, the mind will let go—not through effort, but through understanding.

Final Words

This technique is a path of courage and clarity. From bones to breath, from sensations to consciousness, from emptiness to the unconditioned—it is a gradual peeling away of illusion, until **nothing remains to cling to**.

This is not annihilation. This is **freedom**.

The Blessed One said: *"In seeing things as they truly are, the mind lets go, and what is left is the Deathless."*

May you walk this path not with force, but with stillness.
Not with fear, but with the fire of insight.
And may you reach the end of all becoming.

The Path Beyond the Body

The body is a sack of grains—
bone and bile, sweat and stains.
Not mine, not me, not worth the chain—
a temple carved of mud and pain.

Through sinew, skin, and dripping core,
the yogi sees, and clings no more.
No beauty hides in blood and bone,
just passing forms, not self, not home.

Then mind detaches, light and bare,
floating free in silent air.
But even here, illusion speaks:
"I am the soul, the one who seeks."

The watcher turns to feel and see—
sensation, thought, identity.
"This is perception,"—just a wave.
"This is awareness,"—not to save.

The mind descends to subtler flame,
still whispers soft the self's old name.
But truth inquires with gentle breath:
"Did this arise? Will it know death?"

Then emptiness—so wide, so deep—
where even thoughts fall still and sleep.
Yet subtle pride begins to cling:
"I am the void, the silent king."

So insight sharp as wisdom's sword
reveals: this too cannot be stored.
When sitting ends, it too shall cease—
thus not the self, not final peace.

And when at last all clinging dies,
no watcher lives, no thinker tries—
no form, no sound, no this or that—
just silent sky, forever flat.

No birth, no death, no breath to chase,
no inner light, no outer face.
Just **suchness**, pure, the formless shore—
where mind is still, and seeks no more.

Chapter 39

Will You Start Your Journey?

As you turn the final page of this book, I invite you to pause—not just in your reading, but in your heart.

You've journeyed through hidden longings, sacred struggles, and the tender ache of forbidden love. You've witnessed a monk's heart, not as a polished statue on a pedestal, but as a living, breathing flame—flickering with desire, devotion, doubt, and deep contemplation. You've touched the complexity of human love, and the quiet beauty of renunciation. But this, dear reader, is not the end.

This is your beginning.

🌱 A Question for You

Do you carry within your heart a quiet longing—perhaps unspoken—to have **an elder sister or elder brother**, someone who wraps you in protective warmth and sees your soul beyond

words?
Or maybe a **younger sibling**, someone to care for, to guide, to hold in that unconditional tenderness that stirs so naturally within you?

This yearning, often misunderstood by the world, is not trivial. It is not weak. It is a reflection of your capacity to **love deeply, innocently, and fully**. It is a mirror of a spiritual hunger—for connection, for safety, for a home in another being. And this book, in its own way, is a space where such love is not judged, but understood.

We are now engaged in a heartfelt research project to understand the depth of this emotional connection—what we call **sibling longing**, a hidden thread in many lives. If you've ever experienced this longing—whether in childhood or adulthood—we would be truly honoured to hear your story, even briefly.

You may simply share your thoughts or memories with us.
Your message may help others realise:
"I was not the only one who felt this way."

📧 **Email:** venerableananda@gmail.com
📱 **WhatsApp:** +94 72 444 8 555

Even a few lines from your heart could become a light for someone else walking the same silent path.

□□ And If You Seek Something Deeper…

If this book touched something more profound within you—
If you've ever looked at your own desires, attachments, and inner storms and wondered, *"Is there a way out of all this?"*
If you feel ready, even just a little, to uncover the **reality beneath this dream we call life**…

Then I invite you to take the next step, not into another story, but into the **path of true awakening**.

My first book, *The Liberation Manual – A Guide to Transcend the Mirage of Desires and the Illusion of Mind*, is a step-by-step spiritual manual born from the same heart that wrote this story. It shares not only teachings, but **twelve powerful meditation techniques**, offered with precision and compassion, for anyone who longs to break free from suffering.

This manual is not for Buddhists alone. It is for any human being ready to **stop chasing** and start **seeing**. It is for those who are tired of running and are now willing to sit, breathe, feel, and wake up.

You can find it now on Amazon. If you need help finding it, or if you wish to begin or continue your meditation journey under my guidance, please do not hesitate to reach out. I am not far. My heart is open.

📧 **Email:** venerableananda@gmail.com
📱 **WhatsApp:** +94 72 444 8 555

💫 One Final Whisper…

Perhaps you've never meditated.
Perhaps you've only just begun to understand the depth of your own longing.
Perhaps you've wandered through this life wondering why the world often feels so beautiful and so painful at once.
If so, let this moment be your turning point.

Let this be the place where the story ends…
…so **your real journey** can begin.

You do not have to be perfect.
You do not have to renounce everything.
You do not have to become a monk.

You only need to be willing—to sit, to breathe, to feel, to observe… and to look within.

The rest will unfold.
In silence.
In simplicity.
In truth.

Everything you seek is already within you—waiting to be discovered in stillness, in sincerity, in silence.

Were you my elder sister?

"Apârutâ tesam amatassa dvârâ
Ye sotavanto pamuñcantu saddham"

"The doors to the Enlightenment have been opened for you. Those who have ears, let them hear with faith and be liberated."

Printed in Great Britain
by Amazon

e0b01f4c-42cc-46da-9aa7-c6573a6a28daR01